olly Martin is the bestselling author of eighteen books and lives
 a little white cottage by the sea. She studied media at university,
 hich led to a very glitzy career as a hotel receptionist, followed
 by two even more glamorous years working in a bank. She then
 taught for four years but escaped the classroom to teach history
 orkshops, dressing up as a Viking one day and an Egyptian
 High Priestess the next. The long journeys travelling around the
 UK gave her a lot of time to plan out her stories and she now
 writes full time, doing what she loves.

Follow her on Twitter @HollyMAuthor

ALSO BY HOLLY MARTIN

HOPE ISLAND SERIES
Spring at Blueberry Bay
Summer at Buttercup Beach
Christmas at Mistletoe Cove

TOWN CALLED CHRISTMAS SERIES
Christmas Under a Cranberry Sky
A Town Called Christmas

WHITE CLIFF BAY SERIES
Christmas at Lilac Cottage
Snowflakes on Silver Cove
Summer at Rose Island

The Guestbook
One Hundred Proposals
One Hundred Christmas Proposals
Fairytale Beginnings

HOLLY WRITING AS AMELIA THORNE
Tied Up with Love
Beneath the Moon and the Stars

FOR YOUNG ADULTS
The Sentinel
The Prophecies
The Revenge

Summer
at
Buttercup
Beach

HOLLY MARTIN

sphere

SPHERE

First published in 2016 by Bookouture, an imprint of StoryFire Ltd.
This paperback edition published in 2017 by Sphere

1 3 5 7 9 10 8 6 4 2

ISBN 978-0-7515-7378-7

Printed and bound in Great Britain by
Clays Ltd, St Ives plc

Papers used by Sphere are from well-managed forests
and other responsible sources.

MIX
Paper from
responsible sources
FSC® C104740

Sphere
An imprint of
Little, Brown Book Group
Carmelite House
50 Victoria Embankment
London EC4Y 0DZ

An Hachette UK Company

www.hachette.co.uk
www.littlebrown.co.uk

To all the wonderful bloggers for your tweets, retweets, Facebook posts, tireless promotions, support, encouragement and endless enthusiasm. You guys are amazing and I couldn't do this journey without you.

Summer
at
Buttercup
Beach

CHAPTER 1

Freya Greene stared in wonder at the glorious sight of Rome Lancaster naked from the waist up. They were experiencing the first really hot day of the year with temperatures apparently hotter than Miami. Freya spent quite a bit of time working outside during the course of her job, and she loved it, but even she hadn't been looking forward to working outside in such sweltering conditions today. Now, however, she had changed her mind.

Freya and Rome had been working alongside each other all morning on the roof of a three-storey townhouse overlooking Buttercup Beach. They were replacing the old skylight with one of Rome's beautiful stained glass creations. They had chatted, laughed as they always did, and then suddenly Rome had wiped the sweat off his head and stripped off his t-shirt without any kind of warning. After almost two years of working alongside him, she had seen him topless before, but not as many times as she would like. And as winter had dragged on into a relatively cool spring, his wonderful body had been well and truly kept under wraps. Now it was out for her to enjoy.

He was so broad and muscular, but not from working out in a gym, just years of hard labour instead. His stomach was toned and showed the faint lines of a six-pack. His chest was smooth and hairless though there was a thin trail of dark hair leading from his belly button that disappeared into his shorts. His arms were so strong. Safe. With his dark, curly hair, soft grey eyes and dark stubble that covered his jaw, he was beautiful.

She felt a bit bad ogling her best friend like this, but if his fifty-six thousand followers on Instagram could enjoy his body then it didn't hurt to look for a few seconds surely.

Except it had been a good minute, maybe two, and to her horror she realised that Rome had noticed her staring.

Embarrassed, she took a step back, and toppled straight off the roof.

She plummeted head first down the side of the building and let out an ear-piercing scream, but she fell only a few feet before the safety harness she was wearing kicked in and she was jerked to a halt. Rome had made a big fuss about her wearing one and though at the time she hadn't thought it was necessary, right now she had never been so grateful for his overprotectiveness.

She swung like a pendulum for a few seconds, her heart racing in her chest as she tried to grab onto the scaffolding to pull herself back up, but it was just out of her reach and the swinging motion of her body made it even more difficult.

Rome was suddenly there, leaping onto the scaffolding from the roof, and as she swung back towards him he wrapped his arms round her back and dragged her up. She reached out to grab him too, wrapping her arms round him, which made it even more awkward for him, and as he pulled her to safety, he stumbled back himself and hit the platform with her lying on his chest, his arms tight around her.

For a few seconds, Freya felt only relief, her body roaring with adrenaline as she clung to him, but then she realised her cheek was resting on his warm bare chest; how fantastic he smelt, that gorgeous tang of the ocean, coupled with that wonderful clean sandalwood smell. For a brief moment, she closed her eyes and relished in the feel of lying on his chest, feeling his heart hammering against her cheek and how utterly right it felt to have his arms wrapped round her.

'Jesus Christ, you scared the crap out of me,' Rome said, shattering her moment of bliss. 'What the hell were you doing just staring into space? You should have been paying more attention.'

He slid his hand up her back to cup her neck and all words she had wanted to say to defend herself stalled in her throat. It was such an unconscious gesture, but for her it meant the world.

'It was just the heat,' Freya said, lamely, and then winced. She was not a girl who fainted in the heat and telling Rome that the hot weather had made her feel funny made her cringe.

'It is getting hot up here,' Rome admitted, begrudgingly. 'Maybe we should take a break for a little while. Get some lunch, come back to it this afternoon when it gets a bit cooler.'

'Sounds good,' Freya said, though she made no attempt to move and Rome didn't relinquish his hold on her either. She wondered, not for the first time, whether he was starting to have feelings for her too. There had been many such gestures over the last few months and more frequently over the last few weeks: little looks, comments, touches. She was so confused by it all. One minute she was convinced he had feelings for her and the very next it seemed those feelings weren't there at all, almost as if he had simply flicked a switch and turned them off. If only she had that luxury of turning off her inappropriate feelings for her best friend.

In an attempt to distract herself from how wonderful it felt to be lying on Rome's chest, she shifted her attention to the view. From up here she could see almost the whole of Hope Island, the tiny town with its cute little shops, cafés and windy lanes and almost all of the seven hundred and eighty nine houses. She smiled to herself at that little factoid Rome had told her and the fact that she had remembered it. Stretching out almost the entire length of the island was Buttercup Beach with its golden sands and crystal blue waters and beyond that, out in the sea were the shadows of the other Scilly Isles. Hope Island was the hilliest of all the islands and even though it was the most westerly, on a clear day you could even see the cliffs and hills of Land's End. She squinted at the horizon which was a smudge of purple haze and tried really hard not to focus on the feel of Rome's fingers at the back of her neck.

Eventually, when her heart had slowed and she had probably laid on him for a lot longer than was socially acceptable in these circumstances, Freya lifted her head to look at him.

'Thank you for saving me.'

'Well the harness did that, I just made a fumbled attempt to grab you and ended up falling on my arse. Let's go get something to eat.'

Freya nodded and carefully climbed off him and then stood up. He stood up too, towering over her.

'Are you OK? Are you hurt?' he asked, his hand on her shoulder, his touch searing against her skin.

'No, I'm fine. A little shaken but I'm OK.'

'A little shaken? I don't think my heart will stop pounding for several hours yet.' He leaned forward and detached her harness from the roof, reattaching it to the scaffolding so she could climb down. It was something she was perfectly capable of doing herself but she sensed he was in protective mode now and probably wouldn't even allow her back on the roof later that afternoon, or at least not unless she was attached to two or three safety ropes just in case.

He swung himself over the side of the scaffolding to the ladder, moved down a few steps and then waited for her, clearly wanting to make sure she could manage the ladder without hurtling to her death. She smiled at him, wanting to take care of her. Even though she hated to play the damsel in distress, there was something wonderful about him looking out for her like this.

She climbed onto the ladder with ease and, with him close behind her, they both made their way down the ladder.

Once down on the ground she turned to face him and saw his eyes were still shadowed with concern.

'See, I didn't die.'

'Not from lack of trying,' Rome grumbled, unhooking them both from the scaffolding.

She watched as he pulled his t-shirt back on and then wandered over to the van to put away their tools and lock it up. Not that anything would go missing parked in the private driveway of the house. It was very unlikely that anything would go missing if the van was left wide open in the middle of the town. Hope Island just wasn't that sort of place. There really was no crime on the island, beyond the occasional teenager getting a bit drunk and disorderly, the crime rate was almost non-existent. Everyone looked out for each other here. It was one of the things that Freya loved about the place.

Once the van was secured, Freya and Rome walked down the drive and headed towards the high street, through the tiny lanes, past the whitewashed cottages with blue shutters or houses painted in bright colours, the little shops that sold cute seaside paraphernalia and Rosa's where they'd end up two or three times a week for coffee, great food and wonderful chat with her friends.

'What were you thinking about up there?' Rome gestured back to the roof. 'You were standing there with this big smile on your face. You looked so happy there for a while, before you tried to kill yourself. I thought that whatever it was that had made you so happy, I wanted some of it too.'

But that was the problem. He *didn't* want it. Freya was in love with her best friend and it was that feeling that made her so happy. Sometimes it was hell, but a lot of the time, working with Rome, talking to him, spending time with him, was complete heaven. But despite what he'd just said, he didn't want that kind of happiness, he wasn't looking for love.

After his fiancée had died six years before, he had shut himself off from ever finding love again.

That didn't stop him dating though. There had been too many women to count over the years. And after his mini brush with fame the year before, the queue of women wanting a piece of him had got even longer. But not once had anything ever happened between Freya and him. Though if he wasn't attracted to her, why did she keep catching him staring at her in ways that went far beyond anything that could be classed as friendly?

She knew she wasn't a typical girly girl. She rarely wore a dress, preferring jeans and shirts. She lived in her Timberland boots. Her blonde hair was short, cut in an elfin style and streaked with blue, and she had a tiny nose piercing. If Rome's type was girly and feminine then she didn't stand a chance.

She realised he was still waiting for an answer. 'Just... excited to see the window when it's in. You've worked so hard on this one and I can't wait to see the owners' faces when they see it.'

He smiled, swinging his arm round her shoulders in a way that was more brotherly than anything else. 'I love how passionate you are about our company. You've always been my little cheerleader. The company wouldn't be anywhere near as successful if it wasn't for you.'

'You have no idea how crazy talented you are, the success is down to you, not me,' Freya protested.

'The work you've been doing over the last few months has been outstanding,' Rome insisted. 'I've been so impressed with how quickly you've picked it all up. You really do have a natural talent for this stuff. The success is ours; don't doubt yourself.'

'Does that mean you've forgiven me for posting that video on Twitter?'

He laughed and shook his head. 'I'm never forgiving you for that.'

When she'd started working for him, she'd wanted to increase his social media presence. He'd had no interest in it so she had taken care of it. Every day she would post a picture of one of his stained glass pieces or a work in progress on Instagram, Twitter or Facebook and after a while it started to have an impact. The tweets would get retweeted, the Facebook posts would be shared and they'd started to see a real increase in the number of enquiries and sales. And then, the year before, she had posted a mini video of Rome working on a piece. It had been a hot day and he'd been working topless but Freya had mainly wanted people to see a different side to the company, to see how a piece was made. She hadn't expected the reaction that it got. Within twenty-four hours, it had been retweeted over four thousand times. The comments hadn't been about the piece he had been working on or the beauty of the stained glass as was usually the case, they'd all been about him and most of them were really X-rated. Freya had been horrified and knew that Rome would be furious so she hadn't told him. But the sales over the next few days went through the roof and in the end she'd had to admit the truth.

He'd found it hard to believe that one fifteen-second video of him half naked would have such an impact on sales. So to prove it to him she took a photo of him, topless, holding one of his stained glass panels. The piece had sold within minutes of her posting it on Instagram and by the end of the day they had received orders for fifty more. In the next six months, profits for Through the Looking Glass had gone up by over a hundred percent.

Rome had become an mini internet sensation and, while he thought the whole thing was ridiculous and insisted that most of the time she stick to posting pictures of the pieces and not him, she had compromised that she'd post pictures or videos of him once a week under the hashtag, 'Feel Good Friday'. She had to give the fans what they wanted.

They walked into Pots and Paints, the little pottery painting café owned by Eden, Rome's sister and Freya's best friend. They seemed to end up there for lunch most days. Eden would quite often join them if she wasn't too busy but as the long summer school holidays had just started, she had been rushed off her feet the last few days.

Eden waved at them as they came in and then turned her attention back to some children as she showed them how to use the templates on the side of the mugs they were painting.

Rome walked behind the counter, served two people who were waiting for coffees and then turned his attention to Freya. 'What would you like to eat?'

She smiled at how easily he switched from working on a roof, to patiently teaching her how to work with stained glass, to serving behind the counter at his sister's café. Rome was solid, dependable and generous with his time and money. Some of the many things she loved about him.

'That salmon sandwich looks good.'

Rome nodded and slipped it onto a plate for her before grabbing a bacon and brie sandwich for himself and putting it into the sandwich toaster. He proceeded to make a strawberry milkshake for her and a mango smoothie for himself and then pulled out a twenty-pound note from his pocket and put it in the till, even though Freya knew that was way too much to cover the cost of the lunch, especially when Eden insisted on feeding them for free.

Eden joined him behind the counter. 'Did you just pay for that?'

'Of course not; I know you don't like me paying for my lunch.'

'You bought this place for me, that gives you free lunch and cakes for the rest of your life.'

'I know, which is why I always come in here. I'm not going to turn down free food. Is Clare still on holiday?'

Freya smiled at how quickly he had changed the subject.

'Yes, but she's back next week,' Eden sighed. 'Mum is going to help me for a few days, though I know she doesn't really have time.'

'Maybe Dougie can give you a hand,' Rome said, nonchalantly, though Freya knew there was nothing casual about that remark. Eden had fallen in love with Dougie, who had been her childhood best friend when they were teenagers. And then he'd emigrated to America with his parents. Despite being thousands of miles apart, they'd stayed in touch and he visited regularly and that love Eden had felt for him had never gone away. He was supposed to be moving back to the island in the next few months, something that Eden didn't know whether to be delighted or upset about. 'When does he get here?' Rome asked.

'The weekend.' Eden couldn't hide her grin at the prospect of him coming. 'But he won't have time to help me. He's only here for two weeks and he'll be out looking at houses every day. Anyway, I'm doing OK. How are you getting on at Oakwood House?'

'Fine, we'll be done today. That's if Freya doesn't kill herself first,' Rome said, pointedly. Clearly he wasn't going to let it go.

Freya rolled her eyes and took her sandwich and milkshake and went and sat down in the window while Rome served up his toastie and gave Eden a rundown of how Freya had thrown herself off the roof. He came and joined her a few minutes later.

He took a bite of his sandwich and glanced out the window at the little town square and the multi-coloured bunting that fluttered in the gentle sea breeze.

'So tomorrow is two years since you came to work for me,' Rome said and took another bite of his sandwich.

She watched him in surprise. She hadn't expected him to remember the date. She knew it was exactly two years. The date had been etched on her memory as it was the day she had been supposed to get married to Jake.

After finding her fiancé in the throes of passion with Lizzie, his best friend, two days before the wedding, Freya had fled the little village she had lived in with her fiancé and ended up going on her honeymoon alone, heading to the Scilly Isles where she had spent many weeks on childhood holidays.

On the day that was supposed to be her wedding day, she had headed over to Hope Island on a day trip, wondering what she was going to do with her life. She had no home to return to, no job as she had worked with her fiancé, no friends because all her friends were his friends and no idea what she was going to do next. All she did know was that she was never going to let herself get into that situation again, where her whole life had centred around the man she loved.

She had wandered into Rome's shop and been struck by the complete beauty of his stained glass panels, pictures, mirrors, lamps and boxes. She remembered the sun glinting off the coloured glass in a way that seemed ethereal and magical, as if she had stepped into a different land. She had also been struck with what a state the studio was in, mirrors stacked behind lamps, panels upside down, all the stock in some kind of higgledy-piggledy mess. Rome hadn't even noticed she was there, so intent on his work at the back of the shop that she had quietly wandered deeper between the shelves, admiring each piece.

Then he'd got up and left the studio, unwittingly locking her inside. When he came back several hours later, he'd found the shop had been completely reorganised, with definite sections for each of the products, which were now all displayed beautifully in the best places to catch the light. He had jokingly offered her a job and she had taken it, even though it wasn't really on offer. Unable to backtrack, Rome had offered her a few hours a week, which had quickly extended to a full-time job. She spent the night in the empty flat above the shop since she'd already missed the last ferry off the island and never left. She quickly fell in love with the beauty of the island, the friendliness of the islanders and just how peaceful the place was. Since then, not only had Rome become her boss, he had taught her everything he knew about stained glass. But more than that, he'd become her best friend. He had saved her in more ways than one.

'*I* knew it was two years, I just didn't expect you to remember our anniversary,' Freya teased.

'I first met you on the fourth anniversary of Paige's death. Sadly, I don't think I'll ever forget that date.'

Freya's smile fell from her face. 'Oh God, Rome, I'm so sorry. I never knew that date was so significant to you.'

He shook his head. 'Don't be sorry. It's fine. We were only together eighteen months, she passed away six years ago. I will always miss her and I think I will always carry a piece of her in here but I promise I'm not about to break down in tears because the anniversary of her death is tomorrow. I remember the day me and you met because Paige and I once had a jokey conversation about what we would do if the other died. Paige told me that she would expect me to grieve for her for a certain amount of time and then I had to move on, find someone else, fall in love again. I asked her how long would she expect me to grieve over her and she told me that as she was so brilliant and sexy and funny then four years should do it.'

Freya smiled. She'd never met Paige but, from what she'd heard, she'd been sweet, kind and had a brilliant sense of humour.

'That day you walked into my shop, I'd been down at the graveyard and I told her that even though it had been four years, I still wasn't over her. That nothing had changed, that it still hurt. Every day I'd wake up in our bed and I'd miss her. I'd go to work alone and sit in my studio and I couldn't seem to snap out of it. I… slept with far too many women in an attempt to move on but none of it made any difference. I told her something needed to change and I couldn't see what to do about it. Then I got back to my studio and my whole life changed. There you were, dusting my shelves, rearranging my shop and eating my sandwich.'

Freya laughed. 'I was hungry.'

'I didn't realise it at the time, but you were the change I needed. I looked forward to coming to work, the nights that you came round to my house for dinner made me feel alive again. You've turned my business around, made it a huge success, and I will forever be grateful that I locked you in my studio that day. You make me laugh so much and for four years I never laughed at all. You literally saved me.'

Freya swallowed the lump in her throat, not wanting to tell him that she felt the same way. Was this his way of finally telling her he had feelings for her too? She thought back to the way he had held her after she had fallen off the roof. She remembered when he had cancelled a date the week before so he could look after her when she was ill. In fact, the number of women he dated had been getting fewer and fewer lately; he seemingly preferred to spend time with her instead. Was he finally falling in love with her too? Freya had never imagined that he would feel the same way before but now… Was he trying to tell her he loved her?

'I think we should go out tomorrow to celebrate,' Rome said. 'I have a question I want to ask you and I'd like to do it over a nice meal and a bottle of wine. Will you join me at Envy tomorrow?'

Envy was her favourite restaurant on the island; the food was amazing, the atmosphere was cool, all black and silver and chic, and she always felt like she was at some exclusive restaurant in London every time she went there, instead of the furthest corner of the Scilly Isles.

'I'd love to,' Freya said, unable to keep the excited tremor from her voice.

He smiled. 'Good.'

CHAPTER 2

'So I hear you nearly died today?' Bella, Rome's youngest sister, said as she came back from the kitchen with bowls of ice cream for the three of them. She passed one each to Eden and Freya and sat back down on the sofa.

Freya laughed. 'I did not nearly die.'

She took a big spoonful and let the creamy flavour melt on her tongue.

'The way I heard it was that Rome saved your life,' Bella giggled.

Freya knew what the islanders were like. If there was any kind of gossip floating about, it had already been discussed, dissected, embellished and exaggerated by the time you heard about it. A twenty-inch fish that had been caught in the harbour in the morning had already tripled in size by the time the fishermen had left the pub that same night. It was something that Freya would never get used to. She loved it here on Hope Island and never wanted to leave, but the fact that everyone knew each other's business and felt they were entitled to an opinion on it was something that Freya was not entirely comfortable with.

They were sitting in Eden's tiny cottage having spent the evening chatting and eating pizza. She adored Bella and Eden and she loved how easily the Lancaster family had adopted her as their own. Rome had given her so much more than a job the day they'd first met, he had given her a home, friendship and a family.

'I also heard that Rome is taking you out for dinner tomorrow night,' Eden said, her eyes lighting up with happiness.

Freya choked on her ice cream. 'How on earth did you hear that?'

'Barbara Copperthwaite was sitting at the next table to you two at lunch and she heard him say he wanted to take you to Envy. She said it sounded very romantic.'

Freya sighed. Bella and Eden knew about her inappropriate crush on their brother. She didn't think they knew quite how deeply her feelings ran but she knew they would like nothing more than to see them together.

'It's not like that. Well honestly, I don't know what to think. He said the sweetest things to me over lunch, said how I had changed his life and how grateful he was for me and I got the sense he was talking about more than just work. And I got all excited and thought that perhaps he had feelings for me too, but then we spent the rest of the afternoon as normal, just chatting and laughing and he showed no signs at all of being head over heels in love with me.'

'He adores you,' Eden said. 'And you did change his life. He spent the four years after Paige died barely existing. He moved on autopilot. You changed all that.'

Bella nodded, swallowing a spoonful of ice cream. 'He doesn't have what he has with you with anyone else. He didn't even have that with Paige.'

'He didn't? It sounds like they were very much in love.'

'Maybe they were. But they didn't have that friendship as a base. They had passion and lust. Theirs was a whirlwind affair and I don't honestly know if it would have lasted. They met, fell in love, he proposed after one month,' Eden said.

'A *month*?' Freya was stunned. She knew that things had moved quickly for Rome and Paige but proposing after a month was crazy. But was it? She had fallen in love with Rome within the first few days of meeting him. Maybe for some people you just know. Rome clearly did.

'He was young and they had that crazy, can't keep their hands off each other kind of love,' Bella said.

'You mean like you and Isaac,' Freya teased.

Bella blushed and Freya laughed, knowing that Bella could hardly deny it. They had been together only for a few months but to say their relationship was passionate was an understatement.

'Yes, I guess they were like me and Isaac in the beginning. They had one month together where they saw each other every day, that wonderful honeymoon period where everything is perfect, and then she went off to work in London supposedly for one year but it ended up being a bit longer. So he proposed to her before she left. I think he was scared that she would go off to London and forget all about him. Credit to them both, they kept the relationship going. He'd go up there, she'd come back here on a regular basis. But whenever they'd meet up they would just spend the weekend having sex before returning back to their respective jobs and homes on Monday morning. This kept going for eighteen months before she sadly died in that terrible accident. They never had a proper relationship, never really had the time to get to know each other properly. Never became friends like you and Rome. What you two have is really special. You work with each other, you spend all your spare time together, maybe this could be the start of something more for you two. What better way to start a relationship than two years of being friends?'

Freya stared at her bowl, at the puddle of ice cream as it slowly melted. There was nothing she wanted more than for Rome to fall in love with her too. She had a great job, brilliant friends and lived in the most beautiful place in the world, but her life was missing love and it wasn't just love with anyone she wanted, it was Rome. He was the missing piece that didn't seem like it would ever be filled.

'But he has to want that too and I really don't think he is looking for love,' Freya said.

'I think he is,' Eden said, finishing off the last of her ice cream. 'A few months ago we were talking about love and relationships and he said that, although he preferred to only have casual relationships with women because then he could never get hurt, he said he missed the companionship and intimacy of being in a real relationship. You know what he listed as things that he wanted in a real relationship? Those long, stay-up-late-into-the-night conversations, laughing hard with someone, being with someone you know inside and out. You have all those things and my guess is he's starting to realise that.'

Freya's heart bloomed with hope. Was that really what tomorrow night was going to be about? Could it be the start of a beautiful relationship? She allowed herself to dream for a moment. She imagined him holding her hand and telling her he was in love with her, that he'd always been in love with her. And then they'd kiss. Their first kiss. Would that happen at the restaurant or would they wait until they went back to his place or hers? What would it be like to kiss Rome? Would it be hard and passionate or slow and gentle? Would the kiss lead to something more? The thought of making love to him filled her with so much joy and nerves and excited anticipation all at once. She could be making love to Rome Lancaster this time tomorrow night. OK, maybe that was moving a bit too quickly. If he wanted to date then he might want to take things slowly. But at least they might share a kiss.

Bella took her hand. 'I think Eden's right. This time last year he was going out with a different woman every week. These last few months I could probably count the women he has dated on one hand. And I think it's because no one fulfils what he is looking for like you do. No one makes him laugh like you do. He can't talk for hours with anyone like he does with you. You are everything he needs and wants. My heart says he is in love with you but he just doesn't realise it yet. So if he does ask you out tomorrow night, then take things slowly. He hasn't been in a proper relationship with someone for years and I don't honestly think you could call what he had with Paige a proper relationship either so… be patient with him.'

Freya nodded. She could do that. If he asked her out, she was happy to give him all the time in the world to get used to the idea of being in a relationship again. She would go as slow as he needed.

'You're staying in the same room as him at the Under the Sea carnival next week, aren't you?' Eden asked.

Freya nodded. The Under the Sea carnival happened every year in Penzance with a float to represent every town or village in Cornwall. This year's float from Hope Island had been decked out with dolphins and waves made entirely from her and Rome's glass work so they were going along to help oversee their float in the parade. They had both worked so hard to get the decorations for the float ready. Rome had given her free reign over how she wanted to design the dolphins and she had utilised all the skills he had taught her over the last few years to showcase what she could do. She was so proud of how it had turned out. The carnival was something she was really excited to be a part of.

'Maybe something might happen between you then,' Eden said, her eyebrows wiggling mischievously.

'It was the only room left, and it's a twin. Hardly romantic,' Freya protested, not wanting her heart to get too carried away. She had been looking forward to the Under the Sea carnival for weeks and going away together felt very romantic, even if it wasn't like that. She'd been looking forward to it even more since she'd found out she'd be sharing a room with him. Even though she'd repeatedly told herself it was just work and that they were just friends, it didn't seem to be sinking in.

'The fireworks after the carnival, the sea views from the hotel window, both of you walking around in your pyjamas, or the lack of them. It could be very romantic,' Eden said, dreamily.

'Take protection, just in case,' Bella said, practically. 'You don't want to get pregnant the first time you make love to him.'

Freya cursed the sudden wonderful image of her holding a tiny baby with black curly hair and grey eyes. Talk about not getting too carried away.

'I'm on the pill anyway, so no babies happening here,' Freya said as the image dissolved in her mind.

Just then there was a knock on the door and Bella shot up as if she'd been electrocuted.

'That will be Isaac,' Bella said excitedly, rushing to the door. She answered it and threw her arms around him as if it had been weeks since she had last seen him, not just a few hours. He kissed her briefly, wrapping his arms around her and hugging her tight.

'Hello, beautiful. Did you have a good night?' he said, quietly, staring down at Bella with complete adoration in his eyes.

Bella nodded. 'Always do with these two lovely ladies.'

Isaac tore his eyes away from Bella and smiled at Eden and Freya. 'Evening, ladies.'

Freya waved and Eden got up to give him a hug. Bella was already pulling her jacket on as she came over and gave Freya a kiss on the cheek. 'Let me know how it goes tomorrow.'

Freya nodded.

Bella hugged Eden and then she and Isaac left.

Eden came and sat down on the sofa next to Freya as they watched Isaac and Bella outside. Isaac said something to make Bella laugh and then he kissed her as if she was the air he needed to breathe.

Freya couldn't take her eyes off them. She had never seen two people so completely and utterly in love as Bella and Isaac.

When they parted, he placed a kiss on her forehead and then took her hand and led her off home.

'God, I want what they have,' Freya said.

Eden sighed next to her. 'Me too.'

CHAPTER 3

After running a circuit of the island, Rome paused for breath at the top of the hill. He stood with his hands on his hips as he looked down on Hope Island. The view was incredible from up here, he could see the whole island, from the tree-lined Mistletoe Cove to Blueberry Bay all the way over on the other side. Over in the western corner of the island, the white-domed roof of the observatory glinted in the darkness. The moonlit-covered sea stretched out in front of him and the lights of the town sparkled in the darkness.

He looked up at the endless starlit canopy. There was so little light pollution on the island that the stars seemed so much brighter here. He had studied books about astronomy when he was younger and he could identify most of the constellations in the sky. He could see Ursa Major and Minor, Cassiopeia, Hercules and Pegasus, Draco – which looked more like a serpent than a dragon – and several of the constellations that made up the zodiac signs. Although he held no stock in stars trillions of miles away having any kind of influence over someone's life, he still liked to pick them out. It was one of the things he'd once thought he could impress women with; if they were into horoscopes he thought he would point out the relevant star signs in the sky. Sadly women didn't really like geeks and when he started explaining about light years to them, he could see their eyes glazing over with boredom.

He focussed his attention back on the town. He loved to run at this time of night, when the rest of the island was tucked up in their homes for the night. There was barely a soul to be seen apart from a few stragglers coming out of the pub and going home. It was so quiet and peaceful and it allowed him time to think. He had been doing a lot of that lately, mostly about what he wanted from his life.

Things were going great right now. He had a job he loved and thanks to his best friend, Freya Greene, the company was a huge success. His family were happy, his little sister was in love, which was something he'd never thought would happen, and Eden's shop seemed to be busy and thriving. But his personal life was... was it fair to say it was lacking? That didn't seem right when he had a best friend who he thought the world of. He and Freya spent almost every spare second together and there was no one he enjoyed spending time with as much as he loved being with her. She made him laugh, they could talk for hours and never draw breath. He had gone out on barely any dates recently because he would much rather spend time with her. She made him really happy but he knew in his heart there was something missing from his life. He missed being in a proper relationship.

After Paige had died he hadn't wanted another relationship; had been too fearful to fall in love again because the pain of losing her had been too much to bear. He had guarded his heart and that had worked just fine for him. But recently he had been thinking that maybe it was time to move on from the past.

His sister Bella had been equally protective over her heart, although for completely different reasons. After her parents had abandoned her as a child and she was adopted and raised by his parents, her aunt and uncle, she had shied away from falling in love in case she was rejected all over again. But she had opened her heart to Isaac earlier that year, she had taken a risk and it had paid off; he had never seen her so deliriously happy in his whole life before. He wanted that too, that wonderful feeling of being in love again.

His thoughts turned to Freya again as they had many times over the last few months. If he was honest, he couldn't stop thinking about her. He wasn't sure how he would describe his feelings for Freya. He knew they were far from just being platonic, they never had been. But they were so different to how he'd felt for Paige. His time with Paige had been fuelled by sex, a passion that was fierce and urgent and demanding. It had been six years since she'd died and his memories of her were fading. They'd had a good laugh, they'd talked about the future in that vague way where neither of them really knew what the future would hold for them. They'd spoken about when they would get married but never about having children as if they both knew that was way too serious for what they had. That was telling in itself. Rome had always wanted children. But their conversations had never ventured into anything that could be considered deep. Looking back he wasn't sure if they'd ever really had anything more than amazing sex.

His feelings for Freya went way beyond that. He cared for her so deeply, just the thought of her made him smile, the fact that he wanted to spend all his time with her and missed her when they were apart spoke volumes. He craved her too. He wanted to kiss her, dreamed about making love to her and it scared him to death. If he was honest with himself, he'd always had these feelings for Freya but had never been willing to do anything about it. A fear of getting hurt again, a fear of ruining the beautiful friendship they shared had stopped him from taking it any further. He had denied his feelings to anyone who asked and for the longest time denied them to himself. He knew he had to talk to her about it but he had been putting it off for some time. Maybe it was time to take a risk. Though if he did take that risk, what if she didn't feel the same way? He had no idea what women were thinking and, while there had been many looks or comments from Freya over the last few years that suggested she had feelings for him too, he couldn't be sure he wasn't just projecting what he wanted to see.

Down in the town, he spotted Bella's distinctive red hair as she walked alongside Isaac back towards his house overlooking Blueberry Bay. He knew that the girls had spent the evening together and if Bella had left it probably meant the evening had come to an end, and Freya would be leaving Eden's soon too. His heart leapt that he might see her again and he shook his head. He was behaving like a schoolboy with a silly crush.

He scanned the houses until he found Eden's cottage with her distinctive pink front door and, sure enough, the door opened and he saw the glow of gold as Freya's hair caught in the moonlight. She hugged Eden goodbye and stepped out onto the street.

He ran down the hill and headed towards the high street where he knew Freya would be heading too as she made her way home. Once he was down in the town, he lost sight of her and, as he moved into the high street, he wasn't sure if he was now ahead of her or behind. He cast around the deserted street and then saw her staring through one of the shop windows. As he moved closer, he realised it was the jewellery shop and she was staring at the engagement and wedding rings.

Freya was probably the least romantic out of the three girls and he didn't take her for someone who had fairy tale dreams of love and romance. But of course she would want a happy ending with someone too. He suddenly remembered that tomorrow would have been her second anniversary of marrying Jake and maybe she was thinking about that. How different would her life have been if she hadn't walked in on her fiancé cheating on her a few days before her wedding? Would they have stayed together, would they have been happy?

He swallowed the sudden lump of emotion in his throat. How different would *his* life have been if he hadn't met her?

Would he still have been grieving over Paige? Even if he had managed to snap out of his period of mourning, his life would have been empty without Freya. The thought of not having her in his life made him feel sick. She had given him so much. He had simply existed before, but now he felt alive. She brought so much energy to his life that he knew he would miss her if she was gone.

She suddenly caught sight of him in the reflection of the window and turned round to face him, a huge smile filling her face.

'Hey,' he said, moving closer.

'Hey.'

He gestured to the window. 'Choosing your engagement ring?'

Freya laughed, completely unabashed. 'A girl can dream.'

'Would you really get married after what happened with Jake?'

'Of course. Just because the last guy was a complete tit, doesn't mean the next one will be. I would never be scared of falling in love again. Real love is too precious and wonderful to hide away from.'

He looked at her. She had as much right to be fearful of love as he did. Love could hurt you in so many different ways. Rejection, unrequited love, affairs, death. Being in love was so fraught with possible problems but his best friend didn't see it that way. She was braver than he was.

He stepped closer to the window and peered in. 'Which would you choose if you were to get engaged again?'

'Traditionally, it's the man who would do the choosing. Which one would you choose for me?' Freya challenged.

He chuckled as he looked down at her. Her warm caramel brown eyes were like whisky; flecked with gold they sparkled in the streetlights. With her white-blonde hair, streaked with blue, she was uniquely beautiful.

Realising he was staring, he glanced back into the window at all the diamonds. They glittered and twinkled in the light from the street, but there was nothing special about these rings.

'None of these.'

'Really?'

'They're not unique enough.'

He moved to her other side to look at the antique rings, emeralds, sapphires, rubies, but there was nothing that grabbed his attention. Getting the right engagement ring was a lot harder than he thought.

But then he saw it. At the very bottom of the display, resting in the palm of a plaster-cast hand, was an opal ring. The shoulders of the ring were encrusted with diamonds, but the gold-looking opal was a startling array of colours. He squatted down to get a closer look at it, watching the facets of colour change as he moved. The ring looked like it was on fire as it glowed gold in the streetlights.

'This one.'

He stood up and looked at Freya.

'I love opals. They're so unique and beautiful,' Freya said, softly, looking up at him, and he sensed something had shifted between them.

'They're quite rare, especially ones this colour,' Rome said.

Freya looked back at the ring. 'I love it.'

'Although if I'm honest, I think I would make you an engagement ring from fused glass. I would choose the perfect colours and tones and make something that no one else in the world had, something that celebrates how exceptional and special you really are.'

She stared up at him, her eyes wide with surprise.

'But it depends whether you're a girl that prefers the expense of rubies and diamonds or someone who would appreciate that, although the ring is only made from glass, it's something that was made specifically with you in mind.'

Freya swallowed. 'If it was the right man, it wouldn't matter if it was a cheap plastic ring from the inside of a cracker, because marrying him would be the only thing that mattered. I love the idea of having a ring made just for me.'

Rome suddenly realised how close they were standing. He took a step back. What was he doing? Choosing engagement rings with his best friend? They'd never even kissed and suddenly they had taken a big leap. It felt intimate and terrifying all at once.

'Let me walk you home.'

'Don't be silly, it's completely the opposite direction from your house.'

Rome shrugged. 'It's not far. And you never know what unsavoury characters are hanging around at this time of night.'

Freya laughed, knowing as well as he did that unsavoury characters on Hope Island were as unlikely as aliens coming down and kidnapping her. 'I know. There I was looking at rings and then I see this creepy guy staring at me.'

Rome laughed as she fell in at his side and started walking back towards her flat.

'He was breathing heavily, obviously some right pervert.'

Rome nudged her and she nudged him right back.

They fell into an easy silence and as her hand briefly brushed against his, he had an overwhelming urge to suddenly slide his fingers through hers and hold her hand.

'Did you have a good night with Eden and Bella?' he asked, trying to distract himself from how close their fingers were. He couldn't decide whether he was walking really close to her or if she was walking really close to him. They seemed to gravitate towards each other.

'Yes, I love your sisters.'

'They love you,' Rome said, honestly. 'All my family do.'

'What did you do with your night?' Freya asked.

'Reading, went for a run.'

She looked up at him, a smirk on her lips. 'No hot date?'

Rome shrugged. 'It feels like a waste of my time.'

'Why?'

'Because I want something more than just sex.'

'You never give these girls a chance – you go out once, twice if they're lucky, and you never see them again. Some of them could be something more if you'd let them.'

He shook his head. 'I'm looking for someone special.'

'What is it that you're looking for?'

'Someone who can make me laugh, someone I can talk to and who I enjoy spending time with.'

She went quiet next to him and he realised he had pretty much described what he had with her. Had she recognised that too? He looked up to see that they were approaching the front door that led up to her flat above the shop.

She put the key in the lock and then stepped inside, turning back to face him.

'I'm very much looking forward to our dinner tomorrow night.'

He smiled. 'I am too. Don't be late for work tomorrow. I know what that commute is like.'

'Yes, those thirteen stairs are a killer.'

He grinned. 'Goodnight, Freya.'

'Goodnight.'

He waited for her to close the door and then he turned back towards his own house. What was he doing?

CHAPTER 4

Rome was dreaming. He knew he was dreaming because he'd had this dream many times before. It varied slightly over the years but the basic crux of it was the same. However, knowing it was a dream didn't stop the events from unfolding and it didn't stop the heart-pounding, stomach-wrenching fear he felt every single time it happened.

He was standing in the main high street talking to Freya, the sun was shining, he could hear children laughing and playing, when suddenly he knew he was being watched. And, like in all good horror films, when he turned his head to see, there was a hooded cloaked figure. Death. The grim reaper had come to claim him.

Rome started to run, dragging Freya along with him in a desperate attempt to get away, but every time he looked over his shoulder, Death was getting closer and closer, seemingly with very little effort at all.

'Run,' he urged, panic gripping him, but Freya didn't seem to see the urgency, she didn't seem to see Death either. He kept on running but Death was closing on him with every step.

Death reached out to grab Rome's arm and he quickly pushed Freya behind him out of harm's reach. He tried to fight Death off but his grip was unrelenting as he dragged Rome away from Freya, dragged him away from his home and everything he loved so dearly. He fought as hard as he could but it was no use. In a last desperate bid to stop him, Rome pushed back the hood of the figure and, with sickening dread, stared into the dead eyes and mutilated body of Paige.

He woke with a jerk in the darkness and quickly leaned over and slammed on the bedside lamp.

He was alone in his bedroom and he lay back on his pillow and stared at the ceiling as he tried to slow his breathing back to normal.

His childhood had been plagued by these dreams. His gran had died when he was eight and he'd gone to her funeral, which had been open casket. He'd not been allowed in to see the body, instead waiting outside while everyone had gone in to pay their respects before the main service. But that hadn't stopped him sneaking in while they all filed into the other room ready for the service. He'd stared at the dead body, finding it hard to fathom that his gran, who had been so full of life and spirit, was nothing more than this empty shell.

After the funeral, he'd had a weird fascination with death and did a lot of research on it, how different cultures celebrated the lives or mourned the loss. But the one thing that had stuck with him had been the figure of the grim reaper who came to collect the souls of the living.

For years after he would have nightmares of the grim reaper coming to take him away. He'd eventually grown out of it in his early teens. But after Paige had died, the dreams had returned. Same dreams but this time they always ended with Paige being the grim reaper that had come to take him away. In the dreams she was nothing more than this zombified corpse, horribly disfigured after the rollercoaster accident. He'd had them a lot after the accident – they had become less and less frequent over the years, but he still had them occasionally. Sometimes in the dreams, Paige came to take Eden or Bella or his parents away and Rome would try to hold onto them as Paige dragged them kicking and screaming away from him. There was nothing he could do to stop Paige from taking them.

He rubbed his face and sat up. There was no way he was going to get back to sleep now and he didn't want to if the zombified face of his ex was waiting for him.

Poor Paige. She deserved better than to be remembered as a mutilated zombie. She had been beautiful and so sweet and kind.

He got out of bed, washed his face, got dressed and slipped out onto the moonlit hillside. The island lay in darkness, only the twinkling streetlights showing any sign of life at all. He walked down his small road and then cut down the steps onto Buttercup Beach. The inky water lapped gently on the sand and out on the horizon there was a thin glow of pink as the sun prepared to make its appearance.

He walked along the shoreline and as his eyes became accustomed to the dark he could pick out the bright pinpricks above him, which he knew were planets.

He walked the length of Buttercup Beach and sat down to watch the sun rise. Right on cue, a thin sliver of gold lit up the horizon and then slowly spread out across the sea and the clouds as it chased the nightmares away. It was going to be another glorious day.

His thoughts turned to Freya as they constantly did. She always filled his thoughts; before he went to sleep, when he woke up, she was always there.

He wanted to see her now, partly because just being with her made him feel so much better, but mostly because he wanted to check she was OK, which was completely irrational. It was a dream and he had been the one to get taken away by the grim reaper, not Freya.

He glanced over towards the row of houses that was the start of the high street and looked up to where he knew her flat was.

To his surprise, he could see her light was on. Her window was so easy to spot as it was one he had made himself. Although it was mostly clear glass so it didn't hinder the view, there were blue waves and a dolphin jumping out of the water at the bottom.

He scrambled up and walked up the steps to the high street and followed the little lane up to the door of her flat. He let himself in using his key and walked up the stairs. A feeling of contentment washed over him as soon as he stepped inside her flat – as if he was home, even though he'd never lived there. She was in the kitchen, singing to herself, and as he closed the door behind him, she poked her head out to see who it was. Her face erupted into a huge grin when she saw him. No questions or comments, no look of surprise at having him turn up in her home at six in the morning. He knew it wasn't the first time but he wondered at what point it had become the norm for her.

'I'm just making a hot chocolate, do you want one?'

'Yes please.'

'I have white chocolate or crème brûlée?'

He smiled. No ordinary hot chocolate for Freya Greene. 'White chocolate would be great.'

She disappeared back into the kitchen and Rome followed her in. She was dressed only in a midnight-blue satin robe which finished several inches above her knee, revealing golden bare legs that he had a sudden desire to stroke. His mind was suddenly filled with the possibilities of what she was wearing under that robe.

She turned to face him and his eyes snapped back up to her face.

'How come you're up this early?' Rome asked.

She shrugged. 'I couldn't sleep, thought I'd get up and watch the sun rise.'

'Me too. I love it down on the beach at this time of the day, it's so peaceful and quiet. I had weird dreams and I needed to blow them away in the early morning sea breeze.'

'Yeah, I had weird dreams too.' She handed him his hot chocolate and wandered out into the lounge. She sat down on the sofa and he sat down next to her. 'What was yours about?'

Rome hesitated. There was no way he wanted Freya to know that he was having weird freaky dreams about the grim reaper taking him away or his dead ex, zombified and horribly disfigured. She would get up and run a million miles away from him. He gave an answer which he hoped was appropriate.

'Paige.'

'Oh.' Freya was silent for a while. 'You must miss her terribly.'

He thought about this because he really didn't. Not any more. And what kind of horrible person did that make him? It had been six years but he knew people who had lost loved ones many years before Paige had died and they still missed them. He hadn't known Paige for long, only just over eighteen months, but he had loved her. Well, at the time he thought he had, now he wasn't so sure. He felt guilty about that. And he felt guilty that in his heart he knew he was ready to move on. He decided not to answer Freya's question for fear of losing any kind of respect in Freya's eyes.

'What was your dream about?' he asked.

'Oh… nothing really. You were there. Some other people,' Freya said, vaguely, and he got the sense she wasn't happy talking about her dreams either.

They both took sips from their drinks and lapsed into an easy, contented silence. Rome put his drink down on the table for a moment as he got more comfortable on the sofa and noticed the book on the table. It was his. He always carried a book around with him even though he never got much chance to read at work. He loved non-fiction books, most of them were encyclopaedic in content, facts about sea creatures, animals, history of technology, space, weird cultures or traditions of the world. He loved learning little interesting facts about the world he lived in. His head was filled with completely worthless facts that weren't at all useful to know but, on the rare occasion that he took part in the pub quizzes on the island, his team were almost always guaranteed to win.

He picked up the book, *The Book of Love*. 'Are you reading this?'

Freya blushed a little. 'It looked like it might be an interesting read. I'm more surprised that you're reading it. You don't strike me as a hearts and rainbows kind of person.'

He laughed. 'This is not really a cutesy sparkles and puppies kind of book. This has loads of interesting facts about old wedding traditions and how different cultures around the world celebrate love. It's very interesting.'

Freya turned to face him and curled her legs underneath her. 'Tell me some of the interesting facts you've found out about love.'

'Well in Finland, they have these wife-carrying championships, where the men will carry their wives or girlfriends over their shoulders while they have to complete an array of different challenges and obstacles. The champion wins their wife's weight in beer.'

'I love that. Carrying a really skinny wife means you'd get a lot less beer.'

'That's true, so not always a benefit. In Denmark they give snowdrops to their beloved instead of red roses.'

'That's so cool. I wonder why our culture chose roses instead.'

'I'm sure I'll find that out in the book. There's so many facts in there.'

'What else?' Freya said, keenly, and he loved that she seemed to enjoy listening to these facts as much as he enjoyed finding them out.

'Wales celebrate Valentine's Day but they also celebrate St Dwynwen's Day on January twenty-fifth. I'm sure I'm pronouncing her name wrong. She is the patron saint of lovers and traditionally men would give the women they love a spoon.'

Freya laughed. 'How romantic.'

'They were wooden hand-carved spoons, not just some old teaspoon.'

'Oh that's actually quite sweet.'

'Yes, the Welsh have quite a few sweet traditions. The Chinese though, not so much. An engaged couple will dissect a chicken's liver and, if it's healthy, then it's a good omen and they can set the date of their wedding.'

'Ewww, nothing says love like a dissected chicken's liver.'

'I know. As I said, this book is not exactly cute.'

'I love it, it's so funny. And I love listening to you talk about these things, you get so passionate about your facts.'

He shrugged. 'I'm a geek, I own that.'

'And I love your geekery.'

He smiled with fondness for her. She never seemed to find him boring and he loved that about her.

She finished her drink and put it down on the table and stood up. 'Well, I might try to go back to sleep for an hour or so, before I have to get up for work.'

Rome nodded. 'I'll probably go back home and try to do the same.' He didn't relish that thought. Here with Freya, he felt happy and content.

'You can stay here if you want, rather than going all the way back home.'

Christ, what an invite. He scrambled to his feet quickly before she changed her mind.

'Are you sure?' he asked, softly, and for the briefest of seconds he saw confusion cross her face.

She nodded and walked into the bedroom and he followed her. God, he was suddenly nervous and he didn't know why. They were just two friends who were going to share a bed together. But their friendship had never really been one that was particularly tactile. They didn't really hug like she did with Eden and Bella and they'd certainly not done this before. She disappeared inside her walk-in wardrobe and he took off his shoes, jeans and t-shirt and got into bed.

She popped her head around the door holding what looked like a pillow. 'Do you want—' She stared at him sitting in her bed, her eyes wide for a second, before she seemingly threw the pillow back into the cupboard and hurried across the room so fast she nearly skidded into the wall. She ditched her robe, revealing tiny shorts and a little vest, and climbed into bed next to him and turned off the bedside light.

He lay there in the muted darkness as the pink glow of the early sunrise lit up the room. He frowned with confusion.

'You meant stay on the sofa, didn't you?' Rome said and Freya burst out laughing into uncontrollable giggles.

'Yes I did.'

'Crap. I'm so sorry, I'll go and sleep on the sofa.'

He made a move to get out of bed before Freya suddenly leaned across him, pinning him to the mattress with her weight. 'Stay where you are. We're friends, we can sleep in the same bed as each other without it being awkward.'

'I think we're already past that. I just got undressed and got into your bed.'

Freya giggled again. 'It's fine, go to sleep.'

She was still holding him down and he was suddenly hyper-aware of her warm, beautiful body over his, her leg hooked over his thigh, her hand on his bare chest. If she moved her leg a few more inches higher, she was going to know how turned on he was and this was suddenly going to get a hell of a lot more awkward.

And now he was staying, surely she should let him go and move back onto her side of the bed, but she was showing no sign of moving.

There was no way in hell he was getting back to sleep now. He was so wired he was probably never getting back to sleep ever again. He didn't think Freya was going to sleep any time soon either; her heart was hammering against her chest.

God, this was heaven and hell all at the same time.

If he was any other man, he would have rolled on top of her and, if she was willing, just started making love to her. He wanted that more than anything but this was Freya, his best friend. There was no way he was going to do anything to ruin that.

Though his body didn't seem to agree. Quite without his permission, his hand snaked up to hold her back, his fingers caressing across her bare flesh, just above the top of her vest. That wasn't safe. He slid his hand up further to cup the back of her neck, stroking her hair, echoing how he had held her after her fall off the roof.

'And you're sure this isn't awkward?'

'Not one bit.' Her voice was high with tension. 'Go to sleep.'

He closed his eyes and tried to think of anything other than the woman in his arms, though that still wasn't going to help him go to sleep.

❦

Freya woke a few hours later with the sun streaming through the window, her face resting on Rome Lancaster's bare chest, his arms wrapped around her. She smiled; this was where she belonged.

She lifted her head slightly to look at him and saw he was fast asleep. He looked so beautiful and peaceful as he lay there sleeping, not plagued by the dreams that haunted him. Last night had not been the first time he had turned up at her flat in the early hours of the morning, as if somehow he felt safer being around her. She knew that he had bad dreams about Paige although he'd never gone into the specifics of it. To lose his fiancée in such awful circumstances must have been very traumatic for him, but sadly the nightmares were a sign that he probably wasn't over her yet and maybe never would be.

She remembered her own dreams that had woken her up before Rome's arrival and she couldn't help but smile. She had dreamed about her wedding day to Rome too many times to count. It was silly, she knew that. The little looks and touches he had given her over the last few weeks and months indicated that perhaps he had some feelings for her but nothing to suggest that he was ready to get married to her or that he ever would be. But that hadn't stopped her dreams from acting out that wonderful scenario, from the simple beach wedding surrounded by only a handful of family and friends, the pretty beach dress she would wear, and the way that Rome would look at her with absolute love in his eyes when she stepped up by his side. She knew it was crazy but she couldn't simply turn those feelings off just because they were inappropriate.

She suddenly realised her cheek was wet and she looked down and realised there was a small patch of drool on Rome's chest. Her heart leapt with horror. She never drooled in her sleep, why had her body decided that now was an opportune moment to start? She quickly tried to wipe it off with her fingers, realising, as she was doing it, that what she was actually doing was stroking his chest.

His eyelashes fluttered as his sleeping body registered what she was doing and unconsciously he shifted her tighter against him. And that's when she realised where his hands was. One arm was tight around her back, the other hand was cupping her bum cheek. His hand wasn't even over the top of her shorts, it had somehow slipped beneath the material and was holding onto her bare bum as if his life depended on it.

Freya suppressed a giggle, her body shuddering slightly as she tried to hold it in. Rome was the least likely person in the world to surreptitiously try to grab her arse. Where other men might pretend to be asleep in this situation while they 'accidentally' had a little squeeze, she knew Rome would never do that. He had been embarrassed enough a few hours before when he had misunderstood her offer to stay. He had been so awkward and mortified by it, she just wanted to hug him, which was how she'd ended up in this position in the first place.

She didn't want Rome to wake up and be embarrassed, not least because it would reduce the chance of them ever sharing a bed again. She decided to get up and out of bed before he woke up fully and realised where his hand was.

She tried to extricate herself from his arms but he groaned softly and held her tighter.

'Don't go,' he whispered, still clearly asleep.

He was probably dreaming about Paige and her heart ached for him and hurt for herself in equal measure. Would he always love his ex? Would he ever be able to get over her?

The worst thing was, she'd been here before. There had been three people in her relationship with Jake, her ex-fiancé. Lizzie was Jake's best friend, ex-girlfriend, neighbour and the first person he had ever been in love with. Lizzie had been round their house every day and they were always very close. When Freya had questioned their relationship, Jake had insisted they were just friends, that he had got over her many years before and he simply wasn't interested in Lizzie like that any more. Freya had believed it and even though she often felt like the third wheel in her own relationship as Jake and Lizzie shared all these little in-jokes and history, she had trusted him. Right up until she had walked in on them in bed together. She had been with Jake for eight years and in that time he had never gotten over his ex. He had never loved her as much as he loved Lizzie.

That day she had caught them was imprinted on her mind, walking in on him, clearly having way more fun than she'd seen him have before, moaning and shouting and the words she'd never forget.

'It's never this good with Freya,' Jake had said.

Lizzie had laughed. 'You have *nice* sex with Freya.'

'Yes it's *nice*. Sex with you is always incredible.'

That had hurt. Eight years and Jake had thought the sex was just nice. It had never been incredible for him. It had never been incredible for her either but as he had been her only boyfriend she had nothing else to compare it to. Sex always seemed to be over way too quickly and left her feeling mostly unsatisfied. But clearly the problem had been with her, not him, as Lizzie had been having a whale of a time.

There'd been no one for Freya since. Even the lovely Roberto she'd met on her holiday in Italy, who had been sexy, charming and attentive, hadn't tempted her out of her dry patch. They'd flirted and chatted but one kiss had told her enough. And though she had made it seem more than it was when she'd got home in an attempt to provoke a reaction out of Rome, it had never gone further than that one kiss. She knew why she'd never taken it any further: she had fallen in love with Rome and Roberto simply wasn't him. Also, there was a small part of her that didn't want anyone else to be disappointed by sleeping with her the way Jake had been. But was she a fool waiting around for Rome, hoping that one day he would get over his ex and fall in love with her instead? She had never been enough for Jake, why would she be enough for Rome? And if he was still dreaming about Paige it didn't look like he would be ready to move on any time soon.

Suddenly she experienced a moment of doubt and fear. With Jake she had allowed herself to wrap her whole life around his, living in his house, socialising with his friends, working for him, and though she had vowed she would never let it happen again, she had done the same thing with Rome. How had she found herself in this position again? Her job with Rome was only ever meant to be a temporary thing but then she had fallen in love with him, the island, his family, and she'd never wanted to leave. She never realised before that she was making the same mistake twice. If she gave up on Rome now, she would lose everything all over again.

She sighed and tried to move again as Rome's eyes fluttered open. He blinked in confusion for a second and then when he saw her his face erupted into a huge grin.

'It's been a long time since I've woken up with a beautiful woman in my arms.'

Her heart soared at that wonderfully innocent comment.

'God, I slept so well,' Rome said.

'I slept really well too,' Freya said. Clearly too well if she had been drooling on him in her sleep.

'We'll have to make this a regular thing,' he joked and she resisted saying that she would love to.

He stretched beneath her then suddenly stilled, his face frozen in horror as he clearly realised where his hand was.

She bit her lip as she tried to suppress her smile, wondering how he was going to play this one. To her surprise, he still didn't remove his hand, clearly wondering if she had noticed.

'What time is it?'

Freya smirked. She wasn't wearing a watch so she'd have to sit up to see the time on the clock across the room. She obliged and as she moved he ever so casually let his hand slip out from her shorts.

She snorted and then turned the snort into a cough. 'It's just coming up for nine.'

'Well, we have a ton of work to do today so we better get going,' Rome said and she turned back to look at him, still trying to hide her laughter. 'You knew it was there, didn't you?'

'Yes, you pervert,' she teased.

His cheeks flushed red. 'I'm so sorry. I don't know how that happened.'

'I do.' She stretched and then got out of bed. 'You clearly couldn't keep your hands off me, Rome Lancaster.'

He laughed and rolled on his side, the sheet just above his waist. There was no finer sight than Rome Lancaster lying half naked in her bed. 'Well fair's fair, next time you can grab my arse instead.'

She laughed. 'In that case, I'll look forward to it.'

CHAPTER 5

Freya was sketching out a new design for a mirror while she waited for the phone to ring for the scheduled interview, later that morning. Working for Rome had unleashed this creative side to her that she never knew she had and she absolutely loved it. This job had been made for her and she couldn't ever see a time when she would get bored of it or not want to work with glass anymore. She had started off drawing out designs for him to make but, after months of training, she had recently been making her own. It was a wonderful feeling to see a project through from the very beginning when she was sketching an idea, to choosing the right glass and the right effect and then going on to cutting the glass and making the finished piece. Rome displayed all of her pieces in the shop to buy alongside his own and it made her feel very proud of her achievements.

She glanced over at Rome who was busily cutting out all the glass pieces he needed for a large glass mural that had been commissioned for the local school that sat right on Buttercup Beach. This was a massive project that incorporated all of their skills, from fused glass, to stained glass copper foiling, and even some mosaicking. She was so excited about working on this project and she needed this woman to hurry up and call so she could get back to helping him.

The school had been so enthusiastic about Rome creating a piece for them, but they were super strict on the fact that it had to be ready and fitted for the new school year at the beginning of September when the new building was going to be opened. It was going to be part of the grand opening ceremony with a barbeque on the beach and there was to be a big unveiling with the island's mayor. It was a big deal for Rome to get such an important commission but it was going to take many, many hours to make and, although there were still six weeks until the start of term, she knew Rome was worried about getting it finished on time, especially with some of the other commissions that were coming in.

Freya was worried too but for completely different reasons. This mural was going to be on show to the whole island and any tourists that came to visit as it would be facing out onto Buttercup Beach. It would be there for many years to come and her contribution was a huge part of it. She felt enormously proud to have her work showcased like that in a community that had taken her in and she wanted to do everything she could to make Rome and Hope Island proud too.

Thankfully all the work for the Under the Sea carnival had been finished the week before. It had been carefully packed away into a wooden crate and shipped over to Penzance and, though they were going to Penzance the following week to help set up the float that would represent Hope Island, they would only be gone for two days and then they could really focus on the school mural.

Rome had insisted that she would be in charge of designing the sea parts of the mural and she had spent several days experimenting with fused glass and dichroic glass to get the metallic, sparkly look she wanted for the waves just right. She couldn't wait to get started on that part.

She checked her watch again. Petal, a journalist from a local magazine, was already fifteen minutes late for the interview. Freya got up to go and help Rome while she was waiting but the phone rang before she got anywhere near him. She sighed and went back to answer it.

Petal greeted Freya with a happiness and enthusiasm that was clearly fake and started explaining the article she was writing, which Freya already knew about since it had been discussed via email. Petal clearly fancied her magazine as Cornwall's own answer to *Heat* magazine, though in reality it was a million miles from that. Her finger was so on the pulse that she had only just discovered Rome nearly a year after his mini brush with fame. Petal was doing an article on Cornwall's top ten sexiest men and wanted to feature Rome. Freya knew that Rome had no interest in taking part in such an article even though he was aware of it. He hated doing interviews. While he could talk for hours about stained glass and the process of how he made his pieces, when it came to questions about himself he would often resort to monosyllabic answers. So it was down to her to answer all the questions for the magazine on his behalf. She'd done this several times before, so she knew lots of the answers off by heart.

'Tell me about how he got into working with stained glass?' Petal said.

'Rome was a glazier, he just fitted normal windows in houses across the Scilly Isles and Cornwall but he'd get quite a lot of requests for stained glass panels or picture windows. Coming from an art and design background, it was something he was really interested in doing. He did a few courses in it and started producing his own and it was something he loved.'

'I understand he didn't start Through the Looking Glass, his stained glass business, until after his wife died.'

Freya's heart sank. She hated these journalists who wanted to pry into every part of Rome's life. Talking about Paige seemed so private. Rome didn't mind but Freya did on his behalf.

'His fiancée,' Freya corrected.

'Oh that's right, they weren't even married,' Petal said, dismissively. 'What was the motivation for changing his career *after* she had died?'

Freya cringed, knowing that Rome was probably listening to every word she said. She had no idea why Rome had felt the need to change careers after Paige had died and she wasn't about to ask him either.

'Life is short,' Freya answered vaguely. 'The plans we have may never happen if we wait until tomorrow. So it's best to make them happen today.'

'So, nothing to do with the huge sum of money Rome got from Phantom Rides when they settled out of court for wrongful death?'

Freya sat up straight. 'We are not talking about that.'

Rome looked round, frowning at her tone.

'Oh honey, don't be silly. Of course we are. As a hot, young bachelor, our readers will be very interested to know that Rome Lancaster is filthy rich with it. I heard it was a seven-figure sum. That's quite a large sum considering they weren't even married.'

'This was the woman he loved,' Freya protested.

'And how do you put a price on a life?'

Freya had no words.

'Though I heard her body was so mangled, they had to use dental records to identify her. I guess they paid the big money because of that.'

She sat down heavily on the stool behind her, watching Rome looking at her with concern. She knew that Paige had died in a horrible rollercoaster accident but she didn't know all the details. She also knew that Phantom Rides had admitted full responsibility and paid out millions of pounds in damages to all concerned within weeks of the accident.

'Yes, her whole body was completely crushed. Well, I suppose that might be worth a seven-figure sum.'

Tears immediately filled Freya's eyes. How awful for Rome. No wonder the grief had hit him so badly that he'd never wanted to move on from it.

'Bet that has messed him up spectacularly,' Petal went on. 'Still, our readers will love him even more for that. A widower. Damaged, rich and looking for love. What could be better?'

This was disgusting and Freya suddenly wanted no part of it.

'He's not single,' Freya snapped. 'He's engaged again.'

Rome's eyebrows shot up in surprise.

'Well that's interesting too. Not quite as interesting as the broken widower angle, but still interesting nonetheless. Who's the gold digger?'

'Listen here, you disgusting, vile woman. He has been through hell and you have no right to judge him or to try to exploit this for your gains. We don't want to be part of this article any more. You can find someone else,' Freya said.

'Oh, it's you,' Petal laughed. 'You're the gold digger.'

Freya slammed the phone down.

Rome was immediately there in front of her, his hands on her shoulders. 'Hey, what's wrong? I know these journalists can be a pain in the arse, but I've never seen you react like this before.'

She quickly dashed the tears from her eyes. 'Nothing, they're just arseholes.'

'Tell me what's upset you so badly.'

'God, she was so horrible. They just wanted to talk about Paige and the money that you got. And then she was talking about the accident and how awful it was and how the readers would love to read about it, as if this was some soap opera and not your life.'

Rome's face softened with realisation. 'Don't cry for me honey, that's the last thing I want.'

Tears filled her eyes again. 'I had no idea it was so horrible.'

Rome cupped her face in his strong hands and gently wiped the tears away, his touch making her breath catch in her throat. The gesture was so unexpected and she could see that Rome was surprised too. They didn't really have a tactile relationship, a hand on the shoulder was pretty much as far as it had gone. Sleeping together in the same bed had been a huge step in their relationship and this suddenly felt like another big step. Clearly realising how inappropriate it was, Rome let his hands fall back to her shoulders, a gesture which suddenly didn't seem as harmless as it did before. After a moment he stepped back.

'I never saw her body. They wouldn't let me and in many ways I'm so glad for that but it also made it harder too. As horrible as it sounds, I never got to properly say goodbye. In some ways I needed that closure. I'd seen her the weekend before and we'd made plans for the following weekend when she was coming home for her birthday. But she never did. I didn't find out she'd died until a few days after the accident. Her parents were both dead, no siblings. She had work colleagues there but they didn't have my number. I kept ringing and ringing her phone. Eventually it was the police that answered, having found her phone after the accident. I knew then. I'd seen the accident on the news and knew no one could survive that. The police confirmed that she had died and shortly after the manager of the park rang to offer his condolences and to say how sorry he was. It was the weirdest thing to be told she had died. I kept thinking it must have been a mistake, that she'd walk through the door at any minute, laughing and joking over the whole silly affair. Of course, I never saw her again.'

'How on earth do you move on from that?'

'I'm working on it.' He looked at her then with such affection and adoration that it took her breath away. 'I think the key is finding someone special enough that it's worth taking the risk.'

His words hung in the air between them before he looked away.

'In truth, I think it will always be with me.'

He looked so sad all of a sudden and Freya wanted to step forward and hug him.

'I'm so sorry,' Freya said, wishing that she had lied about what had upset her.

'Don't be sorry for someone else's behaviour. I appreciate you trying to protect me.'

'She kept going on about the money, as if you were wrong for taking it. I wasn't going to stand for that. She said a lot of women would be interested in you because of that money, as if that was a quality to be admired.'

Rome sighed. 'A lot of women *were* interested in me because of the money, nothing stays secret on this island and it wasn't long before word got out. They were disappointed to find it's all gone.'

He sat down on a stool and picked up a piece of red fused glass that was smooth all over. 'It never even occurred to me to take anyone to court for Paige's death. It was an accident. I was still in a state of shock when the cheque arrived a few weeks after her death. Two and half million pounds. It didn't seem enough. I would have paid a hundred times that to have her back. But at the same time it seemed an obscene amount of money and I knew that others involved in the accident didn't get anywhere near that. I didn't know what to do with it. I thought something good should come out of her death. I paid off my parents' mortgage so they could retire, I bought Eden's shop and fitted it out with everything she needed to start her own business, I paid off all of Bella's student debts from the tuition fees and course costs at university and I gave over half of it to an amputees' charity that was helping the other victims of the crash. Several children lost limbs and in many ways that seems harder to deal with than death. Death is final, you have to live with a severed limb for the rest of your life. The practicalities of rehabilitation or refitting your house to cope with a wheelchair or the cost of prosthetic limbs are very expensive and while they all received good sums from Phantom Rides, the cost will always be ongoing. I wanted to do something to help. And spending the money on myself seemed wrong somehow, but after I had helped everyone that I could I started thinking about my own future.'

He flicked the glass over in his hand and it sparkled in the sun that streamed through the windows. 'I had spoken with Paige at length about starting a stained glass business and she was really excited about it for me. She said she wanted to help me make my dream come true and she said she would start putting some money aside to help me make it a reality. You were right what you said to the journalist – when someone close to you dies, it makes you realise how short life is, how it can be taken away from you in the blink of an eye and we shouldn't make plans for the future, but make that future happen now. I realised that she would have wanted me to make this change so I paid off my mortgage, bought this place, the kilns, the tools and started the business. I didn't actively seek customers back then, I was happy to just distract myself from her death with making different pieces. When I'm working with glass, measuring, cutting, grinding, piecing it all together, it allows me to forget about the world for a while and just focus on that. That's why, when you started work here, there were hundreds of different pieces for sale. It was a way to cope with my grief. A lot of what was left of the money dwindled away over the next few years as I sat here, every day, making more and more mirrors and lamps. There's a bit left now, but certainly not the millions that many women think I have. Luckily, thanks to you, this place is now making a huge profit and unfortunately I guess some of that comes from talking to shallow, small-minded journalists, who are hungry for any kind of gossip or juicy story.'

'I'm not talking to her again.'

Rome smiled. 'No, you made that very clear.'

'I'm sorry.'

'Don't be.'

'She thinks we're engaged.'

Rome shrugged. 'Let her think it. Look, we could both do with a pick-me-up. Why don't you pop along to the cake shop and pick up something gooey and chocolatey and I'll go and put the kettle on.'

He pulled out a five-pound note and passed it to her and then walked off to the kitchen, leaving the fused glass he had been playing with on the worktable. She looked at it and picked it up. It was a piece from a part of a mirror that had gone wrong in the kiln but it looked like a red heart. Keeping it in her hand, she walked out and headed towards the high street. When she was safely out of sight of the shop, she looked at it again.

Would Rome ever be able to move on and give his heart to someone else? Petal had one thing right. He was damaged. After losing his fiancée in such horrible circumstances, could he ever get over that? Was she completely misreading what the dinner was that night? But then she thought about how he had held her, when she had cried. That was something that was way beyond friendly. The way he had looked at her when he said he was looking for someone special. She felt sure he meant her.

No, he definitely had feelings for her, she refused to believe that all those looks and sweet gestures were purely platonic. Something was going to happen that night, she was sure of it.

❦

Rome carefully wrapped the copper foil ribbon around the outside of a piece of green glass, smoothing it down with his finger as he quickly dealt with the corners until the whole edge had been covered, then he passed it to Freya who was kneeling next to him so she could fold over the side of the foil onto the edge of the face with the fid, a plastic shaping tool, that helped to get rid of any air bubbles in the copper foil. She simultaneously passed him another piece of glass and, when she had finished smoothing out the foil, she placed her piece of glass carefully back in the right place on the paper design. They were like a well-oiled machine, working alongside each other in perfect harmony. They didn't need to speak, they both knew the process like the back of their hand.

He was so proud of how quickly Freya had picked up the art of working with stained glass. Every step, every method he had taught her she had grasped within a few minutes of watching him and excelled in every way. She'd had no art, craft or design training, coming mainly from an admin background, and that's all she'd done for him for the first six months she had worked for him, sorting out orders, taking care of the marketing and social media, but she'd been so keen to learn she had been an absolute pleasure to teach. She really listened to his explanations and demonstrations and she was so eager to get it right. The company was hers now as much as it was his.

He finished another piece and handed it to Freya and she gave him another piece in return. He smiled to himself; they made such a good team. He wondered, and not for the first time, if they would make a good team in other areas of his life too but that prospect scared him. It wasn't falling in love again that he was scared of, he wanted that in his life again, it was falling in love with Freya. With these other women he had dated, he had nothing to lose. He would go out with them, have some fun and then move on before it ever got serious. With Freya he had everything to lose, she was his best friend and he never wanted to jeopardise that. After he had spent four years waking up with a black cloud hanging over him, she had picked him up. She made him laugh and blew those clouds away. She had changed his life and he owed her so much. He looked over at her, her whisky-brown eyes concentrating on the job in hand. A jolt of desire punched him in the stomach. She was worth the risk.

'I'm looking forward to dinner tonight,' Freya said, taking his finished copper foiled piece and replacing it with another piece of glass to be foiled.

'I am too.' He really was. This could be the night that changed everything between them. He knew how he was going to start the night, where it led from there he wasn't sure but he was hopeful it might at least end in a kiss.

Freya sat back on her heels after she'd placed the last green piece on the design. 'I might even wear a dress for the occasion.'

He smiled and without thinking he reached out to stroke her cheek. 'If you turned up in a bin bag I wouldn't mind. You're beautiful, no matter what you wear.'

Her eyes widened in surprise at his touch, but this time he didn't pull away. Her eyes darkened and then cast down to his lips and for a glorious moment he thought she was going to kiss him but then the phone rang and the moment between them vanished.

'I better get that,' Freya said, her voice hoarse.

Rome nodded and Freya got up and moved towards the phone. She stared at him as she talked to the person on the other end and he smiled. Tonight was definitely going to end in a kiss.

A clatter at the door drew his attention away from Freya and, when he turned, he saw Bella, who had managed to get the strap of her bag caught around the door handle. He smiled with affection for her.

After she had untangled herself, he stood up to greet her, giving her a big hug. She looked so happy he couldn't help smiling at her. Her happiness was infectious.

'Don't normally see you round here during the day,' Rome said. 'Don't you have some big charity event to organise?'

'Always,' Bella said. 'But my boss allows me to have a lunch break.'

'Only because you're sleeping with him,' Rome said. He enjoyed teasing her about the perks of dating the boss as often as he could. Bella didn't even bat an eyelid.

'I don't have long actually. There's still loads to organise for the water obstacle course in London next month, but I wondered if you could make me something.'

'Out of glass?' Rome clarified, though that was obvious as she was standing in his glass studio.

'Yes, a present for Isaac. I'd pay you of course, but you're so talented and I love your art. I know Isaac loves it too.'

Isaac had bought several stained glass pieces for his house when he had moved in a few months before. It seemed Rome had got himself a fan who wasn't after his body.

'This mural is going to take me forever so it might have to wait a few weeks. What is it you have in mind?'

'I'm not sure if I'm honest.'

'Maybe a pink heart with "Isaac and Bella forever" written inside it,' Rome teased.

Bella laughed. 'You can mock me all you want, I'm in love and I don't care who knows it. And no, I don't want a pink love heart with rainbows and sparkles. Would you be able to do a piece with the London skyline in it? I know Isaac loves it here and would never move back to London, but I know he misses it too.'

'So nothing simple then?' He shook his head, fondly. 'I'll do a design for you over the weekend and, once you've approved it, we can talk about colours and the type of glass you want, but as I said, it'll be a few weeks until I can actually start the making of it. But I'll bump you to the head of the queue once I've done this mural.'

'Thank you, you're the best,' Bella grinned at him.

'And I presume you want the London skyline inside a pink heart?'

Bella laughed. 'One day, you'll be happily married, and you'll know what it is to be in love.'

'How did you know you loved Isaac?' Rome asked, not sure why the conversation had suddenly turned serious. But, as it had already taken that path, Rome decided to pursue it. 'You've had a few boyfriends over the years but you never loved any of them. What was different about how you felt for Isaac, how did you know it was love?'

'I'm not sure really. Being with him made me feel warm inside and that warmth spread throughout my whole body whenever I was with him, or thought about him. I just seemed to be walking around with a big smile on my face the whole time. I had never felt so happy with anyone as I did with him. I suppose that's how I knew. I think the thing that made it real in my head was when we were making love – that connection we shared was so much more than just sex. It's hard to describe but if you ever have that connection with someone, then you'll know.'

'Wait, I don't want to hear about my little sister making love,' Rome said, pretending to put his fingers in his ears.

'Then don't ask,' Bella grinned.

'So basically, your advice for when I'll know I'm in love is, I'll know?'

Bella laughed. 'When you put it like that it sounds pretty lame but you will. The connection you share when you make love to the person you love is something so incredible, so rare and beautiful, you'll know it when you feel it.'

'Glad you've cleared that up for me,' Rome said.

'Look for the warmth, that's a big clue,' Bella tried. 'Are you asking about anyone in particular or just love in general?'

Rome was unable to stop his eyes from wandering over to Freya, who was still on the phone, and when he looked back at Bella he knew she had seen him look at her. 'Just a general hypothetical question,' Rome said.

Bella nodded, unconvincingly. 'Right, of course it was. Enjoy your dinner tonight.'

She leaned over and gave him a kiss on the cheek, waved at Freya and walked out.

Rome sighed.

CHAPTER 6

By the time Freya got off the phone, Rome had moved back to the fused glass pieces of jewellery he was making for the summer craft fair that weekend. She moved back to his side, sensing that the moment, if there had indeed been one, had gone completely now, but nonetheless the nervous feeling of excitement bubbled through her about what the night held.

She looked at the pieces he was making. Fusing glass together was a simple thing, but it produced such beautiful results. He had cut out little bits of coloured glass and was layering and gluing them together in different patterns. He would put them in the kiln on a high temperature and all the bits of glass would melt together to make one piece of jewellery that was beautiful and completely unique. Later he might then add smaller pieces or metallic bits and they would be fired at a slightly cooler temperature to add texture to the piece too. He would often use the fused glass and add copper foiling around the outside and then solder gemstones to it as well. He bought a lot of old or broken jewellery from the jewellers and used the gem stones in different pieces. The brooch she was wearing was a daisy that had frosted pearly white glass petals and tiny yellow crystals in the middle.

'I love the brooches you make,' Freya said, fingering the one he had made her a few months before. 'I've seen lots of fused glass jewellery but yours is completely different.'

She passed him the bottle of fusing glue so he could stick his layer together to ensure it would hold in place in the kiln.

'I love making them, they're so easy, but it means I can be completely creative.' He smiled at her as he took the bottle of glue and there was that tension bubbling in the air between them again. 'So I have a question for you, I wanted to have my own stained glass studio for many years and now I'm living my dream. What's your dream, what is on your list of must-do things?'

Freya took the glue bottle back off him for a second as he readjusted the position of the glass. 'I read an article about this the other day, how to improve your life or something. But it said you should have a list of five things you'd like to achieve in your life at any one time rather than a list of a hundred things which never seem achievable. Once you've ticked off those things then you should replace them with new dreams, so you always have something to strive towards. So I had a think about what my five things are. Some of them are quite simple, some of them are a bit harder. I'd like to fly in a plane. I've never been in a plane before, only left the UK on a boat. I'd love to see the earth from up there in the sky. I think that would be incredible.'

He smiled at her. 'That's an easy fix.'

'They get harder. I want to go on safari in Africa. Which would tick my fly-on-a-plane dream if I was to travel to Africa. I want to see lions and elephants, I want to see giraffes galloping across the plains.'

'That's doable.'

'Doable but expensive.'

'What else?'

She liked that he didn't seem fazed by these dreams. Though she was sure he would soon. 'I want to buy my own house. I lived with my parents, my gran, my boyfriend and now I live here. It's always been someone else's property and I've always wanted to have my own house one day, something that is completely mine.'

'The flat is yours,' Rome said.

'Not really. It belongs to you. And you have been kind enough to let me live in it for the last couple of years and decorate it how I want, but if you decided to rent it out properly and make some decent money from it, or even if you wanted to sell it on, I'd lose my home.'

'I'd never do that.'

'Well things change, people change, their circumstances change. I'd want my own house one day and then no one can ever take it from me.'

Rome nodded. 'I understand that. What are numbers four and five on your list?'

'I'd like to travel through space. Go up there and see what the astronauts see, the planets, the moons and the stars, travel to different galaxies, see different worlds. I grew up watching all the *Star Trek* shows and it just looked so wonderful.'

She saw his whole face light up. 'You watched *Star Trek*?'

'Yes, every episode, *Voyager*, *Deep Space Nine*, *The Next Generation*, *Enterprise*, plus all the old ones with Captain Kirk. I loved it. Gene Roddenberry has a lot to answer for. But space travel has been a dream of mine ever since I was a little kid and, although it's probably never likely, the article said never to give up on the impossible dreams. And that brings me on to my last dream. I want to get married. When I was younger I had this life plan, I was going to get married by the time I was twenty-five and have four kids before I was thirty. I'm twenty-nine this year and when I broke up with Jake it seemed like that dream was never going to happen for me. Two years down the line and I'm still no closer but I want that more than anything.' She sighed. 'I told you some were harder than others.'

She didn't know what Rome's reaction was going to be to her dream of getting married. Most men would run a million miles away from a conversation about marriage. But Rome Lancaster wasn't most men.

Rome nodded as he thought. 'Well, given that we don't yet have faster-than-light technology and that most of the nearest galaxies are trillions of miles away, that dream might be a bit tricky. I know Virgin are creating tourist flights through space but I don't think they are ready yet and they won't have the technology to visit the planets in our solar system, let alone other solar systems. At a quarter of a million dollars per ticket it's not exactly affordable or achievable at the moment either but I think it's good to have dreams to aspire to. Just because we aren't there yet, doesn't mean it won't happen in our lifetime. But the other dreams are definitely achievable.'

She stared at him. 'I kind of feel that getting married and having children is more impossible than space travel at the moment. That dream feels very far away.'

He shrugged. 'I don't think that's an impossible dream at all. We could get married, have children together, if that's what you want.'

Her heart galloped in her chest, all words frozen in her throat. Was he actually proposing? They'd never even kissed and now this. He wasn't serious. He'd thrown it into the conversation so casually he couldn't possibly be serious.

'We're best friends, we work together, we hang out in the evenings and at weekends, we already know we get on. You're my favourite person in the world,' Rome carried on.

Freya finally found her voice. 'But… But marriage is supposed to be about a bit more than two best friends living together. Most people get married out of love.'

'And a lot of people marry their best friends.'

'Because they love them, not out of convenience. My marriage to Jake, if that had happened, would have been a marriage of convenience for him. I didn't realise it at the time. I cooked and cleaned the house, I sorted out all the paperwork and admin for his company and occasionally we had some rubbish sex. And when I started thinking there had to be more than this out there, when I started talking about travelling the world, he proposed to me to get me to stay. I thought it was because he loved me but in reality he didn't. I wouldn't want a marriage like that again. I suppose it seems like an impossible dream because I want to get married to someone who loves me, who wants to be with me because of me not because of the work I do. I want someone who misses me when I'm gone and every time they look at me, their heart feels full with the love they have for me. And I want to feel that for someone else too.'

Rome stared at her. If he wasn't freaked out by her dream to get married before, he almost certainly was now.

'Our marriage wouldn't be like what you had with Jake.'

God, he wasn't backing away from this conversation like she thought he would, he was embracing it. But it was all hypothetical, wasn't it? He wasn't actually serious about this, surely?

'I wouldn't marry someone so they could cook and clean for me. I'm perfectly capable of doing those things for myself. And I'm an excellent cook, or so Bella and Eden tell me. I love cooking. And yes, it would be hard at work if you left, but I'd cope, train up a new assistant. I certainly wouldn't marry you for that.'

'So why would you marry me?'

'Because that's what you want.'

'What about what you want?'

'I want to make you happy,' Rome said, softly. 'That's all I want. You make me ridiculously happy, you saved me when I was at my lowest, every day was a struggle but you, you made me smile again. I want to make you happy too.'

She stared at him. She loved this man so much. This conversation, if it was hypothetical, was killing her. She needed him to back away now, laugh it off, talk his way out of it before she got her hopes up, grabbed his hand and marched him down the aisle.

'What about sex?'

He smiled. 'What about it?'

'How would that work?'

'Well I know you said that the sex was rubbish with Jake but I presume you know how that part works. Unless he was completely inept I'm guessing he was doing something right.'

'I meant sex between us? If we were married, would we have sex?'

'Well, I'm not an expert but I think that's how babies are made. If you want four children, we'd have to have sex at least four times.' He smiled a mischievous grin. 'Plus we'd have to practise to get it right.'

God she was getting so hot, whereas Rome didn't seem fazed by this conversation at all. She had no idea whether he was serious or not.

'I want really amazing sex,' Freya blurted out. 'After eight years of sex which Jake classified as nice and I classified as a bit of a chore, I think I deserve some amazing sex. I want that incredible movie kind of sex, fireworks exploding, mind-blowing, phenomenal sex. Every day.'

Rome smirked. 'That's a tall order.'

'That's why it's an impossible dream.'

'Not with the right man. I'm reliably informed that when you have sex with the right person it's pretty bloody incredible every single time.' He stared at her intently and his eyes cast down to her lips for the briefest of seconds. 'I think we would have—'

'Hello!' called a voice from the door and Freya looked around to see Kitty Lane leaning against the frame. Freya turned back to Rome and resisted rolling her eyes. What had Rome been going to say? She guessed she would never find out now as Rome's number one fan had arrived. While Freya had tried very hard to keep her feelings for Rome to herself, Kitty had no such scruples.

She couldn't have been more obvious if she tried. And although Freya didn't think that anything had ever happened between Rome and Kitty, that didn't stop the other woman from trying and Rome did nothing to discourage her.

She watched Rome's reaction and as a big smile spread on his face, she recognised that something felt off about it. This wasn't the smile that he reserved for her, nor was it the easy smile he had with Bella and Eden, this was something completely different.

'Hello Kitty, how lovely to see you again.'

'I miss you, Rome. I never see you at the pub any more,' Kitty pouted as she walked in wearing a tiny denim skirt, a white t-shirt that was way too tight and quite a bit too see-through and bright red high-heeled sandals.

'I'm always busy with work,' Rome said, his smile still fixed in place.

Kitty ran her hand over his arm and shoulder, leaning into him. 'All work and no play makes Jack a dull lad.'

'I wouldn't say it's dull at all,' Rome said. 'If I'm not here, I'm hanging out with Freya and it's fast becoming one of my favourite things.'

Freya smiled.

Kitty gave Freya a fleeting disparaging glance and then leaned into Rome a bit more, whispering in his ear, loud enough for Freya to hear. 'I think time spent with me would be far more… entertaining.'

Freya rolled her eyes. 'Why don't I unload the bottles from your car, I presume that's why you're here.'

'They're in the boot,' Kitty said, dismissively, wrapping an arm around Rome's shoulders.

'I'll get them,' Rome said, disentangling himself from Kitty's grasp and walking quickly outside. Kitty followed him, leaving Freya alone in the shop.

All the women of the island loved Rome Lancaster, and it didn't matter what age they were either. Every single female around Rome's age flocked around him and many of the married ones too. Even the little old ladies adored him. He was charming and polite to them all and, in the case of the women his age, he'd probably slept with half of them. Freya had no right to be jealous but she was. And it didn't matter that she was the one that he would choose to spend almost every night with, it didn't matter that he said she was the only one he could talk to, it still hurt.

She inched closer to the door to watch him with Kitty. She was typically beautiful, with long chestnut hair that cascaded in loose curls down her back and long thin tanned legs. She was a lot closer to Rome's height as well, and all the men seemed to appreciate that she was tall. Freya was tiny in comparison.

Kitty came round at least once a week. Working in the pub, she brought all the empty glass bottles for Rome to use. The prettier alcopop bottles could be broken and used in mosaic pieces and the wine bottles would be put into the kiln and melted to make flat bottle shapes which he would sell as chopping boards or use in some of his more arty lamps or other pieces. The really small glass bottles he had used to make glass bottle bunting, which had proved very popular at the wine festival the island had held earlier in the year.

Kitty was laughing at something Rome was saying to her as he unloaded the boxes from the boot onto the side of the road, using every available opportunity to touch him. When Rome was finished he closed the boot and then walked round to the driver's door which he opened for Kitty. The gesture seemed charming and gentlemanly but Freya couldn't help wondering if this was Rome's attempt to get rid of Kitty as quickly as possible. Rome laughed at something Kitty said and Freya quickly dispelled that idea. Why would he want to get rid of her, she was pretty, funny and obviously into him. Had Kitty been one of the many women he had slept with before Freya came along? There hadn't been that many in the last few years although one was too many in Freya's book, and there had been a lot more than that – she'd heard the rumours that he used to date a different girl every week. Did Kitty and Rome have history?

Finally, with a kiss on the cheek for Rome, Kitty slid into the driver's seat and Rome closed the door. With a little wave, Kitty drove off and Rome waved her goodbye. He turned away to pick up the boxes and Freya saw the smile slide off his face. He heaved two boxes up into his arms and walked back into the studio. She quickly moved back to where she had been standing before, helping to glue some of the glass together that Rome had already layered.

'Did the Rome Lancaster Fan Club leave?'

Rome sighed. 'Yes, she's gone.'

'You should put her out of her misery and sleep with her.'

'That's the last thing I want to do,' Rome muttered, putting the boxes down a little too heavily bearing in mind the contents.

'Why? She's beautiful, funny—'

'And has more notches on her bedpost than she could possibly count.'

'So do you by all accounts.'

He stared at her for a moment. 'I'm not particularly proud of how I behaved after Paige died but, as I've already said, I'm looking for something more than just sex.'

'Why don't you just tell her that you're not interested then?'

'It's easier to smile and be polite than to tell the truth. I don't want to be rude to people.'

'You're rude to me all the time,' Freya protested.

He looked shocked. 'When am I rude to you?'

'Well maybe not rude, but grumpy.'

He smirked. 'I'm different with you than I am with other people.'

'I know. What was that smile that you gave Kitty, I've never seen that before. I was trying to decide if that was your flirty smile or something else.'

'This one?' Rome replaced his frown with the fake grin he had adorned Kitty with.

'Yeah that one.'

The smile faded away. 'Yes, that's the mask I wear when talking to people who annoy me, especially the women who swarm around me like bees around a honeypot. Sadly, you have to put up with the real me. There's not many people who get the full unedited version. You, Bella, Eden, my parents, and Dougie get the warts and all experience; everyone else gets the polite, more charming Rome.'

'Why can't you just be yourself with everyone?'

'Because people don't want to do business with the grumpy sod who is grieving over his dead fiancée, they find it awkward, they don't know what to say to me, so I make it easier for them. With you I can be myself and that's a quality I appreciate more than you could ever know.'

Rome turned and walked back outside to pick up the remaining box and Freya stared after him.

She really liked that he was so comfortable with her he could be completely himself. But had he become so comfortable with her that he'd never see her as anything more? No, she didn't believe that any more. Those little comments, the looks, the touches over the last few weeks meant something, she knew that. Every instinct she had said those gestures meant far more than just friendship. He was just being cautious with his heart after losing his fiancée and that's why he hadn't said anything to her yet. But the conversation about marriage hadn't fazed him at all, neither had the conversation about love and sex. Maybe, over dinner that night, with the fine food, candles, soft music and a view over Buttercup Beach, maybe that would be the right time to talk properly about their future.

❧❀☙

Freya quickly ran out to get some milk before she started getting ready for dinner that night. Rome might come back to hers for coffee or... No, she wasn't going to focus on the *or*. She had got her hopes up, talked her way out of it, got excited, fearful, hopeful and convinced herself many times that nothing was going to happen before changing her mind again. Currently she was optimistically hopeful but she knew that would change again before she got to dinner. Realistically, she knew she was probably projecting, seeing things that probably weren't there just because she wanted to see them.

She glanced in the window of the ring shop as she walked past and looked down at the plaster-cast hand that held the opal ring Rome had chosen for her. Except the hand was empty. She stopped and looked in the window more carefully. It hadn't fallen off the hand, in fact it wasn't displayed anywhere else at all. The display was exactly the same as it had been the night before, except her ring was missing.

Just then Abigail, the owner of the shop, walked out.

'Oh hey, Freya, I was just about to close for the day, did you want something before I go?'

'No... Well, I was just wondering about the opal ring you had in the window yesterday. I was going to buy it for my friend for her birthday, she loves opal,' Freya lied, knowing she couldn't explain to Abigail the real reason. It had been a hypothetical conversation between her and Rome after all. It could merely be a coincidence that the ring was now missing.

'Oh, I'm sorry. Rome bought that this morning. I might have a few others though out the back. If you want to pop by tomorrow, I might be able to help you.'

Freya nodded and Abigail locked the shop door and wandered off down the high street.

Rome had bought the ring. Her ring. He had bought the ring *for her*, there was no other explanation. Hope bloomed in her heart. Did he intend to propose to her? Surely not when they hadn't even kissed. But the ring was gone and that was a bit of a coincidence after Rome had picked it out for her the night before.

No, it *was* a coincidence, nothing more. Rome bought old jewellery from here all the time to incorporate into his pieces. She was not going to get her hopes up for dinner that night, but as she walked towards the shop, she couldn't help the huge smile that spread on her face.

CHAPTER 7

Rome let himself into the shop later that night, walked to the back and up the stairs to Freya's flat. He knocked on the door and then let himself in.

'Freya!' Rome called, making his presence known in case she suddenly decided to walk out the bathroom naked.

'Be right out,' Freya called from the bedroom.

He moved to the window and looked out at the little cobbled street. The sun was just setting and some of the houses on the hills beyond already had their lights on.

He put his hands in his pockets and let out a deep breath he hadn't realised he'd been holding.

He was nervous. He had no idea what he was going to say to her and whether he was going to say anything at all. But he knew if he did he had to get it right. This was too important to screw up. Freya was too important.

'I'm ready.'

Rome turned and burst out laughing. Freya had done her eyes so they sparkled with an electric blue eyeshadow and that gorgeous feline flick of eyeliner. Her shoes matched her eyes and that streak in her hair exactly, but the thing that had made him laugh was she was dressed head to toe in a wheelie bin bag. God, she made him so happy.

Freya did a little spin for him. 'Do you like it? You did say I could wear a bin bag tonight.'

'You look amazing.'

'You'd be happy to take me to the restaurant like this?'

He stepped closer. 'Of course, although I'm rather interested to see what exactly you have on underneath.'

She smirked at him. 'Why don't you find out?'

Intrigued by the challenge, he moved his hand to her shoulder and tore through the plastic, expecting to find the shoulder strap of a dress, but all he found was bare shoulder. Even though that was the only part of her body that had been revealed, it was suddenly hot as hell. He swallowed and repeated the action on the other shoulder, again revealing bare skin. He glanced into her eyes and they were alight with amusement. He returned his attention back to her bare shoulder, resisting the overwhelming urge to bend his head and kiss it. What if she was completely naked under this dress? What would he do if he ripped off the rest of the bin bag and she was wearing nothing but those wonderful sparkly blue high heels? Actually, he knew what would happen if he found her naked under this bin bag: what little restraint he had would snap and he'd end up kissing her, pinning her to the nearest hard surface and not stopping unless she told him to. Suddenly he wanted that more than anything but a night of sex would change everything between them and he wasn't sure he was ready for that change.

He slid his fingers into the collar, caressing only bare skin on the other side, and he felt the tension crackle in the air between them. All humour had gone from her eyes now and he got the feeling she was suddenly regretting this little joke. Without taking his eyes from hers, he slowly tore at the collar, ripping it open straight down her middle. As the bin bag fell away, he glanced down and was equally relieved and disappointed to see that she was wearing a silver strapless dress that sparkled with blue sequins around the top.

'Is this better?'

He took a step back so he could admire the dress properly and swallowed. He had never seen her look so pretty before, as she spent every day in jeans. He'd seen her wear dresses previously, but this was something else. The desire to kiss her hadn't faded at all. 'You look incredible.'

Her face lit up. 'Thank you.'

'Who knew you were hiding those wonderful legs under those jeans and I've never seen you wear a pair of heels before.'

'That's because I never do. I probably won't even be able to walk in them.'

He offered out the crook of his arm. 'Well if you need to lean on me, feel free.'

She grinned at him. 'I might just take you up on that offer.'

She picked up her tiny blue bag and her jacket which she slung over her arm and then he followed her down the stairs and out onto the street. He offered her his arm again and this time she took it, tucking her hand into his elbow and leaning into him as they walked along the street.

Suddenly he wasn't nervous about what the night would hold or what he would say. He was with his best friend and it couldn't get more perfect than that.

***

Freya was practically trembling by the time they got to the restaurant. She'd worn the bin bag as a joke to try to lift her nerves more than anything but that whole moment when Rome had been tearing it off her was so freaking hot. It made her think about him tearing off the rest of her clothes. And then walking arm in arm to the restaurant as if they were a proper couple. Rome had booked a table by the window overlooking Buttercup Beach and the sun was setting into the sea, leaving trails of pink and gold across the sky. It was all incredibly romantic. And she was sitting opposite her best friend and with any luck he was going to tell her he was in love with her.

She looked down at the menu, barely seeing the words, and when the waitress came to take their order Freya ended up ordering the first thing she laid her eyes on. She would probably be too nervous to eat anything anyway.

The waitress left and Freya smiled across the table at Rome. It was awkward, neither of them knowing what to say. It had never been like this before. Was he nervous too? The waitress returned and opened a bottle of champagne, pouring it out into two flutes and then discreetly leaving.

'Champagne?'

'I felt like we needed to celebrate,' Rome said, sliding a square black box across the table towards her. 'I made you something.'

Oh god, her heart was pounding so fast she felt sure that Rome would hear it. Was he really going to propose? This was crazy but she knew if he did she would say yes. She had been in love with this man for two long years, of course she would say yes.

With trembling fingers she lifted the lid and stared down at the pale pink glass orchid brooch that glittered in the candlelight. At the centre was the opal that Rome had clearly taken from the ring. Disappointment hit her in a great wave but she quickly pushed it away. The brooch was beautiful and he had made it with her in mind. Of course he wasn't going to propose. They hadn't kissed, never gone out on a date and he had lost the woman he loved and never been in a proper relationship since. He would want to take things slowly.

'This is stunning, thank you,' Freya said, hoping that he couldn't hear the disappointment in her voice.

'I know you love orchids.'

'I do, thank you.'

'Freya, I have something important I want to talk to you about.'

Freya looked up at him and he was smiling at her.

'Two years ago you came to work for me and you've turned my business around. Sales are up nearly four hundred percent, I have never been so busy. You created a stunning website, handle all my social media, I owe you so much. Because of you Through the Looking Glass is a massive success. But more than that you have worked so hard to train in the art of working with glass. You've been a delight to teach and the work you produce is completely stunning.'

Freya frowned slightly. As lovely as all this was to hear, it wasn't the big romantic declaration she was hoping for. Maybe he was building up to that.

'The business is as much yours as it is mine and I was wondering if you would like to be my partner.'

She stared at him in shock.

He wanted her to be his partner at work.

'That's what you wanted to ask me tonight?'

Rome frowned in confusion. 'Well yes. Well, I wanted to talk to you about a number of things but… mainly that.'

Freya swallowed down the burning ball of emotion in her throat.

'Excuse me for a moment, I just need to go to the bathroom.'

She got up on shaky legs and made it into the toilet cubicle just before the tears came.

How could she have been so stupid? She looked back over the last few weeks, the gestures, the looks, the little touches. Every instinct said that Rome was falling in love with her too. How could she have got it so wrong?

She was his friend, his colleague and nothing more than that. She would never be more than that. She had allowed herself to hope over the last few days and that was a dangerous thing because now those hopes were dashed, it was the most painful, disappointing feeling she'd ever had. She hadn't even felt like this when her engagement to Jake had broken up. There had always been a niggling doubt that something wasn't right between her and her fiancé and, in some ways, finding him cheating on her was something of a relief. This... this was heartbreaking.

Two years during which she'd thought she was getting closer to Rome, during which she'd thought it was leading somewhere, and it had led to this: her crying in the toilets while her friend had no idea that she was in love with him.

Well thank god she hadn't declared her love for him, she could still hold her head up high and continue as normal.

But could she continue as normal? Because even though Rome wasn't in love with her, she was still desperately in love with him. Could she really continue to work alongside him knowing that nothing was ever going to happen between them? It would be torture. And if she did then she would always be hoping, always be waiting for him to one day realise she was there and that he was in love with her too. How long could she wait for that? Another two years? Forever?

But then what was the alternative? Rome was her best friend and she didn't want to lose that. The prospect of not having Rome in her life hurt even more than the thought that he didn't love her. And she loved her job, she didn't want to walk away from that either. She would just have to go out there, graciously accept his partnership and continue working with him, being friends with him, and hope one day she could fall out of love with him.

She stepped out of the cubicle and dabbed a wet tissue under her eyes to get rid of the streaks; luckily the rest of her eye make-up had stayed intact so hopefully he wouldn't notice she'd been crying.

She took a deep breath, fixed a smile on her face and stepped back outside into the main restaurant.

There was Rome, chatting and laughing with a different waitress. She watched his face as he talked to her and he wasn't wearing the fake smile he had used on Kitty that day, this was natural and relaxed. He liked her.

There would always be other women in Rome's life and while Freya could possibly just accept that he didn't love her and never would, it would be impossible to watch him continue going out with all these women for the rest of her life.

Something inside Freya snapped. She wasn't good enough for him, that's what it boiled down to, just like she had never been good enough for Jake. And frustratingly, here she was again, making the same mistake she made with Jake. Waiting for him, pinning all her hopes on Rome falling in love with her too one day, building her life around him. She thought of all the women Rome had been with and how he had not once looked at her in that way. She was friend material and not anything more. She deserved more than that.

Feeling angry, hurt and betrayed, she marched over to the table, Rome looked over at her as she got closer and his face creased in concern.

'You know what Rome Lancaster, I'm better than this, I deserve better. You can stick your partnership up your arse.'

Rome stared at her in shock and she grabbed her jacket and bag and stormed out.

Once out on the street, the chill of the night shocked her back to reality. What the hell had she just done?

CHAPTER 8

Rome ran out onto the street and looked around but Freya was nowhere to be seen. Though wherever she had gone she had done so without shoes as they lay littering the street in front of him. Clearly she had wanted to make a quick getaway.

He needed to speak to her, to put things right, but quite how he was going to do that when he had no idea what he'd done wrong, he didn't know.

He glanced along the street that led back towards the shop and her flat and then in the opposite direction, which led to Eden's house.

He made a snap decision and ran along the street that would lead to Eden's house.

He tried to retrace what had happened. What had he said that had made her react in such a way? Everything had been going so well over the last few weeks, but especially over the last few days. Something had shifted between them and he'd liked the way it was going. There'd been that wonderful sexy moment in her flat when he'd stripped off the bin bag and there had been something in her eyes that said if he'd kept on removing items of her clothes, she would have been more than OK with that. He really thought that she was attracted to him in the same way he was attracted to her. He'd had no idea how he was going to broach the subject of them going out together that night or what her reaction to it would have been if he had, but the one thing he was confident of was asking her to be partner in his company. She loved her job.

That was supposed to be the easiest part of the night, then after that he could move on to the trickier conversations. Her reaction was so surprising and unexpected, he just didn't understand it, but he knew he had to do everything in his power to put it right.

He came to Eden's door and knocked, probably a bit too hard. It took a few minutes but his sister eventually came to the door.

'Rome, I didn't expect you tonight.' Her voice was strained and so he pushed past into the house, not waiting for an invite. There was no sign of Freya inside.

'Is Freya here?'

'No, I thought you two were going out tonight?'

'We were, we did, I really need to talk to her.'

'What happened?'

Rome moved through to the kitchen, not taking Eden's word that Freya wasn't there.

'I cocked up, though I don't honestly know how, but I've done something to hurt her and I need to put it right.'

'She's not here, Rome, but if I see her, I promise I'll tell her you're looking for her.'

He turned back to look at his sister. 'Look, if you see her, please tell her I'm sorry and that I really need to talk to her.'

Eden nodded and Rome looked around again before heading back outside. He had to find her. Whatever it was, he needed to fix it because losing Freya was absolutely not an option.

❦

'He's gone,' Eden called and Freya came back to the top of the stairs and looked down. She didn't think that Eden would sell her out but Rome was her brother so Freya knew she was loyal to him too. Satisfied that he really was gone, she came down and flopped onto the sofa, tears of frustration still brimming in her eyes. She'd only just arrived at Eden's when Rome hammered on the door so she hadn't even had a chance to explain to Eden how stupid she'd been yet.

Eden sat next to her, with her arm round her shoulders. 'What happened?'

'Oh god, Eden. I'm such a fool. I convinced myself that Rome loves me and even in some crazy moment of madness that he might even propose to me tonight after a silly conversation outside the ring shop last night. There have been so many little signs over the last few weeks, little touches, looks, comments. I thought even if he didn't propose he would tell me that he had feelings for me. I was so excited and so nervous. And you know what happened?'

Eden looked sympathetic. 'I'm guessing he didn't propose. I told you, he'll want to take things slowly—'

'He asked me to be his partner. His business partner,' Freya clarified.

Eden stared at her.

'He had no romantic intentions tonight at all. It was always about work. Years of waiting and hoping that he would finally fall in love with me and I realised tonight that it will never happen. I told myself it was fine, that I would accept his offer of partnership and just carry on as normal, but then I saw him flirting with the waitress and I knew I couldn't carry on working for him, watching him turn his attention to every other woman but me. I just snapped. I told him he could stick his job and left. And now, I have no job, no home and I've lost my best friend.'

The tears were coming thick and fast now and Freya had no chance of making them stop. The worst thing was she'd been here before.

'Oh no, Freya. I don't know what to say. I felt sure that he feels the same as you and now I feel bad because we pushed you into thinking that and hoping for that too.'

'Don't feel bad. This wasn't your fault. I wanted to believe he had feelings for me so I started to imagine that his comments and looks actually meant something. We actually had this conversation about getting married and I started to believe in it. I created this picture-perfect scenario in my mind where he would declare his love for me and I couldn't see past that. I've made such an idiot of myself and I don't think I can face him again.'

'Well, I can't promise you won't have to face him at some point. On an island the size of Hope Island, you two are bound to run into each other sooner or later but you can come and work for me – lord knows I need the help at the moment – and you can sleep in my spare room as long as you want. It will help me actually. Dougie arrives tomorrow and as he is house hunting over here, he'll want to stay with me. You staying here will save me the awkwardness of having him sleep under the same roof.'

'I don't want to be in the way.'

'You won't be. I'm looking forward to seeing Dougie and a part of me wants him to stay with me but the sensible side knows it's not a good idea. I really don't need the heartache of him staying here for the next few weeks. He can stay in a hotel, he can afford it.'

Freya looked at her sadly. Eden was as messed up in the love department as she was. Although Eden was even worse; she had been in love with her friend Dougie for over twelve years and even the fact that he had emigrated to America hadn't changed that.

'OK, thanks. It'll just be a few days, maybe a week or two. I just need to figure out what I'm going to do or where I'm going to go,' Freya said, swallowing down the lump of emotion in her throat.

Eden narrowed her eyes. 'You're not thinking of leaving Hope Island are you?'

'I don't know.' The idea had occurred to her. Could she really face seeing Rome every day knowing that he would never be hers? But the thought of leaving him was not one she could stomach and as she thought about it the reality of leaving her job was almost as bad. She loved working with glass and she was good at it too. The school mural was a project she loved being involved in, she didn't want to walk away from that.

'Your home is here, your friends are here,' Eden said. 'Regardless of what happens between you and Rome, even if you think you can't work with him anymore, this is where you belong. Bella's old house is practically empty as she spends every night at Isaac's, I'm sure she would be happy for you to live there and sub-let it off her, or take over the rent completely and pay Finn instead. I know he would be happy to continue renting it out at a cheap price for you and if that doesn't work out then you can stay here indefinitely. I've always wanted a housemate, we'd have fun living together.'

Freya smiled gratefully at Eden for that sign of solidarity. 'But what would I do for work?'

Eden shrugged. 'You set up your own glass studio.'

'Go up against Rome, I couldn't do that to him.'

'He has more business than he can handle and you love working with glass. I've seen your work and you have a fantastic talent for it. Don't walk away from that just because Rome can't see how wonderful you are.'

That was a possibility that she hadn't even thought of. Bella's house had a big shed at the bottom of the garden, she could use that as a workshop and then sell her pieces in some of the craft shops in the town. And although she wouldn't be working on the school mural, she would still be able to work with glass and she could stay on Hope Island.

But she would miss working alongside Rome every day and the thought of that broke her heart although after telling him where he could stick his job, she might not have a choice.

Rome woke up with a sore neck and looked around for a few moments before he realised where he was. After trawling the streets looking for Freya, going to all her favourite spots with no luck, he'd come back to her flat and determined he was going to wait for her there, but she'd never come home and he'd ended up falling asleep on her sofa.

He stood up and wandered to the bedroom, just in case she had come home late and he hadn't heard her come in, but he knew she wasn't there – the flat was too quiet for that.

Where was she? He grabbed his phone and called her again but it rang for a while before he was connected to her answerphone once more. Christ, what if she was hurt somewhere? He should have tried harder to find her the night before.

He looked out of the window, hoping to see her little bouncy walk as she headed back down the street, but there was no of sign of her.

He gave Bella a call to see if she'd ended up there.

'Hey Rome, I'm just off out, you OK?'

'Did you see Freya last night?'

'No, why? What's happened?'

'I'm an idiot, that's what's happened. If you see her, can you tell her to call me?'

'Is she OK?' Bella sounded worried.

'I don't know. I need to talk to her. Just tell her to call me.'

'Of course I will.'

He hung up and paced the lounge. He called Eden, starting to speak before Eden had even said hello. 'Please tell me she came to you last night, I'm so worried, I have no idea where she is.'

Eden hesitated for a moment then she spoke. 'She stayed in my spare room last night.'

'Oh thank god. Is she there? Let me speak to her.'

'Sorry Rome, I can't.'

'I'll come round.'

'No, she doesn't want to see you. She's going to stay with me for a few days.'

Rome stared at the pink orchid brooch sitting on the table in front of him. Freya didn't want to see him?

'Do you know what's wrong, did she talk to you?'

'Yes.'

'I have no idea what I did, or what upset her so much. But I will do anything to put this right.'

'I'm not getting in the middle of this. If she wants to tell you what's wrong then she will.'

'Please Eden, I… I can't lose her.'

Eden sighed. 'Give her a few days. She might be more willing to talk to you then and, in the meantime, I suggest you think about what it would be like if she left Hope Island for good.'

Rome sat down heavily on the sofa. 'She's leaving?'

'I don't know. She was very upset last night and she said she didn't think she could stay here any more.'

'God, no, you can't let her leave.'

There was silence from Eden for a moment. 'You'll come to Pots and Paints for lunch, won't you?'

'What?' He stood back up, his brain whirring. He had to do something, he had to talk to Freya even if she didn't want to talk to him.

'I think you should,' she said, emphatically.

He paused in his pacing of the lounge. Clearly Freya was going to be there too. 'Around one?'

'That will be perfect.'

He hung up and looked at his watch. He had just over four hours to figure out what he had done wrong and what he was going to do to rescue the situation.

❦

Freya was busily serving teas and coffees to Eden's customers, feeling thoroughly miserable. As it was the first Saturday in the summer holidays, it was busier than Freya had seen it in a long time. But at least being busy meant that she didn't really have a lot of time to think.

Her cheeks burned every single time she thought about the night before. Did Rome have any idea of her feelings for him? She knew she had hardly been subtle over the last few days, but it would be mortifying if he did. And what was she going to say to him when she saw him? How could she possibly explain her bizarre reaction to his business offer?

She glanced up with a smile, ready to serve the next customer, but the smile fell from her face when she saw that it was Rome. Of course he would be here, he came here every day. And even if she had hidden out at Eden's house like she'd wanted to that morning, she knew she would have ran into him at some point.

Humiliation flooded her cheeks and the depressing thought that he would never be hers was like a punch to the gut. He was staring at her intently and any words that she wanted to say were lost in her throat.

'What would you like?' Freya said, her voice strangled. She looked around to see if anyone was witnessing her further humili-ation but no one seemed to care.

'I'd like to talk to you,' Rome said, seriously.

'I haven't got time,' Freya objected, just as Eden slipped behind the counter.

'Go and have your lunch break, I can look after things behind here for a while,' Eden said.

Freya looked at her desperately, silently pleading with her to help her, but as she had already given her a roof over her head and a job, Freya could hardly complain.

'Go and talk to him,' Eden urged, quietly. 'You can't avoid him forever and he was so worried about you last night. He deserves to know.'

Freya sighed. Eden was right and though she had no intention of telling Rome the truth about her feelings, having suffered enough humiliation to last her a lifetime, he deserved some kind of explanation. He had done nothing wrong after all.

She took off her apron and joined Rome on the other side of the counter.

'Shall we go for a walk?' Rome asked, awkwardly, and her heart went out to him.

Did she really want to be alone with him? If he pushed her for an explanation she was afraid everything would come tumbling out and then her humiliation would truly be complete. She shook her head. 'I can't talk for long, Eden needs the help.'

Rome nodded and they sat down in the corner of the café. Freya stared at her fingers, not willing to look at him. After they had sat in silence for a few moments, Eden came over with two coffees and two slices of cake then discreetly left them alone.

'I'm so sorry about last night,' Rome said.

She looked up at him in surprise. 'You are?'

He nodded. 'I've obviously done or said something to upset you and believe me that's the last thing I want.'

He had no idea. And in some ways that made it worse. Although if he didn't know then her humiliation was a lot less.

'Was it the money?' Rome said. 'I know we never really sorted out your salary properly. I know in the beginning you insisted that the free rent on the flat was more than enough but that never really sat well with me as you should have been paid a fair wage, not just had the flat for free. I know the salary I paid you initially was nowhere near enough and that I increased it a bit last year when things started taking off but you've never had a proper salary from working with me. I'm so rubbish when it comes to that side of things and I never gave it much thought and you never brought it up. I know you get the money from the pieces you make but that's why I wanted to make you partner so we would both have an equal share from all the profits. We can talk about a deal that you would be happy with. It certainly wasn't my intention that you would carry on working on your low wage when you became partner. Is that what upset you?'

She stared at him. He honestly thought that she had stormed out because of the money? That had never been a factor for her. She got her lovely little flat above the shop for free and no bills as that all came under the bills for the shop. The small wages she did get, plus any commissions from the pieces she had made, helped to buy any food and household things she needed. Rome was always so generous with his money, insisting on buying her lunch and inviting her round for dinner, that her outgoings were tiny.

'It's not the money.'

'Then what is it?'

She had no decent explanation, no words in her head at all. What possible reason could she have for storming out like that?

She picked at the cake, feeling so uncomfortable with him for the first time since they'd met.

Finally she looked back up at him. His eyes were filled with concern.

'I just need some time away from you for a few days.'

He stared at her aghast. 'What did I do? What's happened? You're working here so I guess that means you don't want to work with me any more, you didn't come home last night. Tell me what's wrong. How can I fix it if you won't tell me what's wrong?'

She shook her head. How was there any way back from this? Why couldn't she just accept the partnership graciously and then none of this would ever have happened?

He swept his hair back from his face in frustration, swearing softly. 'I've done something awful, haven't I?'

'No. It's not you, it's me.'

'Everything was fine between us, better than fine, things were going great and I've screwed it all up.'

'No you haven't, I just need some space. I need to make some decisions about my future.'

He stared at her with something that looked like real fear. 'Eden said you were thinking of leaving the island?'

Freya didn't admit it but that was one of the things she had thought about the night before. Could she really leave? Could she really stay and watch Rome date a whole string of women for the rest of her life? Would she fall out of love with him one day or would she be like Eden was with Dougie and still be in love with him in ten or twenty years' time?

'I need time to think.'

'Look, you're my best friend and I don't want to lose you. Whatever it is, whatever I've done, let me fix it, give me the chance to put things right.'

She smiled, sadly. 'Some things can't be fixed.'

She could see he was getting annoyed at the lack of explanation from her and quite rightly so. 'Freya—'

'Look, I promise I'll tell you in a few days. Just give me some time.'

And she would tell him. She owed him that much. And if she really was leaving then it wouldn't matter if he didn't feel the same way. She wouldn't have the embarrassment of seeing him every day. She just had to figure out whether leaving the island was something she really wanted to do or whether she could continue to live here after her declaration of love and subsequent rejection.

He stared at her and then down at his untouched cake. 'If you want space or time alone, then I can do that. But please don't make any rash decisions. And whatever you decide, however long you need, your flat above the shop will always be your home. Don't stay at Eden's to avoid me. You have your separate front door, so you won't need to come through the shop at all and I promise I won't come up there.'

She nodded. 'Thank you.'

He hesitated for a moment and then squeezed her hand and left her alone. As soon as he'd walked out the shop, she put her head in her hands. What a mess.

CHAPTER 9

Rome sat in the shop as he soldered the copper foiling, joining the smaller pieces of glass together for the mural for the school. The shop was quiet, too quiet. Without Freya there to talk to or to listen to her singing along to the radio, he felt like a limb had been severed. He missed her and it hadn't even been a day.

The night before had held so much promise, he felt sure that she had feelings for him too, but it had been over before it had started and he still had no idea why.

But this was what he had been afraid of. He had deliberately held back from starting anything with Freya because he was afraid that if it ended between them he would lose her and he simply couldn't bear the thought of that. It had been better to continue as things were, having her in his life as his best friend, than risk dating her and losing her.

And now he'd lost her anyway.

She wouldn't leave the island, she loved it here. The beaches, the walks over the hills, the close-knit community, this was her home. His sisters had become her friends, his parents adored her, she wouldn't leave. Whatever this was, it was a blip, and in a few days she would calm down and forget all this silly talk about leaving. Even if she didn't come back to work with him, if she stayed on the island then he could cope with that. He looked around the empty shop and knew he was lying to himself, he needed her here.

The shop door opened and his head shot up, hoping it was Freya. He was disappointed to see that it was Dougie, swinging his bag over his shoulder having clearly just arrived on the island. He had a big grin on his face and was obviously ridiculously pleased to be back on his home island again. Ordinarily, Rome would have been happy to see him but he was too fed up about the situation with Freya to spare his best friend a smile. Fortunately, Dougie didn't care.

'Alright buddy, how's it going?' Dougie said.

'Good thanks. Busy.'

Dougie didn't even bat an eye at that subtle attempt to be left alone. 'That's good, nothing better than a successful business. I see your Instagram pictures from time to time. I think your lovely Freya is trying to make you into a sex object. Where is she anyway?'

'She's... taking a break.'

Dougie looked at him speculatively. 'From you or from the job?'

Rome scowled. 'She's helping Eden out for a few days.'

'Oh. So it is a break from you. Well that at least explains the scowl. What did you do?'

'I didn't do anything.'

'Well maybe that's the problem, maybe you need to get off your ass and do something, the poor girl has been waiting around for years for you to do something. She's not going to wait around forever.'

Rome stared at him. 'What are you talking about?'

Dougie shrugged as he dumped his bag on the floor. 'I'm sure you'll figure it out. Just don't take too long about it. I'm going to leave this here. Eden's spare key wasn't where it normally is so I couldn't get in. I'm going to go and see her so I'll come back and collect this later.'

'Maybe she doesn't want you to stay with her,' Rome said.

'Why wouldn't she want me to stay with her?' Dougie said, as if he couldn't possibly believe that someone wouldn't want him around.

'Because you're a pain in the arse.'

Dougie quite clearly let the insult wash off his shoulders. 'Well, if she doesn't want me, then I'll come and stay with you.'

'Or you could stay in a hotel.'

Dougie clapped him hard on the back. 'Where would be the fun in that? I can't annoy you if I'm staying in a hotel. Beer tonight?'

'I suppose.'

Dougie turned and walked towards the door. 'Let's face it, without Freya to occupy you, you'd just be sitting at home with a face like a wet weekend. You might as well come out and sulk rather than sitting alone and being miserable. I'll get Isaac to come out too, so you can bond with your future brother-in-law.'

'Sounds like a great evening,' Rome said, dryly.

Dougie waved one hand in the air and disappeared out the door.

Rome sighed. Dougie was right, he needed something to distract himself, because without Freya he was going crazy.

❦

Freya was sitting with two children, helping them with their pottery painting when Dougie walked in. Having only been on the island for a few years, she didn't know Dougie that well, she'd only met him the handful of times when he'd come over to visit Eden, Rome and Bella. But what she knew of him was that he was laidback, very likeable and absolutely adored Eden. It wasn't hard to see why Eden was still in love with him twelve years after he had left.

'Hey Freya.' Dougie bent down and gave her a kiss on the cheek. 'I've just seen your boss. He looks absolutely devastated.

Would that have anything to do with you working here instead of working there?'

Freya wasn't prepared for such an immediate attack. 'I'm… just helping Eden out for a few days.'

'And that's why Rome looks like his heart has been broken again. When are you two just going to admit that you love each other?'

'He's not in love with me,' Freya said.

Dougie cocked his head slightly, studying her. 'Funny that your first instinct wasn't to deny that you're in love with him.'

Freya stared at him, not having any other words. If Dougie had picked that up so easily did Rome know too?

Eden appeared at Dougie's side. 'Hey, leave her alone.'

Dougie turned to look at her, his face splitting into a huge grin, and he immediately pulled her into a giant hug, crushing her against him.

Eden's face was a picture as she leaned her head against his chest. Her expression was somewhere between pure heaven to be in his arms and pure hell too. Freya watched her subtly inhale his scent, her fingers tightening against his back. Every time Dougie came back, Eden went through this hell, falling in love with him all over again. Nothing had ever happened between them, as far as Freya was aware, mainly because Dougie lived in America and was only ever here for a week or so each time he visited. Eden tried to tell herself that she didn't love him and whenever he went back she always vowed that it was time that she got over him once and for all, but the next time he came over, it happened all over again.

He pulled back to look at her, still with a big smile on his face, clearly completely unaware of Eden's torment. For someone who was so tuned in to other people's emotions, and Freya's feelings for Rome, it was strange that he hadn't picked up on Eden's feelings for him. Unless he knew exactly how Eden felt for him and didn't want to do anything about it because he didn't feel the same way. Was that how it was for Rome – he knew how Freya felt but didn't want to do anything about it? The thought of that was enough to make her want to curl up and die.

'How you doing, buddy, I missed you,' Dougie said, softly. Freya was clearly forgotten, he had eyes only for Eden.

'I'm doing good, I'm glad you're home.'

'Your spare key wasn't under the toadstool like it normally is. I couldn't get in.'

'I have no idea where my spare key is, it disappeared after the last time you stayed with me. You probably took it back to America.'

'Ha. You're probably right.'

'Besides Freya is staying with me for a while, so you'll have to stay in a hotel.'

'I'll sleep on the sofa.'

'Don't be daft. Surely you'd be more comfortable in a proper bed. My little cottage is made for one or two, not three. It will get very crowded.'

'I don't mind crowded,' Dougie said, with a grin.

'Actually, I'll probably go back home tonight,' Freya said. Rome had made it very clear that he wouldn't bother her in her flat and there really was no point hiding out from him on an island as small as Hope Island.

Eden gave her a brief look of despair before fixing the smile back on her face.

Dougie shrugged. 'There you go, problem solved. We can be roomies again.'

'That's great,' Eden said, her voice belying her words. Dougie didn't seem to notice.

'Now we've sorted out that issue, let's sort out Rome and Freya's issue,' Dougie said, sitting down next to Freya. He grabbed a piece of paper and painted a big red heart then looked at Freya with a patient look that a psychiatrist might give a client. 'Tell me your problems, I'm listening.'

Eden clipped him round the ear. 'Go on, get out of my shop. Here's my key. You can cook dinner tonight, I want Chinese so you better go and get the food.'

Dougie grinned as he stood back up. 'Your wish is my command. I promised Rome I'd take him out for a beer to drown his sorrows but I can certainly cook for you before I go out.' He kissed her on the cheek. 'See you later, beautiful.'

He gave Freya a wave and walked towards the door. Freya watched Eden, her eyes filled with adoration for him until he was out of sight, then Eden sat down at the table with a groan, letting her head fall into her hands.

'God, I hate him.'

Freya laughed. 'No you don't.'

'I know, and that's the problem.'

'I can stay with you if you want, force him to go to a hotel.'

'I think Dougie plans on staying with me regardless, so it won't make any difference if you're there. Go home, make your peace with Rome. One of us should be happy.'

She watched Eden for a moment. 'How will you feel if Dougie really does come back here for good?'

'I honestly don't know. Delighted, sad, over the moon, fearful,' Eden said, quietly. 'I love him and to have him back is wonderful and heartbreaking all at once. I suppose ultimately I'll be happy to have him home. He was and still is my best friend above anything else and I need to remember that. It's not his fault that I fell in love with him.'

Freya sighed. Eden was right. She needed to remember that when it came to Rome too. Eden stood up and went back behind the counter and Freya watched her go. They were both a mess when it came to men.

Freya wanted to give Rome a chance to leave the shop before she went home that night. Although she had a separate front door to her flat so she could avoid the shop, she would still prefer not to run into him so she delayed going home after Pots and Paints closed and went for a walk along Buttercup Beach instead. She loved this beach and although it got quite busy in the summer because of all the tourists it was quiet at this time of day and she loved seeing the golden sands stretch out in front of her, curling along the entire length of the island. The sea was calm here, somehow sheltered from the bigger white-crested waves that rolled beyond the reaches of the island.

She kicked off her shoes and walked barefoot along the damp sand until she reached the far end of the island and climbed over the rocks to reach Berry Point. She sat down on the largest, flattest stone that jutted out into the sea. It wasn't long before she spotted the dolphins and porpoises as they crested the waves, swimming in their little pods, some of them jumping clean out of the water. It didn't matter what time of year it was, the dolphins were always there. Most times she came out there she would see Sammy the seal too. There were lots of seals around the island, but Sammy, identifiable by a black spot on his silvery grey head, was a lot tamer than the others and would always hang around where the men were fishing in the hope of being fed any fish heads or smaller fish that had been caught. Why bother trying to catch fish himself if one flash of his beautiful liquid black eyes was enough to make even the hardiest of fishermen cave and hand over any tidbits?

She sighed as she leaned back on her elbows and watched the gold-dappled waves.

She had sworn to herself that she wouldn't make the same mistakes again. She wouldn't build her life around the man she loved because when it all went wrong she would be left with nothing. But despite those promises she had done it again. Though maybe it didn't have to end like it had last time.

It was so beautiful here, could she really contemplate leaving? So things hadn't worked out how she had hoped, did that mean that she would run away again after she had built a life for herself here? The night before she had been in a mess, not sure what to do. The thought of still seeing Rome every day hurt. Even if she wasn't living in her flat or working with him, she'd see him around the island, see him with other women. In a moment of desperation the night before, she had started looking for jobs working with glass and had been surprised to find a glass studio in St Ives in Cornwall that was looking for an assistant to cover maternity leave for six months. They produced mainly glass mosaic work but the skills Rome had taught her were more than enough to equip her to do the job. Feeling at her lowest, she had applied for the job but now she was regretting it. She couldn't leave. Rome was her best friend and she didn't want to lose that.

She stood up and dusted herself down then clambered back over the rocks and up the track that would lead her back to the main high street.

All the shops were closed now, so the street was pretty quiet. There were a few people making their way towards the pubs and restaurants but mostly it was deserted.

She walked by one of the pubs, The Smuggler's Inn, which was quite popular with the younger crowd, mainly because of the large beer garden down the side, with large outdoor heaters taking the edge off the cooler evenings, and pretty lights and fountains that peppered the perimeter.

A loud laugh caught her attention and she immediately spotted Dougie – with his red curly hair, he wasn't hard to miss – and of course he was sitting at a table with Rome and Isaac. Rome had his back to her so she could only see the gorgeous black curls but what held her attention was the pretty girl standing at their table talking to them. She had her hand on Rome's shoulder as she talked and laughed along with them. Freya couldn't see Rome's face to be able to tell whether his expression was the fake one he had bestowed on Kitty the day before or the natural smile he had given the waitress at Envy the night before but she didn't really need to. Jealousy burned in her gut. He would never be hers and every time she saw him with another girl it would be unbearable.

She hurried on before they saw her, making her way quickly back towards her flat.

She couldn't hate Rome for this or be angry at him, none of this was his fault. He was her best friend and for him that hadn't changed.

Remembering how Eden had been with Dougie today made her think. Poor Eden who had never fallen out of love with Dougie in twelve years, always in her heart hoping that one day he would return the feeling. It must have been hell and Freya knew she couldn't hang around for the next twelve years waiting for Rome to fall in love with her too. She needed to fall out of love with him and maybe six months off the island working in St Ives would be enough to do that. Then she could return to the place she called home and just be best friends with him. And maybe, just maybe, it wouldn't hurt any more that she wasn't good enough for him.

CHAPTER 10

Rome carefully removed the fused glass pieces from the kiln. Some of them had worked beautifully, some hadn't. That was always the risk with fused glass. After working with glass in many different ways for too many years to count, he had a pretty good idea what worked and what didn't, but fused glass was always a law unto itself. Sometimes a piece of coloured dichroic glass reacted weirdly with the normal glass and it didn't melt as he thought it would but sometimes the resulting mistake was a lot better than he had intended.

The glass was still warm to the touch so he left them on a tray to cool down and returned his attention to the cut pieces of glass that he was preparing for the school mural.

Even with Freya helping him, he'd been worried about getting the piece finished in time. Now, without her there, he was going to have to work all hours to get it finished, which was why he'd left Dougie and Isaac after two beers and returned to the workshop to work on it some more.

He had been there for several hours, his back was aching and his eyes were getting tired, but as he was manning the table at the craft fair tomorrow, he knew he wouldn't have time to do anything the next day.

He still couldn't believe how badly it had all gone wrong with Freya. Dougie seemed to think Freya had feelings for Rome and he had thought that too, especially given how close they had been over the last few days. But if that was the case why would she quit her job and not even want to speak to him?

He tried to track back over the meal again. She had been disappointed with the orchid brooch he had given her. She had immediately tried to cover up her reaction but he had seen it. But that didn't make sense, she loved his jewellery. She was always going on about how beautiful his brooches, bracelets and necklaces were, and had a large collection of ones he had given her or she had bought from him, insisting that she pay for them as she knew the amount of work that went into them. Why would she be disappointed by the orchid? Orchids were her favourite flower.

He was rubbish with women. He had no idea what was going on in their heads. Growing up he'd not had much experience with girls. Being so tall, even as a child, he had stuck out like a sore thumb in his class. He looked like he had been stretched he was so gangly and for some reason that meant that no one really wanted to be his friend. Apart from when they played basketball, then everyone wanted him on their team. He had taken refuge in books, spending many hours in the library reading non-fiction books about everything.

Fortunately he had grown into his body as a teenager but he never really dated. The girls who suddenly started to take interest in him were the same ones who had made Bella's life hell when her parents had abandoned her. A fierce loyalty to his adopted sister meant he could never date any of them. But even the girls he did date, he had no idea what to say to them. Dougie seemed to have a way with the opposite sex that Rome could never achieve. He was a charmer and the women loved him. Dougie told Rome to chat to the girls like they were his friends but that was a lot harder than Dougie made it sound. None of them were interested in *Star Trek*, *Lord of the Rings* or the ancient history books he used to love to read. Girls weren't interested in boys who could draw, they wanted boys who smoked or rode motorbikes.

Equally, he had no interest in famous people and who was dating who according to the celebrity magazines the teenage girls of the island loved to read. He didn't care about the latest fashions, which seemed to hold their attentions so avidly. Some boys would take the girls they were dating out on their parents' boats. He'd take them down to Berry Point, his favourite part of the island to watch the dolphins and the seals, and they'd be bored after a few minutes. That set the pattern for many of his girlfriends – they soon got bored of him.

It didn't seem to matter when he got older. Sex was apparently one thing he was good at. Who needed to endure awkward, tedious conversations when you could just kiss a girl and then take them to bed? He had spent his late teens and early twenties enjoying the physical side of relationships.

And then, at twenty-four, he'd met Paige. She was the first woman who he had clicked with on much more than a sexual level. She made him laugh. She even loved *Lord of the Rings*. When she had told him she was moving to London for twelve months with work, he'd known he couldn't lose her. He had proposed to her a month after they'd first met and she'd said yes. For the next eighteen months their relationship had survived on weekend visits that primarily revolved around sex. They'd never gone past that physical honeymoon phase. As her time in London approached its end, Rome did worry whether they would be able to maintain a proper relationship once she came back to Hope Island for good. What if she got bored of him? What if sex and a mutual appreciation for Tolkien were the only things they had?

He'd never found out. She'd died shortly before she came back to Hope Island. And there had never been anyone he had remotely felt that connection with since.

Until Freya.

Freya was different to anyone he'd ever met. They'd spent two years working alongside each other every day, they'd spent almost every night together and their days off. They would talk and laugh and talk some more. He would never get bored spending time with Freya and it seemed she hadn't got bored of him.

When he used to date other women, he'd find himself comparing them to Freya and being disappointed when they didn't measure up. He wanted someone like Freya until he'd realised he didn't want someone like Freya, he wanted Freya and that was problematic in itself. She was too important to lose, too important to screw it up with.

And look at how easily he had screwed it up. He'd given her a brooch that he thought she would love and now she was barely speaking to him.

He realised he was hammering the wooden frame he was making too hard, the nails poking through the other side.

'Do you not have a home to go to?'

He looked up to see Freya standing at the foot of her stairs, dressed only in a tiny pair of shorts and a vest. Her hair was mussed up, as she had clearly been woken up, and her eyes were screwed up against the bright lights of the studio. He had never seen anyone look so sexy before in his life. He'd had no idea she had come back home. Surely that was a good sign. God, she was here and she was talking to him. Should he push her for answers, should he just carry on as normal?

'I'm sorry, I didn't realise you were here. Did I wake you?'

'It's one o'clock in the morning, what do you think?'

He stared at her and he decided he'd just act normal. Maybe if she didn't feel defensive or embarrassed around him then maybe things could go back to how they were before.

A thought occurred to him. Maybe he could persuade her to stay and help him and then when she was relaxed and happy working with the glass, maybe he could talk to her then.

'Sorry. I'm just panicking slightly about getting this mural done in time. I thought I'd put a few extra hours in." He deliberately picked up a blue piece of glass. "Go back to bed, I'll be done soon.'

She edged closer as if she couldn't stay away. He knew she was loving working on this project and would want to help even if she didn't want to be with him. 'Which bit are you working on?'

'I've just finished the sky but I was thinking of making a start on the sea. I know you were going to do fused glass for that but I thought for ease I would just do larger curved pieces of silver and blue pieces and then solder them all together.'

She looked horrified at that prospect, just like he knew she would.

'No, I'll do the fused glass, don't get rid of that bit, it will look amazing once it's done. Here let me help you.'

He smirked at how easily she had caved. But he had to keep this light between them.

He arched an eyebrow at her. 'In your pyjamas?'

'You're standing there with no top on, I don't think you're in any position to lecture me on my clothes.'

He grinned.

'What would you do if I wandered around without a top on?' she asked.

He dropped the hammer he was holding as that wonderful thought crashed into his mind and it narrowly missed his foot.

He bent to pick it back up. 'I don't think that would be a good idea.'

'Why is there one rule for health and safety for me but a completely different rule for you?' Freya asked, picking up some of the small pieces of turquoise glass and layering it on top of the deep blue pieces ready for fusing.

He grabbed a silvery blue piece and started copper foiling that. 'It's nothing to do with health and safety, I just wouldn't get any work done.'

She paused in her work and he cursed himself. If he'd been more awake he wouldn't have said that.

She smirked. 'Typical man.'

'Hey, you upload pictures of me to Instagram every week, a lot of them are topless ones.' He finished copper foiling the piece he was holding and placed it inside the frame. 'I've seen the hashtag, "Feel Good Friday". The implication is looking at my body makes people feel good. If anyone is guilty of sexual objectification, it's you.'

She giggled and he loved the sound of it. Maybe they were going to be OK after all.

'Sex sells, what can I say?' she said.

'So you wouldn't object to posing half naked with one of our lamps and then we'll see how many orders we get for it. Equal opportunities and all.'

'I think we'll leave the posing half naked for you, you have a much nicer body than I do,' she said.

He stalled in his work. 'You think I have a nice body?'

She looked at him and her cheeks coloured. Her eyes cast down his body appraising him. For a brief second, he saw her tongue slide out ever so slightly and lick her lips. When she looked up, her eyes were dark. She *was* attracted to him.

She shrugged. 'You'll do, I suppose.'

He burst out laughing.

'The important thing is that fifty-six thousand followers on Instagram think you're pretty hot so we'll keep feeding their desires.'

'I feel used.'

'I'm sure you'll get over it.' She sprinkled tiny silvery shards of glass over the top of her blue layer of glass which would melt into tiny sparkles. Rome picked up the last piece in the section he was working on and started copper foiling that. 'Did you hear there were apparently UFOs over St Mary's last night?'

He laughed. 'I didn't hear that.'

'You get all the gossip working in Eden's pottery café. Everyone comes in there. A couple of fishermen saw them and apparently some of the islanders from St Mary's saw them too. Golden lights in the sky that seemed to move without any kind of real purpose or direction. They were heading over in this direction and then they just disappeared.'

'So we had aliens visiting Hope Island last night? I wish I'd known, I would have tried to sell them some stained glass windows for their spaceship.'

Freya giggled. 'I never said aliens, I said UFOs. Unidentified Flying Objects. It could have been anything. But maybe the aliens saw your Instagram account and wanted to check out the hottie of Hope Island themselves.'

'The hottie of Hope Island?'

Freya shrugged. 'It could work.'

'If you put that on any of our social media, me and you will be having words.' He placed the piece of glass down inside the frame. 'Right, I think I'll leave the soldering for tomorrow as I have to be up early to do the craft fair. And I'll stick your pieces in the kiln to be fused first thing in the morning. Thank you for your help.'

She shrugged. 'No problem.'

She turned to walk back towards her flat but he caught her arm. She turned to look at him. 'Come back to work with me.'

'Oh god, I want to, I really do, this mural means so much to me but…' she trailed off and he had no idea why. If it wasn't the job, then it had to be him but they got on so well so what was it that made her want to stay away from him?

She picked up a piece of glass and held it lovingly in her fingers, caressing the smooth edges. 'I know I've left you in a bit of trouble since I've left, with the school mural to finish and the other commissions. I'm not working with Eden tomorrow, her Sunday girl, Daisy, will be there so I have the day off. I could do the craft fair while you stay here and get on with the mural.'

He stared at her. 'That would be a great help but I didn't mean I wanted you to come back because I'm so busy, though I won't deny I need the help. I want you to come back because I miss you. I miss chatting with you, laughing with you, working alongside you. I miss you, it's as simple as that.'

She stared up at him and then suddenly she stepped closer, running her hand over his cheek. Desire slammed into his stomach at her gentle touch. God, he wanted her so much.

'You're making this so hard,' Freya whispered before she stepped back.

He had no idea what that meant. 'I'm not going to make it easy for you to walk away.'

She didn't say anything for a moment before she took another step away from him. 'The craft fair starts at eleven, doesn't it? I'll see you here at nine and we can go and set up together. Then you can come back here to work on the mural.'

'OK.' He watched her disappear back up the stairs leading to her flat. He had to figure out a way to get her to stay because losing her was not an option.

CHAPTER 11

Freya was on her way back from the craft fair, the last few lamps that she hadn't managed to sell safely stored in the back of the van. She had sold almost everything that she had taken, all of Rome's beautiful jewellery, his wall panels and most of the lamps, and she had even sold a good few pieces that she had designed and made. Rome was quite insistent about showcasing her work at the fair under the Through the Looking Glass studio name and, though she didn't think they were as good as Rome's, people seemed to love them. She'd also had quite a few people interested in commissioning the studio for bespoke pieces. It had been a good day for the business and she felt proud to be a part of it. She frowned. She *had* been a part of it. No, she was still going to be a part of it, she just needed some time away to fall out of love with him.

She joined the beach road at Berry Point and automatically glanced out to see if she could spot the dolphins or seals.

She spotted Sammy the seal and frowned in confusion. He was on the beach. She looked back at the clear road and then glanced back to Sammy again. The seals never came up on the beach. They sometimes came on land to rest, but they preferred the rocky islets that were a little way out in the sea where they wouldn't be disturbed by tourists or a curious dog. This was very strange.

Acting on instinct, she pulled over onto the side of the road and got out. She moved quickly down onto the beach and soon realised that something was wrapped around the seal's neck. He was moving round on the beach, desperately trying to get it off.

She slowed her pace, not wanting to startle him, and as she moved closer she saw it was a Chinese lantern. The wire frame seemed to be embedded into his flesh.

Freya gasped, tears forming in her eyes as she inched closer, but Sammy noticed her there and waddled out into the shallows. Freya froze and the seal didn't go too far.

She needed some help with this. Even if she could get close enough, she doubted she would get the wire off on her own.

She quickly grabbed her phone from her pocket and called Rome.

'Rome, I need you,' Freya said, her voice breaking.

'Are you OK? What's happened? Where are you?' She could hear the urgency in his voice.

'At Berry Point.'

'I'm on my way.'

'Wait, bring some wire cutters.'

Rome didn't even question the odd request. 'OK.'

He rang off and Freya inched closer to the seal. 'Come on Sammy, let me help you.'

The seal didn't move any further away but didn't come any closer either.

Just then Rome's dad, Finn, came climbing over the rocks, fishing rod in one hand and a large bucket in the other. He was whistling to himself, obviously on his way home after a day's fishing.

He waved when he saw her, but his smile fell off when he saw her face. He came rushing over and Sammy sploshed even further away.

'What's wrong?'

'It's Sammy,' Freya gestured. 'He has a Chinese lantern wrapped around his neck and I can't get to him to help him.'

Finn stared at Sammy and then down at his bucket of fish. 'I have twelve mackerel, maybe we can tempt him to come closer.'

'Good idea.'

Finn picked out a small fish and tossed it out into the sea. Sammy was used to eating the fish guts that the fishermen would throw out into the sea once they had caught and gutted the fish. Despite his predicament, Sammy swam close enough to eat the fish and Freya handed Finn her phone and inched out into the water as Finn threw another fish into the sea. Each time Finn threw the fish, he would deliberately do it closer to the shore and Freya made slow progress out into the sea.

'That's it, I'm out of fish, love,' Finn said. 'Let me go grab the guys.'

Freya watched as he climbed back over the rocks and disappeared round the corner. Sammy stayed where he was, obviously hoping for more fish. Freya moved a bit closer.

Finn returned with four more men, all of them carrying the fish they had worked hard to catch. Slowly, one by one, they started throwing the fish towards Sammy.

'Don't throw them all in, we'll need some for when I try to get the wire off,' Freya called and the fishermen slowed in their throwing. 'Do any of you have any wire cutters?'

'I have a knife,' one of the men said and a few of the others nodded their agreement. She shook her head – a knife wouldn't cut the wire and she could end up hurting the seal.

Suddenly she spotted Rome, running down the road towards them. She waved both hands in the air and he ran towards her.

'Are you OK?' he said as he approached.

'I am. Sammy has a Chinese lantern round his neck, we are having trouble getting to him though.'

Rome looked at Sammy and at the fishermen who were slowly throwing their fish into the sea. He walked up to the nearest one and grabbed an armful of the fish and waded out into the sea to join Freya. Sammy must have smelt the fish he was carrying because he didn't move away. Rome handed her the wire cutters and held one of the fish out in front of him.

It was clearly too much temptation for Sammy as he swam closer to take the fish. Freya put her hand out to touch Sammy and to her surprise he didn't pull away. His skin was soft and smooth to touch. As Rome reached out to offer him another fish, Freya ran her hand up to his neck and tried to loosen the wire but it held fast.

Sammy clearly didn't like being touched – his neck was obviously very sensitive where the wire had dug into the flesh – and as Freya tried to remove it, he turned and swam away, though luckily not too far.

'Damn it.'

'He'll be back,' Rome said, quietly. 'This is too tempting for him to ignore.'

The fishermen on the land started throwing their fish into the sea to encourage him back and, after a few moments, Sammy swam within reach of Rome and Freya again.

As Rome reached out with another fish and Sammy came to take it, Freya didn't waste any more time, she slipped the wire cutters under the wire and snipped the wire apart. The lantern still didn't come away, but it was looser now, and very carefully she was able to untangle it from his skin and then remove it completely.

'What should we do, should we try and capture him and bring him to shore to have his injuries looked at?' Freya asked.

Rome shook his head. 'He's too big for us to be able to try and manhandle and we could stress him out.'

He was right; at nearly two metres Sammy would be much too heavy to lift and she couldn't see him being compliant.

'We can call the Cornish Seal Sanctuary in Helford, near Lizard. They might come out and look for him. If they need to take him in, they can do it safely.'

Freya nodded and with Rome and the other fishermen's fish now depleted, Sammy started to drift away.

Rome offered his hand and she took it and he helped her ashore.

'Thank you all for helping,' Freya said to Finn and the other fishermen. 'I'm sorry you lost all your fish.'

They all shrugged, clearly not bothered. 'We couldn't leave Sammy to suffer,' Finn said and they all nodded their agreement.

Finn handed her phone back to her. 'Well done, love.'

Freya smiled and realised she was shaking, though she wasn't sure if that was because she was wet.

'Let's get you back home,' Rome said, his hand on her back searing against her skin. He escorted her back to the van. 'Here, I'll drive.'

Freya didn't even argue, her hands were shaking too much to be any good. She got into the passenger side and Rome climbed into the driver's seat, throwing the remains of the Chinese lantern into the back.

'Well at least we know what the UFOs were now,' Rome said as he started the engine and headed back towards the shop.

Freya stared at him. 'Oh god, the golden lights. I didn't even think of that. But the reports said there were several lights in the sky. That means there's more of these bloody lanterns floating out there in the sea.'

'We'll get word out to the fishermen on the boats. Tell them to be on the lookout for them.'

A moment later Rome pulled up outside the shop and got out. Before she'd even reached for the door, he was already opening the door to her flat.

She climbed out the van and he ushered her inside and up the stairs. She felt so tired all of a sudden. The day had been so fun, with so many people taking an interest in the studio and for it to end like this was heartbreaking. That poor seal.

'God, poor Sammy. The wire was dug into his flesh so deep. He must have been in so much pain,' Freya said, tears forming in her eyes again as she thought about him.

'And you saved him. Their skin is pretty thick, he'll probably be OK,' Rome said, pulling her into his arms and holding her tight.

It was such a surprising gesture from him that it took her mind a few moments to catch up and then she wrapped her arms round his back and leaned her head against his chest. Oh god, she needed this right now. After the disappointment and stress of the last few days, after finding Sammy like she had, she needed to be hugged by her best friend. And he had come. She had called him and he had dropped everything and ran to the opposite side of the island to come to help her. She was supposed to be falling out of love with him but right now she loved him a little bit more.

'Thank you for being there,' Freya said, against his chest.

He pulled back a little to look at her. Cupping her face in his hands, he kissed her on the forehead. 'Always.'

This man was going to ruin her.

She realised she was still shaking and she knew it was only partly due to the cold.

'You need to have a shower to warm up,' Rome said.

She just managed to stop herself in time from suggesting that he joined her. She quickly rephrased it, leaving the ball in his court. 'You need a shower too.'

He nodded. 'Yes, I do. I'll go home and get changed and I'll see you back here in half hour.'

The ball dropped to the floor.

She nodded and he disentangled himself from her arms and left her alone. She stared after him as he disappeared down the stairs.

How was she ever going to get over him?

CHAPTER 12

Rome let himself back into Freya's flat a while later, calling out to her as he climbed up the stairs. She appeared at the top of the stairs wrapped in her dressing gown.

'I didn't think you'd be coming back,' Freya said, her eyes alighting on the large paper bag he was carrying.

'I thought you deserved a treat after your heroic act today.'

Her eyes lit up. 'Is that curry?'

'From the Mulberry Bush. I know it's your favourite.' He frowned slightly, suddenly unsure if it was her favourite. Giving her a brooch based around her favourite flower certainly hadn't worked out the way he had wanted. He hated that he was now second-guessing himself. He had never doubted what to do or say around Freya before but this whole episode had him doubting everything.

'Oh thank you so much. God, I love their food. I was just thinking I couldn't be bothered to cook. I feel so tired.'

'I'm not surprised, the adrenaline rush of dealing with a traumatic event will always leave you feeling exhausted afterwards. I'll… erm, join you if that's OK?'

'Of course. I'll get some plates.'

She went through to the kitchen area and he followed her. Everything seemed back to normal between them but he couldn't help feeling he was treading on eggshells around her. The row, if he could even call it that, seemed to have almost been forgotten, but although she had helped him out with the craft fair that day, she hadn't made any mention of coming back to work for him permanently. He had already asked her to come back to him and she hadn't given any indication whether she would but he wasn't going to let her go without a fight.

'I got the Goa Delight you love so much and I bought the Lamb Saffron for me, but we can share both if you like.'

'Oh yes, I love their lamb.'

He lifted the containers out of the bags and Freya started sharing them out between the two plates, then they carried the food through to the dining table that sat in the tiny window overlooking Buttercup Beach.

'I heard back from the Cornish Seal Sanctuary. They were able to find Sammy quite easily. They think he's OK, but they've taken him in to check him over and monitor him for a few days.'

'Oh, that's good," Freya said. 'Poor Sammy, I hope he's OK.'

'The guy I spoke to said he was gorging himself on a ton of fish so I think he'll be fine.'

Freya smiled and then turned her attention back to her food. 'How did it go at the fair today?'

'We did good, we sold nearly everything I took, including all of my pieces. I have several people that are interested in you creating an individual piece for them too. Our company is becoming well respected.'

He was encouraged by the words of togetherness from that sentence. 'We' and 'Our' were all good signs that she still considered herself a part of Through the Looking Glass. He wouldn't push her on that though, well not yet.

'That's fantastic and I had no doubt that your pieces would do well, you have a wonderful talent for it.'

She blushed. 'I had a great teacher.'

He swallowed a mouthful of food before he spoke, considering his words carefully. 'We make a great team.'

She stared at him and he wondered, not for the first time, what was going on behind those pretty whisky-brown eyes.

'I've always thought so,' she said, eventually.

'I'd hate to lose that,' Rome said, softly.

She looked down, playing with her food for a moment before she returned her attention to him. 'That's the last thing I want.'

He nodded and concentrated on his food for a while. Maybe there was hope for them yet.

❦❧☙

'All this wine is making me sleepy,' Freya said, resting her head on the back of the sofa.

Rome smiled at her, fondly. It hadn't been his intention to get her drunk, but he'd thought with a few glasses of wine inside her she might be more agreeable to coming back to work or at the very least telling him what really had gone wrong that fateful night. But she'd quickly passed from the talkative merry stage, through the giggling stage, and now into the sleepy stage, and he knew he wasn't going to get any coherent answers from her tonight.

'You had a busy day being a hero, no wonder you're tired. I'll leave you to go to bed. I need to do a bit more work before I go home anyway.'

She sat up and grabbed his arm. 'Don't go.'

'No?'

'I'm enjoying talking to you. I always enjoy talking to you.'

'I enjoy talking to you too.'

'Not enough though.'

He frowned. 'What do you mean?'

'Oh never mind. Go get the glass and I'll help you with some copper foiling for a while, before I go to bed.'

He stood up and walked downstairs. Maybe she was in the mood to talk after all. He needed some answers because he didn't have a hope of fixing this unless he knew what he'd done wrong.

He gathered all the yellow, orange and gold bits of glass into a box that would eventually form the sun. He grabbed two rolls of copper foiling, some scissors and a few other tools and put them all in a box so it was easier to carry back upstairs. He walked into the lounge and saw Freya curled up on the sofa fast asleep.

He sighed and put down the box then carefully scooped her up into his arms. Her eyes fluttered open and she wrapped her arms round his neck, pressing her face into his throat.

'What are you doing?'

'Taking you to bed.'

She giggled. 'And there are four words I never dreamed I'd hear you say. Pretty much every woman on the island dreams of you saying those words to them but I'm the only one who hears them in a non-sexual way.'

He moved into her bedroom, not sure what to make of that.

'We're friends, aren't we?' Freya muttered as Rome laid her down on her bed.

'Of course we are.'

'And that is never going to change?'

'No, never.'

She sighed and snuggled into her pillow. 'I knew it. So no night of hot passion for me then?'

He swallowed. 'Would you like us to have a night of hot passion?'

'If I said yes would you climb straight into bed with me?'

'No.'

'God that's depressing. I offer myself to you on a plate and you still don't want me.'

'Trust me, this has nothing to do with me not wanting you, nothing could be further from the truth. I just prefer the women I sleep with to be conscious.'

She closed her eyes.

'It's never going to change,' she whispered, drifting off to sleep.

He stared at her in confusion. Did she really want to sleep with him or was that just the drink talking? But in reality, even if she was sober and she asked him to spend the night with her, he knew he couldn't do it. A night of amazing sex would be incredible and something he wanted more than anything but she was too important to him to want to mess this up.

He needed to talk to her, properly, because this second-guessing was driving him mad.

CHAPTER 13

Freya woke the next morning and stretched and smiled, the sun streaming through the windows. She could hear a radio playing softly downstairs. Rome was obviously working early and a flash of guilt surged through her at leaving him when he was so busy. She glanced over at the clock and sat up in confusion, her head pounding with the sudden movement. The clock read half past nine. It was Monday morning and she was supposed to be helping Eden at the pottery café. She hadn't set the alarm the night before. Her mind tracked back… Why hadn't she set the alarm?

Rome had been there, they'd ended up drinking a bottle of red wine. Horror slammed into her stomach. Had she really asked Rome to go to bed with her? And he'd turned her down.

She quickly got out of bed. It was fine, she had been drunk and if he asked her about it she would just laugh it off.

There was a glass of water next to the bed and a strip of painkillers and her heart swelled with love for Rome. She was never going to get over him if she was seeing him every day. But what was the alternative? If she got offered this job at the glass studio in St Ives at least that would mean she could get off the island and away from him for a little while, but could she afford anywhere to live in St Ives on the salary they were offering? It was such a mess and there was a huge part of her that never wanted to leave Rome anyway.

She drank the glass of water and took two tablets and then had a quick wash and threw some clothes on. She grabbed her bag and ran down the stairs into the shop.

Rome looked up at her when she came tearing through.

'I'm late and I'm hungover and I hold you entirely responsible,' Freya said, jokingly, hoping to smooth over any embarrassment from the night before now so she wouldn't have to face it later.

Rome stood up. 'Wait, Freya, we need to talk.'

Freya cringed inside. Did he really want to talk about the night before? It was random drunken ramblings, surely he wasn't going to take any notice of it.

'I'm late for Eden.'

'This won't take long.'

Freya sighed, conjuring up her best defence for offering to go to bed with him.

Rome walked towards her. 'Listen, I'm not sure what went on the other night when you quit your job and stormed out of Envy. I have no idea what I did to provoke such a reaction but the fact is you have a job to do here and if you want to leave you are contractually obliged to work a notice period and the standard practice is one month.'

She stared at him in shock. That wasn't what she expected him to say at all. 'Wait, what? I've never signed a contract with you.'

'That doesn't matter. I've looked into it and by law you are required to work a notice period. You are responsible for me getting this commission for the school, you are also responsible for the increased workload and these are projects I would never have taken on if I thought I would have to do them alone. There is no way this mural is getting done in time without your help and that was something they were very clear about, that it had to be finished by the end of the summer holiday. If I postpone the deadline, that will look bad on my company and could be detrimental to future commissions. I understand if you don't want to work with me any more. Well actually, I don't understand – we've worked together for two years and not once fallen out, you seem to love your job so I honestly don't get why you would just walk out like this. But I do respect your decision to move on, maybe you want a change in career or a job that will pay you more than what you earn here, lord knows you deserve it, but you need to work your notice before you leave.'

'I… we're best friends and you want to pull some legal rubbish on me.'

'Yes we are best friends, so I don't know why you would leave me to struggle and possibly ruin the company you've worked so hard to build up. I'm asking for four weeks, Freya. As my best friend I would think you could give me that.'

'Eden is my best friend too and she needs the help as well.'

'I appreciate that, but you work for me, not her. Clare will be back this week to give her a hand and Dougie will no doubt help her out until Clare comes back. I spoke to her this morning, and she understands.'

Freya had no words, her mouth flapped open and closed while she thought of a suitable response. But he was right. That school mural was going to take forever to finish and she did feel bad about landing him in trouble like that. The mural was also something she really wanted to work on, loving being part of such a huge community project. They were supposed to be going to Penzance tomorrow to help with the Under the Sea carnival, she didn't want to leave him to do that on his own either. What difference would four weeks make to her in her attempts to get over him? She'd worked alongside him for two years while she'd been in love with him, another four weeks wasn't going to make any difference. The maternity cover job in St Ives didn't start until September anyway, so if she did get the job, her notice period would be over by then. What choice did she have? Any job she applied for would want references and what kind of reference could Rome honestly give her after she walked out and left him in the lurch like this, apparently for no good reason?

'I need to talk to Eden,' Freya muttered.

Rome handed her his mobile phone. 'Go ahead.'

He walked back to his desk and she reluctantly dialled Eden's number. She glared at Rome though he didn't seem to notice. With her pounding head, this was the last thing she needed. But if she thought she could avoid any awkward conversations with Rome today, he clearly had other ideas.

❦

Rome placed a mug of tea down in front of Freya. She had spoken to Eden, who he knew would back him up as he had already primed her early that day, and then she had gotten on with the mural. She had barely spoken to him all morning other than to ask questions revolving round work. He knew she was angry at him for pulling the boss card and demanding she work her notice. Legally, he didn't have a leg to stand on, forcing her to work four weeks. She had never signed a contract and they both knew he would never take her through any kind of employment tribunal. He knew she was there because he had guilted her into it and he felt bad about that but he didn't know what else he could do. Although things seemed to be back to friendly again – well they had been before that morning – it was quite clear, from talking to her the night before, that she had no intention of coming back to work for him. He couldn't lose her. She was his best friend and he couldn't even contemplate what life would be like without her. He now had four weeks to persuade her to stay for good and he was going to use every tool at his disposal to get her to do that.

'Shall we go to lunch? I'll treat you to a slice of cake,' Rome tried.

'You want me to go and have lunch at Eden's after I left her to struggle?'

'Yes. She's your friend, she understands that you need to work your notice before you can leave. No offence to Eden's shop but she can get anyone to help her serve coffee and teas, the kind of job you are doing here requires a very special skill and months or even years of training. And if you hadn't stormed out and left me the other night, then you would still be working here and Eden would still be struggling, as you put it. But as I've already said, Dougie is more than happy to help out so I don't think you're going to be on Eden's barred list just yet.'

Freya stood up. 'Fine. But I want a slice of that white chocolate and strawberry cake.'

He relaxed a little. 'Of course.'

He waited for her to walk out onto the street then followed her out and locked the door behind them.

'So we're going to Penzance tomorrow to help with the setting up of the Hope Island float. Are you going to be angry with me the whole time we are there, or are you just not going to talk to me?'

Freya sighed. 'No, I'll talk to you.'

'Good.' He snagged her arm and pulled her to face him. 'Look, I'm sorry for forcing you to work with me when you clearly don't want to but… but I can't lose you and I'm going to do everything I can to get you to stay. And I don't mean your work, which is incredible by the way, I mean you.'

She stared up at him, her whisky-caramel eyes wide with surprise.

She swallowed and when she spoke her voice was croaky. 'When you talk like that it makes me think you want something more from me than just friendship.'

Did he want something more than friendship? Did he want to fall in love again, to lay himself open to getting hurt all over again? Did he want to push his relationship with Freya into the something more category and risk his wonderful friendship with his best friend if it all went wrong? He was too scared to take that step. Over the last few days he'd seen how tentative their friendship actually was, how easily he could lose her over something that was entirely out of his control, just like the rollercoaster accident that took Paige's life. He just wanted his friend back and he wasn't going to risk losing her completely, no matter how tempting it was to kiss her or make love to her.

He took a step back from her and saw the briefest flash of hurt wash across her face before she turned away and started walking towards Eden's pottery café.

Is that what she wanted? She had hinted at that the night before when she'd had a few drinks but he'd put that down to drunken ramblings.

God, he really was rubbish with women, he had no idea what they were thinking and whereas before it hadn't mattered with Freya, he could just be himself, suddenly it mattered more than anything. He had to get this right.

They walked into Eden's pottery café and immediately Freya went over to hug Eden.

'I'm so sorry.'

'Hey, you have nothing to be sorry for,' Eden said. Pulling back slightly from Freya, she fixed Rome with a teasing glare. 'You, on the other hand.'

He laughed, knowing that Eden didn't mind.

'Honestly, Freya, it's fine. Clare will be back tomorrow and as you can see Dougie is earning his keep.' Eden gestured over to Dougie who was wearing a pink cupcake apron as he served teas and cakes behind the counter. 'Rome is right, he needs you. He would be lost without you.'

Rome nodded. In more ways than one.

They moved to the counter and Dougie looked up at them and grinned as they approached.

'Nice apron,' Rome said.

Dougie pointedly ignored him. 'Freya, you're looking beautiful today, Rome… still ugly as ever. What are you still looking grumpy for anyway, you got Freya back?'

'Temporarily.' He willed Dougie to stop talking but his friend took no notice.

'You should have seen him, Freya, he looked like he'd had his heart ripped out after your row. I still don't know what you two fell out over?' He looked between them, obviously hoping they would enlighten him. But Rome had no idea either.

'Nothing,' Freya muttered.

'Well if it was nothing, then it's high time you two kissed and made up.'

Rome was just trying to decide if it would be bad for Eden's business if he reached across the counter and throttled Dougie when a voice piped up behind them.

'Go on Rome, give her a kiss.'

Rome turned round to see Barbara from the chemist with her friend Mary, both of them smiling at him hopefully.

Mary nodded encouragingly.

'Go on,' Barbara urged. 'Poor Freya bought condoms from me for your big date on Friday evening, such a shame for the poor love that she never got to use them.'

Rome turned to look at Freya who was looking at Barbara in horror.

'It doesn't always have to be the man that makes the first move,' Dorothy Pippin chimed in from a nearby table. 'Freya honey, if you want to kiss him, you go right ahead and do it, don't wait around for him to do it. Life is too short for what ifs and maybes. Kiss him, then you'll soon find out if he feels the same way.'

Good lord. All he wanted was a sandwich and a cappuccino.

Freya cleared her throat. 'Thank you all for your encouragement, but Rome and I are just friends and that is never going to change.'

His words from the night before came back to haunt him. Was that what she had meant when she asked him whether they would always be friends? Had she been asking him whether he saw a future where that friendship would change?

'Just kiss her,' Mary urged.

He glanced back at Dougie, who had a big grin on his face at this turn of events. He passed him a glare that he hoped was suitably scathing enough and then bent down and kissed Freya on the cheek. He lingered for a second or two too long, relishing in the feel of her soft skin on his lips, the scent of her wrapping itself around him before he pulled away. She blinked in surprise, her cheeks flushing pink.

'Freya, I'm sorry, I truly am for whatever it was I said or did that upset you, will you find it in your heart to forgive me?'

'On the lips,' Barbara insisted.

Freya giggled at the absurdness of the situation.

'Now I know why you wanted to leave the island,' Rome muttered. 'In fact, let me get my bag and I'll come with you.'

Eden finally came over to rescue the situation, a little too late for Rome's liking.

'Thank you ladies, I think you've humiliated them quite enough.'

Grumbling at having their fun thwarted, they begrudgingly returned to their own conversations.

'Let me get you some lunch, I presume you'll want it to take away now,' Eden said, slipping behind the counter and cuffing Dougie round the back of the head.

'Ow. What was that for?' Dougie laughed.

'You know what.'

'I'll take the ham, please,' Freya said.

'I'll take the tuna,' Rome said. 'And a slice of white chocolate and strawberry cake please. And yes, we'll have them to take away.'

Eden dished up the food into containers and paper bags and handed them over, waving away Rome's attempts to pay.

'Why does he get free food and I have to pay?' Dougie protested.

'Because I like him,' Eden said.

Dougie grabbed her and pulled her into his arms and she half-heartedly tried to escape. 'Ah but you love me really, deep down, I know there's love in there somewhere.'

'Never,' Eden giggled.

'Hey, get your hands off my sister, she can do a lot better than you,' Rome said and Dougie reluctantly let her go.

'So you're going to miss our dinner tomorrow night?' Eden said, referring to their siblings' dinner he, Eden and Bella had every week at Rosa's restaurant. He always brought Freya along and Dougie would of course invite himself and lately Isaac had started coming to a few of them too.

'Sadly, yes, we're getting the early ferry tomorrow and trying to get into Penzance as early as we can. We were supposed to go this morning but Cal, who is helping to build the float, said he and his team have it all under control. But we'll get there tomorrow morning and help with any last-minute bits – the parade doesn't start until four so we'll still have plenty of time. All the work, from our side of things, was done weeks ago, so for the most part we get to just enjoy the parade.'

'Well, why don't we shift dinner to Wednesday night instead? It won't be the same without you two there. You'll be back by then, won't you?'

'Good idea. Yes, we'll be back Wednesday morning. We're only staying at the Bay View Hotel for one night.'

'In the same room?' Dougie asked, innocently.

Annoyingly the hotel had only had a twin room available and all the other hotels in the area were fully booked because of the carnival. Freya had insisted it would be fine but Rome was wondering whether it would be awkward. Dougie already knew their sleeping arrangements as Rome had mentioned it to him the other night. Dougie had insisted it would be the night when things would finally change between the two of them, though Rome had told him it wasn't going to happen.

Rome cleared his throat and passed Dougie another glare. 'Yes, a twin room, that was all they had available.'

'Oh, romantic.' Dougie waggled his eyebrows obtrusively and, as he turned away to make a coffee for another customer, he started singing, '2 Become 1' by the Spice Girls.

'Oh maybe Freya will have use for those condoms after all,' Barbara piped up from behind them.

Rome rolled his eyes.

'Thanks for lunch, we'll see you Wednesday,' Rome said. Waving goodbye to Eden, he ushered Freya out onto the street.

As soon as the shop door closed behind them, Freya burst out laughing.

'They don't give up, do they? The love lives of the young folk, or the lack of one, seem to be the most interesting thing that goes on around here. And I didn't buy condoms, before you ask. She must have me confused with someone else,' Freya said, awkwardly, even though Rome knew that Barbara was very unlikely to make mistakes and get confused. 'And I appreciated the kiss, even if you were coerced into it.'

'Believe me, it was no hardship.'

She stopped and stared at him and he immediately regretted that statement.

'What does that mean?'

He sighed. 'You seem to think I'm not attracted to you, but nothing could be further from the truth.'

'But… But it's been two years and nothing has ever happened between us.'

'And that's because of a ton of different reasons, none of which have anything to do with me not wanting to. Come on, we have a load of work to do today before we take a day off tomorrow.'

He walked away before she could question him any further. Dougie was right, it was going to come to a head between them sometime soon. He just wasn't sure he would be happy about the end result.

CHAPTER 14

The sun had barely broken above the horizon the next day when there was a soft knock on Freya's front door. Freya was already up, dressed, packed and ready to go. She was nervous about this trip and had spent the night playing out different scenarios in her head.

After returning to the glass studio after lunch the day before, she and Rome had fallen back into how they always were with each other, laughing, chatting and working well alongside each other. She liked Rome too much to stay angry at him and Eden was clearly very happy to be working alongside Dougie, so there didn't seem much point in being upset about Rome pulling rank any more.

She hadn't brought up his cryptic comment about being attracted to her again and he hadn't mentioned it either. But tonight they were going to share a room, albeit not a bed, but the room had wonderful romantic views over the sea so maybe, just maybe, something might happen between them. It was wrong to hope, she knew that. It would only end up hurting again if nothing happened but if she really was going to leave the island then it didn't hurt to try one last time. And Dorothy was right, this time she wasn't going to wait for him to make a move, she was going to instigate it herself. Maybe she wouldn't be brave enough to kiss him or tempt him into bed, but she would tell him how she felt. If she was going to leave then he deserved to know why. After everything he had done for her, she owed him that much.

She opened the door and Rome was standing there with a cup of takeaway coffee from Rosa's in his hand. He was looking sexy in his long woollen coat, his dark curly hair peeping out from the beanie hat he was wearing. He looked like a celebrity.

He smiled. 'I didn't expect to see you up and dressed. I expected to have to drag you out of bed. I brought coffee and pastries to make up for the early start, I know you're not really a morning person.'

'I'm not.' Freya took the coffee and sipped at it, smiling to herself that he had got the hazelnut coffee for her which she loved so much. 'But I'm excited about our trip. I haven't been to Penzance in years and I'm excited to see our hard work come to life in the Hope Island float. And to see the rest of the parade too.'

'The weather is supposed to be glorious so there'll be a lot of people there to see it.'

'Any clue what the other towns and islands have done for their floats?'

'No, but Cal said he's seen a lot of them and ours is by far the best.'

Freya laughed. 'Cal would say that.'

'The man has got some talent when it comes to pneumatics and animatronics. Last year was his first year making the Hope Island float. Obviously we didn't have any part in it last year, but it was brilliant. He probably would have won the parade if he'd had more time but he ended up stepping in at the last minute to do it when the man who normally does it fell ill. Cal wants to bring the trophy home this year so I know he's pulling out all the stops.'

'Has Hope Island ever won it before?'

'Never, but then before Cal came along we never did anything inspiring with it. We stand a really good chance this year.'

'I can't wait to see it.' She quickly glanced at her watch. 'Oh, we'd better go, what time does the ferry leave St Mary's for Penzance?'

'We're not taking the ferry, we're flying from St Mary's,' Rome said.

Her heart leapt. 'We are?'

'Is that OK? You said you've never flown before and I thought you might enjoy it.'

Her heart filled with love for him at that wonderful generous gesture. 'Oh my god, that's fantastic. Thank you so much. Oh god, I'm so excited. We need to go then, we can't be late for the plane.'

He smiled at her and offered her the paper bag. 'We have time. Eat your pastry first and then we'll leave.'

She took the bag and saw it was her favourite, an apple and pecan puff.

'Wow, I feel thoroughly spoiled today, hazelnut coffee, apple puff pastry and a flight to Penzance. Anyone would think you're trying to butter me up.'

'That's exactly what I'm trying to do, Freya. I want you to know how important you are to me. I want you to stay and I'll do whatever I can to make that happen.'

Her heart melted and she put her hand up to touch his face. She was gratified when he didn't pull away. 'There's only one thing you can give me to stop me leaving.'

'Name it, it's yours.'

She sighed and let her hand briefly trail down to his heart. 'It's not something that you can buy.'

He stared at her in confusion. 'Tell me, whatever it is, I'll get it somehow.'

She bit her lip as she thought. Now was not the time to tell him. It'd be awkward for the whole day when she really wanted to enjoy the parade. 'I promise, I'll tell you tonight, after the parade. I'll explain everything then.'

He nodded, seemingly satisfied that he was finally going to get some answers. She could only hope the answers he got were the ones he wanted.

She took a bite of her pastry, closing her eyes at the wonderful sweetness. 'Do we need to get some tools?'

Rome patted the rucksack he was carrying. 'I have some glass cutters, pliers, soldering irons, solder and copper foiling, along with a few pieces of blue and green glass just in case we need any spare bits, though I don't think we'll need them.'

Freya nodded and took another bite of her pastry.

'Let's go then. I don't want to be late.'

She grabbed her rucksack, turned off all the lights and followed Rome down the stairs. They stepped out onto the street and she closed and locked the door just as the postman walked up the road towards them.

'Morning,' Andrew said, handing Rome an envelope.

'Hi Andrew, looks like it'll be a nice day later,' Rome said, shoving the letter in his coat pocket.

'Let's hope so, I've got some vegetables that need digging out at the allotment.'

He waved goodbye and moved onto the next shop and Rome and Freya set off towards the harbour.

❧

'I can't believe we're doing this, I can't believe I'm sitting on a plane about to take off,' Freya said, almost bouncing up and down in her seat as she looked out of the window onto the small runway.

Rome smiled at her fondly. He loved being able to do this for her. He wanted to make her dreams come true, and while there were a few things on her list that might be a bit tricky to make a reality, he was working on the others.

He took her hand. 'You're not nervous?'

'No, I'm so excited.'

The noise of the engines suddenly intensified and the plane started hurtling down the runway, picking up speed, and they were momentarily forced back into their seats. The nose of the plane started to lift and Freya let out a little scream of joy followed by a laugh that was pure adrenaline-filled excitement.

Rome looked around. The plane had six other passengers sitting behind them, some locals popping over to enjoy the parade, a few tourists. Some of them were amused by Freya's squeals of delight, some less so. Rome didn't care. The squeals and laughter continued until the plane levelled out in the sky and Freya didn't take her eyes from the view out of the window the whole time as the islands disappeared from view and were replaced with the turquoise and gold of the sea.

Freya was silent for a long time, taking it all in.

'God, it's so beautiful,' she whispered. 'I never imagined it would be like this. We're so high up.'

Rome leaned over her to look at the view. 'That's Wolf Rock Lighthouse. See that weird cone shape near the foot of the lighthouse, that was the original beacon that was built in 1836. The lighthouse itself took nearly ten years to build and was the first rock lighthouse in the world to have a helipad built on top. And over there is Longships Lighthouse,' he pointed. 'There's been a lighthouse there since 1791.'

'That's over two hundred years old?'

'No, the old lighthouse was too short and the waves would crash over it in storms and block out the light so they built a taller tower in 1875. And on a clear day like today, you can see all the way down the coast to the Rose Island Lighthouse which was very nearly demolished last year but was saved by a shark.'

'A shark?'

'An angel shark actually, which is quite appropriate considering how it saved the tower. It's highly endangered and when they found a resident shark near to the lighthouse the council was stopped from pulling it down.'

Freya stared at him with a smile.

'God, sorry, I let my geeky side have full rein there for a while. I have hundreds of history of Britain books in my bedroom, I spend hours reading this kind of thing before I go to bed. I find it fascinating, I forget that it's boring for other people.'

'I don't find it boring at all.'

'You don't?'

'No, you could keep me entertained for hours with all your facts. It's like having my own personal tour guide.'

Rome smiled. He was sure she was just being kind but it was nice that she didn't seem bored by it.

The plane started to drop in the sky and the pilot called out that the plane was coming into land though it was quite hard to hear her over the noise of the engines.

'We're coming into land already?' Freya looked so disappointed.

'Yes, it only takes fifteen minutes from St Mary's to Land's End, but we're flying back too and I promise I'll take you on a plane again in the future, a much longer journey next time. There are lots of sightseeing flights round these parts.'

'Thank you for doing this for me,' Freya said, squeezing his hand which she had held for the whole journey.

'It was my absolute pleasure.'

He looked out the cockpit window ahead of them and could see the pilot was lining the plane up with the runway ready for landing. The sun was still rising in the sky, painting the clouds

with a wonderful candyfloss pink. He looked back at his best
friend who was staring out the window again, still holding his
hand. It was going to be a good day.

❦

Freya got out of the taxi at the disused football field, which was
now filled with a multitude of brightly coloured floats as the
representatives from each town made last-minute adjustments to
their creations. She knew that everyone's designs had been kept
under wraps until that day when they had gathered together for
the first time on that field. This was where the parade would start
from later as it wound its way through the streets of Penzance.

Rome joined her and to her surprise took her hand again as
he led her through the different floats, trying to find Cal. It was
an Under the Sea themed carnival and as such there were floats
with every sea creature imaginable, from Nemo-type clownfish,
whales, sharks, crabs, octopus to even the imaginary or prehistoric
creatures like the sea dragons, mermaids or the megalodon. They
were all beautiful, clearly having been created with many days
or probably weeks' of hard work. Most of the floats had opted
for the traditional wire frames covered with sheets of paper or
some kind of papier-mâché. Some had used brightly painted
wood panels and, in the case of many of the other islands from
Scilly, their floats were made mostly out of flowers to celebrate
the biggest export from the Isles of Scilly.

It wasn't hard to spot the Hope Island float as it was the
only one made almost entirely out of glass. It was stunning and
completely unique. Six life-size dolphins jumping out of the
waves had been made with large pieces of glass that had been
placed over a mould and heated to get them into the right shape.
Freya knew that Rome had spent a while teaching Cal how to

solder the pieces together using copper foiling as there was no way the dolphins could be transported as one whole piece and arrive safely. The waves were a mixture of sheets of fused glass and mosaic work that were mounted onto wood. And judging from what Rome had told her, she knew that many of these parts would move once the parade was underway.

It had taken her and Rome weeks to get all the pieces ready and as much of it as possible had been joined together before it was carefully packed into containers and shipped over to the mainland with 'Fragile' stickers placed all over the boxes. A lot of Rome's pieces were sent all over the UK and the staff at the ports knew to take extra care with anything that was sent out with the shop's logo emblazoned on it. According to Cal there had only been one breakage once the container was unpacked but it was a clean break and something that was easily fixed by soldering the two pieces back together.

Freya spotted Cal and waved as he came hurrying over. He gave Freya a kiss on the cheek and hugged Rome as if they were best friends. This made Freya giggle – Rome was never a big hugger.

'Cal, this looks amazing,' Freya said. 'It was so hard to imagine what it would look like when we were cutting out all these tiny bits of glass. You've done an incredible job.'

'Thank you, but none of this would have been possible if it wasn't for you two.'

'It's fantastic, Cal,' Rome said. 'Is there anything we can do to help?'

'There's a few bits of soldering you can do here and there. We're nearly finished. Rome, can you go and see if Tiffany needs a hand?' He pointed to the young girl at the back of the float.

Rome nodded and left Freya alone with Cal. As soon as Rome was out of hearing distance, Cal turned to her.

'Have you and Rome finally got together?'

Freya blushed. Was everyone on the island rooting for them to get together? Did they all know her inappropriate feelings for her best friend?

'No, what makes you think that?'

'You were holding hands.'

'Oh, that. I'm not really sure what that was about. We were holding hands on the plane because it's the first time I've ever flown and it's sort of continued since then,' Freya tried to dismiss it but she had been delighted by the hand-holding herself.

'I thought you two had your big date on Friday?' Cal said.

'Jesus, you weren't even on the island then, how did you know about that?'

Cal laughed. 'This is Hope Island we're talking about, nothing goes unnoticed.'

'Well it wasn't a date, Rome wanted to ask me to be his business partner so the jungle drums on Hope Island got that wrong.'

'But you wanted him to ask you out?' Cal said.

Freya hesitated too long while she thought about an appropriate answer. She liked Cal, had chatted to him quite a bit in the past, and especially over the last few months as he had talked through his design for the float, but she'd never considered him someone she could confide in before.

Cal pounced on her hesitation eagerly. 'You leave it with me, honey, I'll sort it out.'

'You will not. I don't need any interference. I can cock things up nicely on my own.'

'I'm not going to interfere. Much. All I'm saying is that part of the prize for the winning float is a night in the Under the Sea themed room at the Bay View Hotel tonight. There's a four-poster bed, a Jacuzzi, a giant aquarium, the room is beautiful. Very romantic. If we win, or should I say when we win, the room is yours.'

'No way, you did all this work—'

'What am I going to do with that room?' Cal said.

'Take your husband, have a romantic night together,' Freya suggested.

'Honey, Travis and I have romantic nights together every night, we don't need some fish tanks and a four-poster bed to inspire romantic moments. You two, however, need all the help you can get. Oh look, here's Travis now, I'll tell him the plan, he'll be delighted.'

Cal rushed off to greet his husband and Freya sighed. Tonight was either going to be completely magical or completely cringe-worthy and as she refused to hope for the former she resigned herself to the latter. But regardless of whether they won the parade or not, no matter what happened, tonight she would tell Rome the truth.

CHAPTER 15

The parade was well underway and the thousands of people that lined the streets of Penzance seemed to be enjoying it. But Rome could barely take his eyes off Freya, who was clearly enchanted by the whole thing. She was standing in front of him watching the floats go by and he was so charmed by her huge smile and enthusiasm that all he wanted to do was wrap his arms around her and hug her. He resisted but he was finding his reasoning and willpower getting weaker and weaker.

The floats had been amazing. Seahorses, starfish, seals, basking sharks had all drifted sedately past, the floats all lit up with strings of fairy lights which looked magical in the setting sun. There were even floats with a yellow submarine, scuba divers and *Baywatch*-style lifeguards. Most of the floats had moving parts or enthusiastic dancers to make up for the lack of movement. The Hope Island float had caused quite a few *ooohs* as the sunlight and fairy lights had glinted off the glass and the dolphins had seemingly leapt out of the waves.

In between each float was a troupe of dancers in different colours, performing the parts of waves, or fish. Dancers dressed entirely in green boogied past now, with great swathes of green ribbon protruding from every limb that were obviously supposed to be seaweed. Small children dressed as multi-coloured fishes darted between them. There was a Chinese-dragon-style whale that weaved and bobbed and opened its oversized mouth, fire breathers, mermaids, ballet dancers, stilt walkers, and even the animals had got involved, with several dogs and pigs in fancy dress. The event was a huge success.

As the last float and dancers drifted past, Rome and Freya joined with the crowds and followed the procession to the nearby park.

'This has been fantastic, I'm so glad we came,' Freya said, slipping her hand back into his as they walked along. Surprisingly, it felt right there.

They had worked alongside each other for the morning, helping with last-minute modifications and soldering, though there hadn't been a lot left to do. Everything had been wonderful between them again, as if the tension of the last few days had never happened.

Cal had been as bad as the ladies in Eden's café the day before, giving Rome looks that he would have found almost comical had he not been on the receiving end: wide eyes, winks, waggling eyebrows, twitching his head in Freya's direction whenever she wasn't looking. It was something of a relief when Cal deemed the float to be finished and they were sent off for the rest of the day to enjoy Penzance before the parade started.

They had crossed the causeway and explored St Michael's Mount and then come back and explored the cliff-side gardens and beach around Lamorna Cove. And Freya's hand had been in his almost the entire time. He wasn't sure whether it was him holding her hand or her holding his and whether it actually mattered. They just seemed to gravitate towards each other.

He realised she was still waiting for some kind of comment from him about the carnival. His head was filled only with her and he had no idea what he was going to do about it.

He cleared his throat. 'Everyone has worked so hard, I think the judges will have a hard time picking a winner.'

'Cal seems to think we have this in the bag.'

'Ours was unique, but there were others that were really good. I hope Cal wins, the trophy will be a big coup for Hope Island.'

'There are other prizes too,' Freya said.

'Oh yes, there's some kind of hamper I think.'

'And a night in the Bay View Hotel's Under the Sea themed suite. Cal said if we win, we can have that room.'

Rome laughed at Cal's not-so-subtle matchmaking. 'What would we do with it?'

Rome knew exactly what he wanted to do with it, but he had no idea if Freya felt the same way. Holding hands with him did not mean she wanted to make love to him and, even if she did, it didn't mean he should go ahead and do it.

Freya shrugged. 'We can at least go and have a look at it. We were going to share a bedroom anyway, this won't be that different.'

'Except we would be sharing a bed.'

Freya shrugged again, trying to appear nonchalant but not quite managing to pull it off. Could it possibly be that she wanted to share a bed with him.

He swallowed. 'And what would happen if we were to share a bed?' he asked, his heart thundering in his chest. He waited for her to laugh it off and say that she intended to sleep and nothing else but she didn't. She didn't say anything for the longest time. Though she was still holding his hand she didn't seem able to look at him.

Eventually she spoke. 'I guess we can cuddle.'

Cuddle?

He suddenly wanted nothing more than to strip her naked and *cuddle* her in bed until she was screaming out his name.

He tried to make his voice sound normal though he knew it was anything but. 'I like the sound of cuddling very much.'

'You do?'

'I can think of no better way to end our night. And even if we don't win, we could still cuddle in one of the single beds.'

Freya looked up at him, a smirk fighting on her lips. 'There wouldn't be much room in a single bed. One of us might have to go on top of the other.'

His heart roared against his chest. They were actually going to do this. They were going to make love. He wanted this more than he'd ever wanted anything or anyone. It terrified him because, after one night, it would change everything between him and Freya. He didn't want to lose her but his desire for her, his need for her, was taking over every thought in his mind right now and there was not a single bone in his body that could stop him.

'Who would go on top?' Rome asked. If they really were just going to cuddle it would be ridiculous for him to lie on top of her. She was so small and he was so big, he easily weighed four or five stone more than she did. He would crush her.

'I think I'd quite like you to go on top. To start with, after that we could swap over,' Freya said.

He couldn't believe they were talking about it like this in the middle of the street, but so many people were talking and laughing around them, the sound of the music from the floats still filling the air, he very much doubted anyone could hear them.

'You make it sound like there would be more than one cuddle?' he said.

'I'm hoping there would be multiple cuddles.'

'Then I think I'd like to go on top too, to start with.' He dropped her hand and slung his arm round her shoulders, pulling her against him. 'We could skip the fireworks if you want. Go back to the hotel room, see which method of cuddling works the best.'

Her whole face lit up into a big smile. 'I actually really want to see the fireworks.'

He groaned. 'You're killing me.'

She burst out laughing as she slid an arm round his waist. 'Now just in case you don't have anything…um… appropriate to… um, wear for our cuddle. I have some…something in the front pocket of my rucksack.'

He grinned. She'd planned for this, that was even hotter. And even though he always carried protection with him, he probably only had the one. As if she was reading his mind, she snuggled in closer.

'I have enough for multiple cuddles.'

He laughed.

They walked into the park and followed the crowds down to the front by the lake.

'I hope these fireworks start soon,' Rome said, not really caring if he missed them all.

Up on the podium the mayor of Penzance was talking about how wonderful the floats were and thanking everyone for coming. A cool sea wind blew in off the coast. Next to him Freya shivered a bit.

'Are you cold?'

'A little.'

He undid his coat and held it open for her. She smiled and stepped up against him and he wrapped the coat back around her, trapping her against his body. She looked up at him as she wrapped her arms round his back. He couldn't take his eyes off her.

He was vaguely aware that somewhere in the distance the mayor was doing a countdown to the fireworks that everyone else was joining in with.

Rome stared at the beautiful girl in his arms and bent his head down and kissed her.

Fireworks exploded in the night sky above them and Freya didn't take her lips off his for a second. He kissed her gently at first, the feel of her lips against his was divine. He moved his hands up to cup her face, stroking her soft skin with his thumbs. God, this kiss. There had been many women since Paige's death but none of them had felt like this when he had kissed them. This was something different. This was something so special and unique that he was almost fearful of it. Afraid of taking it any further in case he ruined it. She wrapped her arms round his neck as the fireworks lit up the inky sky above them and when she let out a tiny moan of need he was lost to her, he knew there was nothing he could do to stop where this was going. He slid his tongue against hers, stroking his hands down her back and pulling her tighter against him.

She eased back ever so slightly, breathing heavily against his lips, and he realised she was trembling in his arms.

'I never thought this would happen between us, I always hoped it would but I didn't think you saw me that way,' Freya said.

The fireworks were reaching a crescendo up above them, lighting up the air around them with red, green, blue and gold. He looked up briefly and then back down at his best friend, a sudden need to take her back to the hotel and show her exactly how much she meant to him.

'Let's get out of here.'

She nodded and he released her from his coat and took her hand, practically marching out of the crowd as the last firework exploded in the sky and a momentary silence fell over them before they all erupted into cheers. Rome didn't even falter in his stride.

Suddenly Cal was in front of them, blocking their path.

'Where are you going? You can't leave yet. They're about to announce the winner.'

Rome gritted his teeth, resisting saying that he didn't care. Cal had worked his arse off to get the float ready and showcase Rome's glass work. He owed it to him to at least cheer him on if he did win.

He glanced at Freya with exasperation and she smirked at him.

The mayor was back on the podium applauding the fireworks and again thanking all those involved. Finally they got on to the judging of the floats.

'The judges and I have deliberated long and hard over the floats this year and who should walk away with the coveted trophy. This year the standards were higher than ever but we have reached a decision.'

The mayor paused for dramatic effect and Rome resisted shouting to him to get on with it.

'In third place is…'

Third place? Did anyone care? He just wanted to get out of there and spend the rest of the night making love to his best friend.

'… Polperro with their basking shark float.'

There were cheers and claps and the representatives from Polperro went up to receive their flowers and wine.

Finally the claps died down and the mayor moved on to second place, while all Rome could think was if they had had left before the fireworks, they'd be back in their hotel room by now, probably hot, naked and sweaty.

'Second place goes to…'

Rome let out an audible sigh of frustration and Freya giggled next to him, leaning into him. He wrapped his arm around her, kissing her forehead.

'Tresco with their mermaid float.'

There were great whoops of delight from the representatives of the tiny island as they went up to collect their prizes. Finally the crowd quietened down.

'And the judges were unanimous about the winner, who brought us something we've never seen before. I'm sure you'll all agree that Hope Island and their float of glass dolphins is a well-deserved winner.'

Cal cheered and whooped and, as Rome turned to congratulate him, Cal ushered both him and Freya and the rest of the team up onto the podium.

Rome shuffled to the back of the group, not keen to be in the limelight, but given his size, he still towered over the top of everyone else.

Cal took the mic, even though the mayor didn't seem keen to give it up.

'Thank you so much, this was months of hard work and planning and I'd just like to say a big thank you to all my team who made it all possible, but especially I want to thank Rome and Freya from Through the Looking Glass, who painstakingly measured, cut and soldered every piece of glass together. If you loved the float, please check out their website, Through the Looking Glass dot com, for more beautiful glass pieces.'

Rome smiled with gratitude for Cal.

There were claps and cheers for Rome and Freya and Rome ducked his head in embarrassment.

The mayor subtly wrestled the mic back from Cal. 'Thank you. I'm sure we'll all agree that the float was one of the best we've seen here for a long time.'

The mayor handed Cal a small silver cup which seemed a bit of a let-down after all the pomp and ceremony, though Rome knew that the fact they had won was a big coup for Cal, the glass studio and the island.

'First prize also comes with this hamper of food and wine and a stay in the Under the Sea themed suite at the Bay View Hotel tonight.'

The crowd ooohed predictably as the mayor handed over a voucher and one of the mayor's staff struggled on stage with a very heavy hamper.

Cal took the voucher and immediately passed it to Rome with a wink. Rome took it without hesitation.

A few more words of thanks and Rome, Freya and the rest of them were allowed to leave the podium.

Cal moved over to Rome and shook his hand as the mayor continued to talk up on the podium.

'Congratulations,' Cal said.

'Thank you and you too. And thanks for the mention of Through the Looking Glass.'

'My pleasure.' Cal eyed the voucher in Rome's hand. 'Now go and enjoy yourselves.'

Rome grinned, not prepared to deny or acknowledge what he and Freya would be getting up to that night, though if Cal had seen them kissing he would have a fair idea.

Cal dived into the hamper and handed Rome a bottle of champagne and Rome laughed and took it.

'You ready to call it a night, Freya?' Rome asked.

Freya fake-yawned. 'It has been a long day.'

'Yeah whatever,' Cal laughed. 'I saw the two of you during the fireworks. I'm happy for you that you've finally got together.'

Rome didn't say anything, just nodded then took Freya's hand and walked out of the park. The walk soon turned into a run until they were practically sprinting back towards the hotel.

They managed to slow down and walk into reception but Freya was giggling helplessly as he handed over the voucher and got the room key.

They quickly went up to the twin room they had checked into earlier and grabbed their bags and then went back in the lift up to the top floor.

Rome put the key in the lock, let them in, dumped their bags and the champagne and immediately pulled Freya into his arms, kissing her hard. He needed her so much right now. The gentleness of the previous kiss was gone, this was filled only with desire. His hands snaked under her jacket and slid it off her shoulders and she stepped back away from him.

'Sorry, I'm so nervous, I can barely breathe. I just need a minute,' Freya said, brushing her hair back from her face in frustration. 'I've been waiting for this for such a long time and now it's going to happen I'm too nervous to enjoy it.'

'There's no rush. We won't do anything you don't want to do. We really can just cuddle if that's what you want.'

'Believe me, we're going to make love tonight. I'm not walking away from that. Just give me a few minutes.'

She walked away from him and for the first time he noticed the room with its incredible view over the sea. There was a huge aquarium that ran the length of the room, dominating the whole wall, with tropical fish of every size and colour swimming gently through the water. The four-poster bed was covered in a satin blue throw with pale blue chiffon curtains and the velvet sofa was a deep blue too. Around the room there were lots of sea paraphernalia and pictures of shells, starfish and other fish. It was all rather lovely but his eyes were drawn back to the beautiful woman standing at the window staring out at the sea.

'I had things I wanted to tell you tonight, I had a big speech prepared and I just don't know if any of it matters now. I mean, of course it matters, you deserve to know the truth but maybe, for one night, we forget all of that.'

He had no idea what she meant, but he just wanted her to be happy and relaxed even if that meant they didn't get to make love that night.

'Why don't we sit down on the sofa? We can have a glass of champagne, watch a little TV if you want, have a cuddle and a kiss and if you want to we can talk.'

She nodded though she still didn't turn round. He took his coat off and slung it over the chair and something white fell out of his pocket. He bent to pick it up and realised it was the letter that Andrew had given him that morning just before they left.

As Freya still hadn't moved and he wanted to give her the time to calm down, he opened the envelope and shook out the letter inside.

He read the letter, then read it again to make sure he was reading it right, anger filling him as he read it a third time.

He looked up at Freya, still standing in the window. 'What the hell is this?'

CHAPTER 16

Freya turned round to see Rome standing there brandishing a letter and looking furious. To her surprise, he was clearly angry with her. Their hot, romantic evening suddenly seemed to be slipping away.

She stepped towards him. 'What's wrong? What's happened?'

He thrust the letter towards her and then walked away across the room, digging out his phone as he started typing something furiously on it.

Freya watched him for a second then looked at the letter. Her heart sank as she realised it was from the glass studio in St Ives asking Rome for a reference for her.

'I applied for this before I came back to work for you,' Freya said, knowing it wouldn't make any difference to his mood.

He held the phone up, clearly having looked up the job online. 'This was why you wanted to leave Through the Looking Glass? I thought perhaps you wanted something that was bigger and better. But now I find out that you want to leave being a partner in your own glass studio to work in a different glass studio on a temporary six-month contract with a lot less pay.'

'Rome, let me explain.'

'So it wasn't that you wanted a change in career, it wasn't that you wanted more money, it really was that you just wanted to get away from me. What the hell did I do?'

'It wasn't you.'

Rome paced back across the floor, clearly not listening. 'Am I really that awful to work for, I know I'm grumpy sometimes, is it that? Or is it that I'm boring, you find me so mind-numbingly dull that you can't bear to be around me any more.'

Freya was horrified. 'Rome, no, that isn't it at all.'

'You were happy to kiss me, you wanted to sleep with me, so obviously I couldn't be too abhorrent for you. Or is it like some of the women on the island say: good at sex, not really good for much else. And you just thought you'd have a piece of that before you left?'

'If you shut up for a second, I'll tell you why I wanted to leave.'

'So tell me?'

Freya sighed. She had never envisaged having the conversation like this. She had imagined that it would eventually happen over much more romantic circumstances. Maybe over a meal and a bottle of wine she would tell him that she loved him and she needed time away from him to finally get over him. And there was a tiny sliver of hope that he would then say it back. After the kiss that night, after their conversation about cuddling which was very obviously about making love, she had begun to think he did have feelings for her after all, that she hadn't imagined those feelings over the last few days and weeks that had led up to that fateful night when she had stormed out on him. But now she had hurt him and the chance of a romantic night making love in this incredible room was gone.

She watched him standing there, so angry, and she didn't know if what she was about to say would make any difference to him.

'Why are you doing this?' he asked.

'Because…' She stepped closer. 'Because, you blind silly boy, I'm in love with you.'

Rome stared at her. That clearly wasn't the answer he'd been expecting.

'I love you, I have been in love with you for so long. I love your humour, your kindness and your intelligence, I love all your

geeky little facts. I love you. I love you to the moon and back.'
She let out a little giggle of relief at finally being able to say it
after all this time.

He pushed his hair back from his face, clearly at a loss for
words.

'I applied for that job because I couldn't do this any more.
Because every day I worked with you or every evening I spent
laughing with you, it was torture because all I really wanted to
do was kiss you and make love to you and tell you how I really
feel. Because every time I see you go off with another woman…'
her words caught in her throat '…a little piece of me dies inside
and I couldn't do it any more.'

All the fight went out of him. Rome took her hand. 'Oh god
Freya, I had no idea. I thought you might be attracted to me, I
had no idea you loved me.'

'That night, at Envy.' Freya swallowed down the humiliation she had felt when she had stormed out. 'I thought you
were going to tell me that you loved me too. I even somehow
stupidly persuaded myself that you were going to propose after
that silly conversation about engagement rings and then your
casual platonic offer to marry me. I'm such an idiot. And then
you gave me this beautiful brooch instead of an engagement ring
and asked me to be your business partner. I was so disappointed
and it hurt so much that you just didn't see me that way. It hurt
more than when I found Jake cheating on me. And when I came
out of the bathroom and saw you talking and flirting with that
waitress, I knew that I would always be watching you going off
with other women, and I realised if I didn't leave I would always
be waiting for you to eventually turn your attention to me and
I couldn't do it any more. I've been there with Jake, I waited for
eight years and he never loved me. I wanted to stay on Hope
Island, I wanted to stay working for you, I love working with

you and working with glass but I knew I just needed time away from you to try to fall out of love with you. I thought six months working in St Ives, six months where I wouldn't get to see you any more, maybe it would be enough. Then I could come back and just be friends.'

He reached out and stroked her face. He looked absolutely devastated by this news. 'I can't believe I hurt you, I'm so sorry, that was never my intention.'

'But today, we were holding hands, you kissed me, we were going to come back here and make love. Was that really just sex? Did it mean nothing to you or do you have feelings for me too?'

'Of course I have feelings for you. I adore you. I love spending time with you, you make me laugh, I can talk to you for hours and every night my dreams are filled with you and believe me they're pretty X-rated.'

'You dream about me?'

'Every night. Which makes me feel all kinds of creepy, having those thoughts about my best friend. I think about you like that all day too.'

She stared at him. 'But if you have these feelings why haven't you done anything about it?'

'That night, I wanted to talk to you about it, but I wanted us to be equals first. I didn't want to be your boss asking you out. I wanted to give you half of the company and then I was going to talk to you about being partners in other aspects of our life. But you walked out before I got that chance.'

Emotion clawed at her throat. She'd got it all wrong. 'You were going to ask me out?'

He shook his head. 'I don't know. I was going to talk to you about it. In some ways I was relieved I never got that far.'

Disappointment crashed through her again. 'I don't understand. You changed your mind. You didn't want to ask me out?'

'You're my best friend and you mean the world to me. I value our friendship so much I didn't want to ruin it just for the sake of having sex.'

'You're my best friend too and that will never change.'

'I don't ever want to lose what we have. I don't do relationships. I'm useless at them. I never know what a woman is thinking or what to say and I would end up doing something that would hurt you and then I'd lose you.'

'But for the last two years we've practically been in a relationship. We spent almost every hour of every day together. I fell in love with the man you are when we're alone. Not the fake persona you show to everyone else. The real you. We talked, we laughed, I was never bored by you. You never said the wrong thing or upset me. The only thing missing from our relationship was the intimacy. Sex wouldn't ruin us, it would complete us.'

He shook his head. 'But I did hurt you. By not doing anything I upset you. These last few days when you walked out on me, I realised that I can't live without you. Six years ago I lost someone very close to me and it broke me, I can't go through that again.'

'So what was tonight about?'

'Desire took over. I wanted you so much.'

'You can have me.'

'It's a bad idea. We're better off as friends.'

'And how would that work? We stay as friends. Do you think I'm going to be OK watching you date other people, because I won't. Will you be OK if I start dating other people, marry someone else?'

Rome scowled.

'So you don't want me but you don't want anyone else to have me either. This is ridiculous. I get you're scared of getting hurt. But you can't hide yourself away for fear of what might happen. There are no guarantees in love but it's better to try than to live a half-life where you'll never experience love again.' She slid her hands round his neck. 'Why don't you show me what your dreams look like?'

'Freya, this isn't a good idea. It would change everything between us.'

'Only for the better.'

'What happens if it ends?'

'What happens if it doesn't?'

Rome still didn't look convinced and Freya stepped back, hurt. She obviously wasn't worth the risk and she certainly wasn't going to beg.

'I'm going for a shower. Fill in the reference form for me, that's the least you can do. Let me go so I can try to get over you. Why don't you take the twin room tonight and tomorrow we can just pretend that this conversation never happened. We'll just carry on as normal until I've worked my notice.'

She walked away from him and into the massive bathroom, barely noticing the huge hot tub and the large walk-in drench shower that was big enough for several people to take a shower all at the same time. The tiles were an inky metallic blue that sparkled in the spotlights. She stripped her clothes off and stepped into the shower, letting the hot water pour over her, closing her eyes against the water as it splashed across her face.

What a mess. She didn't know what she imagined would happen when she told him she loved him but it wasn't this. She cursed herself because if she hadn't got nervous and freaked out, they would be making love about now. And maybe that would have been all that she needed to get over him, maybe they'd have had no chemistry at all and one night would have completely cured her of any inappropriate feelings for him. Though she doubted that to be the case. If their incredible first kiss was anything to go by, they had off-the-wall chemistry. But now she'd never find out.

What was it going to be like over the next few weeks? She presumed it would be awkward at first but they would eventually be able to work alongside each other fairly normally while they completed the work on the school mural and they would just dance around the elephant in the room.

She leaned her hands against the wall and lowered her head so the water could pour over her neck and down her back.

Suddenly she was aware of a heat behind her that had nothing to do with the shower. Her breath caught in her throat, not wanting to turn round and find out she was wrong, not daring to believe she could be right.

She opened one eye, just as a large hand snaked around her stomach and Rome pressed a kiss to her shoulder and then another kiss just below her ear.

'I'm not letting you go.'

Just in case there were any doubts of his intentions, he placed a condom on the shelf in front of her.

Her heart thundered in her chest as he slid another hand over her breast and the hand that was around her stomach slid lower, his hot mouth on her neck the most wonderful feeling in the world. She didn't say anything as he curled himself around her back, possessing her in every way, but she laid her head on Rome's shoulder, arching back against him.

He stroked across her most sensitive area with sure, strong fingers, somehow knowing exactly where to touch her.

He ran his fingers across her nipple, kissing across her collarbone, and to her surprise he brought her tumbling over the edge very quickly, as she let out a guttural moan.

He turned her round, his eyes devouring her hungrily. She ran her hands over his shoulders, relishing in the feel of silky skin over rock-hard muscle. Her eyes cast greedily over his body. He was such a glorious sight and for tonight at least he was hers.

She ran her hands down his chest, across his stomach and further down between his legs, making him take a sharp intake of breath as she held him. He kissed her hard as she continued to stroke him and he groaned against her mouth.

He suddenly pulled back slightly. Sinking to his knees, he placed a loving kiss on her stomach then dipped his head lower. She cried out as he kissed against the area that was still so sensitive from the last time. She stroked her fingers through his gorgeous black curls, caressing the back of his neck as he worked his magic on her. There was something so glorious about seeing him on his knees, taking care of her needs, and it was that thought that sent that feeling crashing through her again. He sat back on his heels, staring at her, the hunger in his eyes for her so raw and urgent, she knew instinctively what he needed.

As she caught her breath she grabbed the condom and passed it to him and he quickly slid it on. He hooked his hands behind her knees and pulled her down on top of him so she was straddling him as he knelt on the floor of the shower, the water pouring over them both.

He cupped her face and kissed her as he thrust up inside her, she gasped against his lips and he stared at her as they moved against each other. He didn't take his eyes off hers for a second as he slid his hands down to her hips, holding her tight against him. They held that connection, not talking, their breathing shallow, just eye to eye as if they both knew this feeling between them was something special and they didn't want to break it. Sex had never felt like this before. This was something incredible and they both knew that.

He ran his hands down her legs, caught her knees and shifted her into a slightly different position so every thrust hit that sweet spot inside her.

She leaned forward and kissed him, sinking her fingers into his shoulders as that wonderful feeling built in her again. He slid his tongue across her lips and as she let out a little gasp of need, he slipped his tongue inside her mouth, colliding with her own.

Tension and need built in her stomach and she pulled back slightly to look at him.

'I'm never letting you go, Freya,' Rome whispered against her lips and it was these words of need from him that sent her hurtling over that peak and he quickly followed.

For the longest time, Freya didn't move, her arms wrapped tightly round his neck, her face pressed into his shoulder as she was too scared to look at him. He was stroking his hands up and down her back as both of their breathing returned to normal but all Freya could think of was what things would be like between them now. Would he regret it? Would he try to talk his way out of it and tell her it could never happen again? They had shared an incredible connection and for Freya it had been the most intimate moment of her life. But what if he simply hadn't felt that? What if it had just been *nice* for him?

'Let's get dry and go to bed,' Rome said and Freya sighed a little. There were no soft words of endearment, no whispers of, 'I love you.' Was it really over before it had even properly begun?

She pulled back slightly and he kissed her on the forehead, which filled her with a tiny sliver of hope.

She stood up, her legs shaking, and watched as he got up too.

He moved out of the shower and grabbed two towels and came back to her, gently towelling her hair dry and then drying her body. He wrapped the towel around her and then quickly dried himself.

She wanted him to say something, anything that would indicate they were going to be OK, but he didn't.

To her surprise he came back to her and scooped her up and then carried her through to the bedroom. He lay her down then climbed into bed with her, pulling her into his arms as he kissed her sweetly. Her heart soared and he pulled back slightly to look at her, his eyes filled with adoration for her. Almost all of her fears faded away. She could see how much she meant to him and he didn't need to say a word.

'You're very quiet,' he said, his eyes clouding with concern.

'So are you.'

He smiled and she reached up to stroke his face.

'I'm quiet because that was quite possibly the best sex I've ever had and I just wasn't expecting it to be like that,' he said.

His honesty completely disarmed her.

'So no regrets?' she asked.

'No. None. Not for one second. You?'

She shook her head. 'I've been waiting for this for years and now it's finally happened it was everything I wanted it to be and more.'

He smiled and kissed her again then pulled back again to look at her as if he was seeing her for the first time.

'So what happens now?' she asked, finally finding the courage to ask the question.

'Well, give me half hour and I think I'll be ready for round two.'

She laughed. 'That sounds like a perfect plan.'

CHAPTER 17

Freya sat next to Rome as the plane taxied down the runway ready for take-off. They were sitting at the back of the plane, he was looking out of his window and she was looking out of hers, almost as if they'd had a row. He was holding her hand again, just as he'd done on the way over to Penzance, but he was quiet, retreating back into himself again. The plane powered up and hurtled down the runway and up into the sky. As the passengers in front of them got excited about the flight, Freya tried to concentrate on the excitement of flying and the incredible views but every second that passed was a step closer to beautiful Hope Island, a step closer to returning to their old lives where they would just be friends again.

They had made love three times the night before, each time sharing this incredible emotional connection, and she'd known that Rome had feelings for her too, feelings that went way beyond friendship or even just desire. But she got the sense that once they were home he would want to draw a line under what happened. What happened in Penzance, would stay in Penzance.

Although she didn't want that to happen, she wanted to make it easy for him. He hadn't wanted a proper relationship, despite being attracted to her, he hadn't wanted things to change, so she would give him the out he so obviously wanted.

'Things don't have to change between us.' Freya leaned over to talk to him so he could hear her over the sound of the engine.

He turned to stare at her. 'Everything has changed.'

'Only if we let it. You're my best friend, I don't want to lose that.'

'I think we lost that the moment I kissed you underneath the fireworks,' Rome said.

'It was just a kiss.'

He smirked at her. 'It was a lot more than a kiss, honey.'

She smiled. 'So what are we now then if we're not friends?'

He shifted the hand that was holding hers slightly, stroking her palm gently with his thumb. It was such an innocent gesture but the touch sent need spiralling through her stomach. 'I'm not sure how to categorise what we have now. Friends who have incredible sex, friends with benefits…' He arched an eyebrow. 'Lovers.'

She looked at him in surprise. 'You make it sound like you want to carry on where we left things last night.'

He frowned in confusion. 'Why would I want to stop? Freya, last night was incredible. I'm not sure what I was expecting but it wasn't that. I knew we would have great chemistry, but last night was so much more than that. Yesterday when I left the glass studio, all I was thinking about was coming home as early as we could today so I could carry on with that mural, and now all I want to do is take you home, strip you naked and make love to you until the sun sets. And then tomorrow I want to do exactly the same, and the day after that and the day after that.'

Her heart soared. He wanted this as much as she did.

'We're not going to finish that school mural if you want to spend every day making love.'

'No, I know. So I'm going to have to limit myself to early morning and evening sex and maybe a quickie at lunch times.'

She burst out laughing. 'I'd be happy with that.'

He leaned over and stroked her face. 'Not today though. When we get back, I'm going to take you up to your flat and make love to you there and then tonight you can come round to my house for dinner and then I'm going to make love to you in my bed. One more day won't hurt. We can get back to work tomorrow.'

She smiled with relief. 'Sounds like a great plan, apart from one tiny detail.'

'What's that?'

'We have dinner tonight with Eden and Bella.'

Rome groaned. 'As much as I love them, I really wanted to keep you to myself for just one more day.'

'Well you'll have to learn to share. They already moved it from last night to tonight just for us. You can have me all to yourself after dinner.'

'OK, but we're not stopping for dessert.'

She laughed and he bent his head and kissed her. For the rest of the journey, and even as the plane touched down on the runway in St Mary's, she didn't take her lips from his even for a second.

※❦֍

Rome rolled onto his back and pulled Freya on top of him so she was lying on his chest. She was breathing heavily and he knew he needed a few minutes to catch his breath before he could speak.

Sex with Freya was incredible. It was not like anything he'd ever experienced before and he had no idea why it was so different. Sex was pretty basic and he'd been with a lot of different women. Sometimes it had been great and sometimes not so much and while he was quite happy to accept responsibility for the times when it had been below average, he knew largely it was about the person he was with and just not being compatible with them. Freya was in a different league. He felt like he was tasting some new amazing food for the first time. For the first time in his life, he felt like he finally realised what sex should be like. He didn't know why it was so amazing, and he didn't want to think about what that showed about his relationship with Paige, but he knew he never wanted to go back to plain ordinary sex ever again.

Freya shifted slightly on top of him, her silky soft skin sliding against his as she leaned over and placed a gentle kiss over his heart. She leaned up to look at him and he cupped her face in his hands.

He knew this face, every freckle, the tiny scar above her eyebrow, the length of her eyelashes, the gorgeous whisky-caramel colour of her eyes. He knew her so well and that, he realised, was the reason why sex was so fantastic. The intimacy of making love to his best friend, of being with someone he knew inside and out. That's what it was. There was no other reason. He ignored the voice in his head that said there was obviously one other reason.

'We need to get ready soon to go to dinner,' Freya said.

'I need to go home and get changed,' Rome said. After getting off the boat, they had come straight back to Freya's flat and not left her bed since. The sun had been shining through the open windows, bringing with it the salty tang of the sea air, and it had been a glorious day. He certainly didn't want it to end now.

'Will we tell the others about us?' Freya asked, quietly.

'Hell no.'

Freya looked surprised by his conviction but he also saw the hurt there too as she laid her head back down on his chest.

Women were such tricky creatures. Did she really want everyone to know about them? She had been there at Eden's café the other day when Barbara and her friends had been meddling in their affairs, encouraging him to kiss her. It had been embarrassing. Surely she didn't want that again? It wouldn't be long until the islanders found out anyway but he didn't want to come right out and tell everyone.

'Hey, it's not that I'm embarrassed by us or anything like that,' Rome tried. 'Eden will be arranging our wedding before we've even finished telling her, Bella will want to know all the details, Dougie will have something inappropriate to say, and as for the rest of the island, you know what the jungle drums are like. This is something special and something private and I just want to keep it that way for a little longer.'

She looked up at him and smiled. 'It's OK, I understand.'

He rolled her over and pinned her to the bed and she let out a little squeal. 'Don't ever doubt that I don't want this.'

She grinned at him, looping her arms round his neck. 'OK.'

He bent his head and kissed her briefly. 'I better go. Save me a seat at the table.'

'I will.'

He rolled out of bed reluctantly and threw on some clothes. 'And tonight you can stay at mine.'

She nodded and he ran down the stairs and out of the flat. Tonight couldn't come soon enough.

❦

Freya arrived at Rosa's to find that Bella, Isaac, Eden and Dougie were already there. No sign of Rome yet though she knew he would be there soon.

Bella and Eden leapt up to hug her when they saw her, then she sat down in the booth.

'How was the parade? I heard we won,' Eden said.

'News travels fast,' Freya said.

'Hell yes it does,' Dougie said, grinning and nudging her. Eden took a swipe at him but that didn't stop the eyebrow waggling.

'We heard that the winner won a night in the Under the Sea suite at the Bay View Hotel,' Eden said. 'And Dougie's imagination is now running wild.'

'The parade was fantastic, all the towns had worked so hard, but our float was definitely the best,' Freya said, deliberately avoiding the question about the room. 'Here, I took some photos.' She dug out her phone and found the photos and showed them to the rest of the table.

Dougie took the phone from her and started scrolling through. 'These floats look great, though I agree the Hope Island float is by far the best. You and Rome outdid yourselves.'

'Cal was responsible for putting it all together, we can't take all the credit,' Freya insisted.

'Whoa, what's all these naked photos of Rome?' Dougie said and Freya flushed scarlet and snatched the phone back, despite knowing there were no photos of Rome naked in her phone. But she could see that Dougie had found the topless ones she had taken of Rome for the social media promotions.

'These are just the Instagram photos, he's not naked,' Freya said, wishing her cheeks hadn't gone quite so pink.

'So what did happen about that room? I looked it up on the website, it had a hot tub, a four-poster bed... Are you telling me that you two didn't utilise the room's facilities?' Dougie nudged her again.

'Leave her alone,' Isaac said.

'Yes, leave her alone,' Bella said, scowling at Dougie before turning her attention back to Freya. 'Well, did you?'

'No. Of course not. Cal insisted we take the room but nothing happened. As we were supposed to be sharing the twin room we had booked, we took a room each. Rome had the suite and I took the twin room.'

They all looked disappointed with that answer and she hated lying to Bella and Eden but she knew, despite Rome's wishes, that she would probably tell them the truth later. They would be discreet, she knew that, and as she had trusted them with her inappropriate crush on their brother, she knew she needed to tell them the next development in their relationship.

Thankfully she was saved from any further interrogations by Rome's arrival.

He stood at the edge of the table as Eden and Bella hugged him, nodded his hello at Dougie and Isaac and then turned his attention to Freya.

'You're looking beautiful tonight Freya,' he said, softly, and her heart did a little jig in her chest.

She cleared her throat. 'Thank you.'

'I'm just going to wash my hands,' Rome said and disappeared off towards the toilets.

Isaac and Dougie were talking about some computer game they were designing and Freya fiddled with her napkin for a moment or two before looking up at Bella and Eden, knowing they were staring at her.

Eden leaned across the table and Bella joined her. 'Something did happen, didn't it?' Eden whispered.

Freya glanced at Dougie and Isaac but they were still too busy talking to notice what was going on down their end of the table. She looked back at Bella and Eden. They were her best friends and there was no way she could lie to them any more. She nodded subtly and they both grinned. They both knew now was not the time to ask questions but she knew she would get a proper grilling later.

Rome returned to the table then and squeezed into the booth next to her, much to Dougie's annoyance at having to move round to make room for him.

'Why aren't you sitting next to Eden, there's plenty of room?' Dougie protested as he shifted round the corner.

Rome flashed him a glare and he returned to his conversation with Isaac, clearly unperturbed. Dougie had known Rome so long that any scowls, glares and comments just washed straight off his back.

Rome shuffled further into the booth, filling it with his enormous frame, and as Freya moved up to make room for him, for a brief second, so fleeting it could have been accidental, Rome squeezed her hand.

'Freya was just telling us about the parade,' Bella said.

'It was fantastic, we had a great day, the floats were all wonderful and winning is a great coup for the island, Cal and the glass studio.'

'The floats all looked so good,' Eden said. 'I've only been to the parade once, many years ago, and the floats were nowhere near as good as the ones I saw from yesterday. The towns have really upped their game this year.'

Freya smiled with love for her friend. Eden was not even mentioning the room or hinting that something had happened between them. Hopefully soon they would stop talking about the parade altogether.

Dougie and Isaac stopped talking and Dougie turned his attention to Rome.

'So how was the suite? We heard you won a night in the sea-themed suite at the Bay View. Did you enjoy the hot tub?'

'Oh, no, erm, Freya slept in the suite, I slept in the twin room.'

Freya glanced at Rome and tried to indicate that she had given the exact opposite answer, but she was obviously having trouble conveying that message with just her eyes as Rome was looking at her in confusion. She only hoped that Dougie hadn't noticed.

'Hang on, Freya said you had the suite and she had the twin,' Dougie said.

Freya shook her head. 'No, I had the suite.'

'That's not what you said before.'

'That's exactly what she said,' Bella lied. 'You need to wash your ears out, cuz.'

'I still can't believe you two are actually cousins,' Eden said, deftly changing the subject.

Bella had recently found out that her biological father was Dougie's uncle. She and Dougie had grown up together and had always been close; now they had an extra reason to be friends.

Freya leapt onto the change of subject. 'Is that weird for the two of you?'

Dougie shrugged. 'I always knew she was my cousin, I just wasn't allowed to talk about it as Bella was the product of my uncle having an affair. I still love her, always have.'

Eden practically swooned across the table at that wonderfully honest and sweet statement from Dougie.

Bella smiled with love for him. 'It hasn't changed things between me and Dougie, I still find him annoying.'

Dougie laughed.

'But I do think about my half-brothers sometimes,' Bella went on. 'The ones I never even knew I had until a few months ago. It'd be nice to meet them at some point. Although I have no idea how to initiate that meeting as doing so would mean telling them that their dad had an affair. I don't want to sully his name after his death, especially when he's not around to defend himself.'

Freya understood that need for family, to feel like she belonged. Her own parents had died when she was young and she'd been raised by her gran. When her gran had died when Freya was eighteen, she had ended up moving in with the boyfriend who she was dating at the time and later became engaged to him. She'd worked with him, socialised with his friends, been adopted by his family. When it all came to an end, she had no one. That was until Rome had taken her under his wing. And she knew that she was stupid to let the same thing happen again with him, but she knew she belonged here, this was her home.

'You can always come over to meet them next time I go over there to see my cousins,' Dougie offered. 'You could just be my friend. We don't need to tell them who you are. Though you do look a lot like your dad, they might figure it out.'

Bella smiled. 'Maybe that would be enough, to at least meet them.'

Isaac squeezed her hand. 'I could come with you. I still have friends on St Mary's, so we have a reason to be there.'

Bella nodded. 'I'd like that.'

The waitress came over then to take their order and the conversation moved on. Thankfully there was no more mention of Rome and Freya's relationship or who had the suite. They could just pretend everything was normal between them. Well, she would try to pretend everything was normal between them, though it was a bit tricky to concentrate on being just friends when Rome's hard thigh was pressed against hers.

CHAPTER 18

Rome stared down at Freya's hand in his. Her fingers had been entwined with his all night. The waitress had taken their order and left and the need to touch Freya had been too much, which was ridiculous since he'd spent the day in bed with her. As he had slipped his hand into hers, it had thrown her, she had been mid-conversation and she had stumbled over her words as he stroked his thumb over her hand. But she hadn't taken her hand away. Thankfully, where Dougie was sitting meant he couldn't see that they were holding hands and, if Eden and Bella noticed that both he and Freya had spent the whole night eating and drinking with just one hand, they hadn't said anything.

God, he needed to be with her now.

'Shall we get dessert?' Bella asked when the plates had been cleared away.

'It's been a long day for Freya and me,' Rome said. 'We were up early to get the plane back from Penzance, so I might call it a night actually.'

'Me too,' Freya said, a bit too quickly, feigning a yawn.

'I'll walk you back home,' Rome said, standing up.

Freya stood up too and he helped her to put her jacket on, innocently brushing his fingers against her neck as he adjusted the collar.

Dougie had seen the gesture, Rome could tell by the subtle way he arched an eyebrow at him, though for once he didn't say anything.

Bella and Eden shot up to hug them both goodbye, delaying them leaving by precious seconds. As Freya fumbled in her purse to pay for her food, Rome threw enough money down on the table to cover them both before ushering her out onto the street.

'You don't have to always pay for me,' Freya said.

'You can pay me back later,' Rome said, taking her hand again and hurrying along the streets towards his house. He ignored the curious glances of a few of the locals who were interested to see that he was holding Freya's hand.

'You know my house is the other way. If you're walking me home, you're doing a terrible job.'

'I want you in my bed.'

'That's very caveman of you. Is that what you say to all the women you date? "I want you in my bed" and then throw them over your shoulder and carry them back to your cave?'

'No, I believe in equal opportunities, I always go to the woman's cave,' Rome said, cursing how far away he lived from the main high street. He had chosen the house because of the incredible view of Buttercup Beach, but now it was something he could do without.

'You never take anyone back to your house?' Freya said, breaking into a jog to keep up with his long-legged stride.

'No, never.'

'But I've been to your house a hundred times.'

'You're different.' He ran down the steps onto Buttercup Beach where the streetlights didn't reach and the only light was the glow of the moon over the sea. It was a hot night and the warm sea breeze enveloped them. He pulled her into his arms and kissed her hard. God, the taste of her against his lips was heaven. She wrapped her arms round his neck and kissed him back, her body melting against his. He pulled back slightly so he could stare into her eyes. 'You're different in every single way.'

'So I'm the first woman you've had in your bed?' Freya giggled and then the smile fell off her face. 'I mean since Paige.'

'First woman in this bed. I got rid of the last bed as I couldn't even contemplate sharing it with another woman after Paige had died. Though it didn't make any difference, I still couldn't bring any woman home.'

Freya was quiet and he cursed himself. He was just about to make love to his best friend, he didn't need to bring up his ex.

'Why now? Why me?'

'Because you're important,' Rome said, stroking her face. 'Because for the first time in forever, I'm going to make love to someone I really want to be with, rather than just having sex with someone to dull the pain or pass the time. What we have is special, you know that.'

She smiled, sadly. 'It's special for me because I love you.'

He needed her to know how important she was to him. He couldn't tell her he loved her – he was so confused by his feelings for her but he knew it was something rare and incredible.

He pulled her closer. 'I have never in my life felt what I feel for you.'

She smiled. 'And what is it that you feel for me?'

Was it love? His feelings for Freya ran so deep and he knew he had never felt like this before, not even with Paige, and that confused the hell out of him. Because if this was what love really felt like, what had he felt for Paige? He thought he had loved her, they'd been planning to get married. To admit that he had never loved her felt like a huge betrayal. But if this wasn't love he felt for Freya, what was it? And labelling it as love scared him, because last time he had been in love, or at least thought he was, he had lost her. The universe had seen that he was happy and came along and ripped that away from him. It seemed safer, somehow, to keep his feelings locked away because he couldn't lose Freya too. There would be no getting over that.

His silence caused her to frown slightly. 'I love you. I've been in love with you for years. I'm hoping that one day you can fall in love with me too.'

He kissed her, not sure what he could say. He pulled away slightly. 'Let me make love to you.'

She hesitated for a moment and that worried him.

'Make love to me here,' Freya said and he felt his eyebrows shoot up into his hair.

'Someone might see,' Rome said.

'And we wouldn't want that, would we,' Freya said, pointedly.

She pulled away from him completely and let her jacket slide off her shoulders onto the sand. To his surprise and his delight she pulled her dress over her head and let it drop to the ground too. She was wearing nothing but a pair of black lacy knickers and her sandals, which she immediately toed off.

She stepped out into the shallows of the sea, looking over her shoulder at him. He had never seen anything as magnificent as her, watching her body lit only by the glow of the moon. Then she turned and dived into the waves, disappearing into the inky blackness. She surfaced a few metres away, sweeping her hair back from her face and laughing.

'Come and join me,' she called.

He looked around, hesitant to get naked in case anyone saw them.

Suddenly Freya threw something soft and black at him. When he caught it, he realised it was her knickers.

Forgetting any of his inhibitions, he quickly stripped off his clothes and waded out to join her.

The water was cool, heated by the sunshine of the day as he swam out towards her. Freya was lying on her back, staring up at the stars. He scooped her up into his arms and she wrapped her hands round his neck, caressing his damp curls as she kissed him on the forehead. She wrapped her legs round his hips and kissed him. She pulled away slightly, leaning her forehead against his; her soft breath against his lips was an incredible feeling.

'I really do care about you Freya, I—'

'Stop talking.' She pressed a finger against his lips. 'No one wants to hear that someone *cares* about them. You care about your sisters, or your parents, or an elderly neighbour. You shouldn't *care* about the woman you're about to make love to. Next you'll be telling me you see me like a sister again. There's nothing guaranteed to put a dampener on a romantic moment than being told you see me like your sister, so if you're even thinking of uttering those words, don't, not if you want to get laid tonight.'

'OK,' he said, quietly. God, he was so rubbish with women. He never knew what to say to them. 'I definitely don't think of you as my sister.' He ran his hands up her sides, stroking her breasts and running his thumbs over her nipples to illustrate his point. She gasped softly against his mouth.

'Look, I know this is just sex for you, and I'm not complaining, it's been incredible. And I'm guessing it's pretty good for you too judging by how you can't keep your hands off me. But don't give me platitudes and pretend that it means something more to you. If you want to say nice things to me, tell me you find me attractive, tell me you think I'm beautiful, don't give me false hopes that this is anything other than sex.'

He swallowed down the ache in his chest. The very last thing he wanted was to hurt her and this was why he'd never wanted to get involved with her – hurting her would mean losing her. But he was already involved now and walking away would hurt her anyway. Not that he could do that. She was right, he couldn't keep his hands off her.

He kissed her and he was gratified when she kissed him back, pulling herself tighter against him as the cool inky water lapped around them. He slipped his hand between them, stroking her, and she moaned against his lips.

'Freya, I find you very attractive.' He moved against her so she could feel just how attractive he found her. He kissed her again, lifting her slightly and then sliding inside her. He let out a noise that was guttural at the feel of her surrounding him. She arched against him, taking him in deeper, and as she tipped her head back, he moved his mouth to her breasts. 'I think you're the most beautiful woman in the world,' he whispered against her skin. 'But I have never lied to you. I have never pretended to be anything other than who I am with you.'

She brought her head back down to look at him.

'When I tell you that this is something special and incredible between us, when I tell you that I have never felt like this with anyone before, then you should know that it's absolutely the truth.'

She moved slowly against him and he held her tighter.

'This is a hell of a lot more than just sex. I told you before that I didn't just want sex any more, I wanted something more and I would never risk our friendship just for a quick shag. You're way too important to me for that.'

Her eyes were soft now and she kissed him briefly. He felt her tighten around him, her breath starting to quicken, and he shifted her slightly to slow her down.

'I know how hard it must have been to tell me you love me and how much it must hurt that I never said it back to you. I just need some time to figure all this out in my head. You asked me not to lie to you and I won't, so you know that, when I say it for the first time, it will be the truth. And while I can't say it yet, you should know that I do cherish you, I adore you, I need you, I'm crazy about you, I idolise you and I fancy the arse off you.'

Freya giggled. 'OK.'

He ducked his head to look properly into her eyes. 'OK?'

She nodded, a big smile on her face. 'Now stop talking and make love to me.'

He grinned and guided her back towards the shore, laying her down where the waves were lapping gently onto the sand. She stared up at him as he moved against her and a feeling of utter contentment washed over him. He wanted this feeling to last forever and as she found her release and clung to him, moaning out his name, it was the need to be with her always that gave him that wonderful release.

CHAPTER 19

Freya pulled her dress back on as Rome quickly got dressed. Although no one could see them from the street as they were hidden in the darkness, she didn't want any late-night dog walkers or fishermen to suddenly come across them. She had never had sex outdoors before and wasn't entirely sure what had possessed her to instigate it but to hear Rome say all those wonderful things made the whole risk factor worth it. Making love to Rome was always going to be wonderful and exciting, she still couldn't quite believe that it was happening after all this time, but maybe she would stick to indoor sex from now on.

Rome picked up her jacket and draped it round her shoulders, kissing her sweetly on the forehead. God, this man. If it ended, if he decided that he didn't or couldn't love her after all, would she ever get over him?

Suddenly there was a noise which sounded like someone falling over behind the rocks close by, followed by a soft curse.

Her heart leapt as she and Rome froze. 'Oh god, someone's there,' Freya whispered. 'They must have seen us.'

'I'll handle this, bloody perverts,' Rome said, leaving her side and climbing over the rocks towards the noise.

Freya hugged herself, feeling shaken at the huge invasion of her privacy.

'Dad!' Rome said from behind the rocks. 'What the bloody hell are you doing here?'

Rome's dad? Freya felt her cheeks burn. It had just got a hundred times worse.

'I was fishing, son, you catch some absolute beauties at night. You don't need to worry, I didn't see anything, I had my eyes closed the whole time.'

Freya watched as Rome helped Finn over the rocks and onto the sand.

'Hello Freya dear, it's lovely to see you again. I've been telling everyone about your heroic deeds the other day with Sammy the seal. Everyone is very grateful. You might even get some kind of medal,' Finn said, clearly as embarrassed about the whole thing as she was.

'You… you were there the whole time?' Freya said. 'You saw me naked?'

'Oh no dear. I never saw that. I didn't even realise you two were there, until I saw you swimming. I thought it might have been Sammy at first, my eyesight isn't what it used to be, and when I realised… um, what was happening, I closed my eyes straight away and put my fingers in my ears for good measure. You don't need to worry.'

'Why didn't you tell us you were there?' Rome asked.

'Well I didn't want to interrupt. The whole island has been rooting for the two of you to get together and now you finally have, well I think it's simply wonderful. I didn't want to be responsible for stopping it before it started. So I thought it best that I just stay out of the way and keep my eyes closed until it was over. I didn't want to embarrass you.'

'Oh god, it's safe to say I'm embarrassed,' Freya said.

'There's nothing wrong with it my dear, nothing to be embarrassed about. Me and Lucy used to have sex outdoors all the time when we were younger,' Finn said, desperately trying to make Freya feel better. 'You're not hurting anyone and it's not technically illegal, providing you don't get caught. Me and Lucy were caught having sex in the park once. The police had got some tip-off that someone was selling drugs in the park and a whole squad of them turned up ready to bust some illegal drug ring and there was Lucy and I, stark naked. She was on her hands and knees and I was—'

'Dad, for the love of god, stop talking,' Rome said.

Finn blushed. 'Yes, quite. Maybe you don't need to know the full story. But my point is, there's no harm in it, two young, single, healthy, consenting adults, why shouldn't you have sex whenever the mood takes you.'

'Dad!'

Freya let out a little giggle.

'Well, why don't I leave you two love birds to it and get off home,' Finn said, clearly deciding to stop making a bad situation even worse.

'We'd appreciate it if you didn't tell anyone about this,' Rome said and Freya felt another little kick of disappointment. Of course she didn't want the whole island to know about her and Rome's late-night naked swim but she also didn't know why Rome was so reluctant for people to know about them being involved either.

'Of course, I'll be discreet,' Finn said. 'I mean, I'll have to tell Lucy, she'd have my guts for garters if I kept that from her, but we won't tell anyone else, I can assure you of that.' Finn turned away and then immediately turned back, embracing Rome in a big hug. 'I'm happy for you, son, you deserve to be happy and find love again and I can think of no one finer to do that with than young Freya here.'

Rome patted his dad awkwardly on the back, probably not wanting to tell him that this thing between Rome and Freya wasn't love. She wasn't sure what it was, but it wasn't love and Rome knew that.

Finn pulled away from Rome and grabbed Freya into a big hug too. 'We always have the children round for dinner every Friday, we didn't last week because we were away, but we'd love you to come round for dinner this week.'

Finn pulled back to look at her.

'Oh thank you, that's so kind, but it wouldn't be right to intrude on your family dinner.'

'Don't be silly. You're family now too. Isaac will be there and Dougie always comes whenever he is in town. You must come.'

'Thanks Dad, we'd love to,' Rome said.

Finn nodded and walked away. Rome slipped his hand into hers and started walking towards his house.

Freya looked up at him in surprise. 'You didn't want to tell anyone and now you want to go to a family dinner and be outed as a proper couple in front of your parents and sisters?'

Rome shrugged. 'We probably have twenty-four hours until the whole island knows. Finn will tell Lucy and Lucy will just have to phone my aunt Cassie and she will tell everyone whether they want to know or not. I'm pretty sure Bella and Eden already know from the looks they were giving us all night and if they don't I'm sure you will tell them, I know how close you are. Dougie definitely knows. There doesn't seem much point in trying to keep it a secret any more.'

Freya frowned slightly. It sounded like he was resigned to his fate rather than happy about being outed. While Freya wanted to shout it from the rooftops. And if he really did love her, wouldn't he want that too?

She sighed. She had said she would give Rome time and she knew she had to do that. This was so new to them both and just because she had been in love with Rome since she met him, it didn't mean that he felt the same way yet. Up until the day before he had been quite happy being friends with her, it was her that had changed things between them. She couldn't expect him to suddenly fall in love with her overnight just because they'd slept together a few times. She had to remind herself that Rome had slept with several women since Paige died and although he insisted this was a lot more than just sex, it would take time for him to make that transition between friendship and something more.

'So now I'm part of the family?'

Rome grinned down at her. 'Seems like it.'

'Does your dad make that kind of fuss with all the women you date?'

'I don't date.'

'Sleep with then. Do they all get invited round for dinner?'

'No, Dad knows how important you are to me, that's why he's inviting you round and practically organising the wedding already. No one else has ever been invited round. You're the only one… Apart from Paige. But she only met them a few times,' he quickly clarified. 'She was away in London a lot and when she was back up here for the weekend we'd spend pretty much the whole time in bed.' He looked down at her. 'I'm making this worse, aren't I? You're my best friend and I have spent two years talking to you about everything, it's hard for me to get my head around that I need to censor my thoughts from now on.'

Freya shook her head. 'Don't censor your thoughts. I never want you to do that. Paige was a big part of your life, you loved her, you were going to get married to her. I'm not expecting you to just forget all about her because we're sort of seeing each other.'

'Not "sort of",' Rome muttered.

'Well, whatever this thing is between us. If this relationship goes the way I want it to, this will be the first relationship you've had since she died and I know that will be hard for you, so talk to me about what you're thinking and feeling, it'll help me to understand. Just because we're lovers now, doesn't mean we're no longer friends. So your relationship with her was very physical?'

He looked down at her in confusion. 'You really want to know?'

She nodded, even though she didn't. But she needed to know whether she actually stood a chance with him. Was the relationship she had with Rome anything like the one he had with Paige?

'Sex with Paige was… frantic, a desperate need for each other.'

Freya looked away over the moonlit sea. She was wrong, she didn't need to hear this. But Rome showed no signs of stopping now.

'I've never had that with anyone since. I often wondered whether our relationship would last when it was only built on amazing sex. We didn't have a lot of time to talk. She was in London all week, so we'd only see each other at weekends. I worked as a glazier during the day and she was out working at night so we barely had time to catch up over the phone during the week either, and the only catching up we did at weekends was purely physical. We rarely talked and actually I was always quite thankful for that. I was always afraid that once she got to know the real me, she wouldn't want to be with me any more. Thank god we had amazing sex.'

Freya felt a bit sad about that, that Paige had never got to know the real Rome. 'You talk about the real you as if there's something wrong with you, when I don't see that at all. There's a lot more to you than your ability to make a girl scream in bed. I fell in love with you long before we had sex. I fell in love with your kindness, the way you really listen, your protectiveness, your intelligence. I fell in love with your humour, you genuinely make me laugh. I fell in love with how easy it is to talk to you, your wonderful talent for working with stained glass and the way you taught me with so much patience. You are a wonderful man, Rome Lancaster, and if you and Paige had ever married, then she would have been the luckiest woman in the world.'

At the foot of the steps that led up the hill towards Rome's house, he stopped and pulled her into his arms, kissing her sweetly. 'What did I do to deserve you?'

'Well, I'm guessing the god of love or Cupid, or whoever is in charge, looked down and saw how many women you made happy in the bedroom and decided you needed a bit of happiness yourself. I could make you happy, Rome. I know our sex is probably nowhere near as amazing as the sex you had with Paige but—'

He frowned. 'Wait a minute. I've never said that. And I want you to know there is something incredible about making love to your best friend, that intimacy of knowing each other so well is something really special. I never had that with Paige.'

He took her hand and led her up the steps towards his house as she digested that. Was he saying it was better with her? She didn't dare ask that question for fear of the answer but it gave her hope.

He let them into the house and immediately pinned her to the door as he kissed her again.

She moved her hands over his chest and started working on the buttons of his shirt then slid it off his shoulders and let it drop on the floor. She ran her hands over his arms and shoulders and then round his bare back.

'Make love to me in your bed,' she whispered against his lips.

'Is that all you think about?' Rome muttered, sliding his hands under her dress and then pulling it over her head. He filled his hands with her breasts, kissing her again. She moaned against his lips, she was never going to get enough of him. His hands slid back to her waist and then down to her bum and he lifted her. She wrapped her arms and legs around him and, without taking his mouth from hers, he carried her up the stairs.

CHAPTER 20

Freya woke the next morning as Rome walked back into the bedroom carrying two mugs of tea. He was wearing only pyjama bottoms and she admired that glorious, huge smooth chest and those strong arms for a moment as he walked around the bed and placed her cup on the small chest of drawers next to her. Then he walked back around the bed and climbed in next to her.

'Morning beautiful,' Rome said, kissing her sweetly on the lips.

She sat up and leaned into him as he wrapped his arm round her shoulders.

'What time is it, it feels really early?'

He grinned. 'You just didn't get enough sleep last night. It is a little earlier than I'd normally get up but, having had the last two days off work, I feel we have a lot to catch up on. The tent around where the mural will be is going to be erected today, so we can start putting it together on the wall without the prying eyes of the public seeing it before the big reveal. So we could go over there this afternoon and work for a few hours. I also have a meeting with my solicitor this morning.'

'Oh, that sounds very official.'

'Just a few things I need to get sorted out,' Rome said, vaguely.

She slid her hand down his chest, heading towards his pyjama bottoms. 'So we haven't got time to hang around here for a bit longer.'

He laughed and extricated himself from her arms as he got back out of bed. 'No, we haven't. Don't tempt me. Besides, I was thinking about what you said yesterday, about how you think this is only physical for me. I want to prove to you that this is a hell of a lot more than that. I want to have a proper relationship with you. So for one week, we're going to talk and kiss and spend time with each other and go out on proper dates but no sex.'

Freya sat up as if she'd been electrocuted. 'No sex?'

'I want to do this properly. Paige and I never had a deep relationship. I'd like to think that when she eventually moved back here after her job finished in London we would have got married and things would have worked between us but if sex was the only thing keeping us together, I wouldn't have fancied our chances. I don't want to fall into that kind of relationship again where we are just tearing each other's clothes off at every available opportunity.'

'Why not, that sounds pretty good to me,' Freya teased. She couldn't believe after waiting for so long she'd finally made love to him and now he was slapping some kind of weird sex ban on their relationship before it had really got started.

'I want to see if we work without it.'

She got out of bed and enjoyed the darkening in his eyes as he appreciated her nakedness as she approached him. She slid her arms round his neck and his hands immediately went to her waist. 'You know we work without it, we have worked together and socialised together perfectly well for the last two years without the sex.'

'But we weren't in a relationship. We can still kiss and spend the night together but I don't want it to be all about sex and I know you don't want that either.'

Freya resisted telling him that she was quite happy for it to be all about sex. She was under no illusions that this was going to end with their happy ever after, happily married with four little children running around their heels. He didn't love her. Real love didn't appear slowly and take years to build. Real love knocked you off your feet, it was crazy and hedonistic and unstoppable. Bella and Isaac were proof of that. Real love wasn't, 'Let's see how it goes over the next few months and I'll try and fall in love with you too.' Real love was falling head over heels with someone so much that they ask you to marry them after only a month, the way he had with Paige. And although he had asked for some time and Freya was quite happy to give him that, in her heart she knew that eventually this thing between them, whatever he wanted to call it, would come to an end. She wanted to make the most of what they had now and make love to Rome as many times as she possibly could before that day came. A sex ban was the very last thing she wanted.

'I thought we could go to Envy again tonight, do the date that we should have had,' Rome said. 'And then tonight you can stay here again. I like having you in my bed. Having you sleep next to me… it made me feel complete.'

She stared up at him, emotion clogging in her throat. 'You say the sweetest things sometimes. It makes me fall in love with you a little bit more.'

'Hey, don't go telling anyone I'm sweet, it'll ruin my reputation as the grumpy sod on the island.'

'Your secret is safe with me.'

He laughed and bent his head to kiss her briefly and then pulled back slightly to look at her.

'Will you go out with me tonight?'

She smiled and nodded.

'Good, now get dressed. We've got work to do.'

He kissed her on the forehead and left the room.

If he wanted to date her, then she was more than happy with that, but this sex ban would have to go.

Rome was busy packing everything into boxes ready to go down to Buttercup Beach so he could start work on the mural that afternoon while Freya was busy copper foiling the last few pieces of the current batch of red glass that would be part of the school building in the mural. Things had ticked along at work that morning as they always had, with them both working seamlessly alongside each other, chatting and laughing as normal.

He'd been worrying about how it would be at the studio, whether it would be awkward after spending almost two days making love to each other, but nothing had changed. It made him wonder if they could really make a go of things. Most couples would end up killing each other if they had to work alongside each other all day and then spend all night together too, but they had never got frustrated or annoyed with each other in the past and he didn't see why that would change now they were dating.

Freya glanced up and out the window and he watched as the smile fell off her face.

He turned to see what had made her sad and saw Kitty Lane getting out of the car and heading towards the shop.

'Here comes the Rome Lancaster fan club,' Freya said.

He turned back to look at her. 'You don't like Kitty coming round?'

'Of course I don't. It's bad enough seeing her draped over the man I love and flirting with him, but now that you're my boyfriend it makes it worse.'

He grinned as he stepped up to her. 'Boyfriend?'

She looked unsure for a second. 'Well if we're dating properly then I'm not sure what else I could call you.'

He slid his hands around her waist and she responded by putting her arms round his neck. He bent his head and kissed her briefly on her lips. 'I like it.'

He saw the delight on her face just as Kitty walked in. As Freya tried to shift back out of his arms, he held onto her and kissed her again, this time taking his time, enjoying the moment. Kissing Freya was so sweet, so wonderful, he could honestly do it all day.

A cough interrupted them and Rome pulled back slightly, kissed Freya on the forehead and then slowly turned and faced Kitty as if he'd only just noticed her.

He plastered on his fake smile. 'Hello Kitty.'

She didn't look pleased at all and he took a small amount of pleasure from that.

'I'd heard the rumours that you two were together, I have to say I didn't believe them.'

Freya pulled out of his arms and carried on working with the red glass, deliberately ignoring Kitty.

'Why wouldn't it be true?' Rome asked.

'Because…' Kitty gestured to Freya and then trailed off, smart enough not to answer that question, but her intention was quite clear. Why would he have Freya when he could have Kitty?

He let the fake smile drop from his face. She could forget being polite.

'Do you have glass in the car?' he said coolly. 'I'll get it out.'

Kitty nodded and he walked past her and out onto the street. She tottered after him in her heels.

'So you and Freya? That's sweet,' Kitty said, dryly.

'Yes, I couldn't be happier,' Rome said, opening her boot and lifting out two boxes of glass.

'Believe me, I could make you happier,' Kitty said, cutting to the chase.

He lifted the last box out and placed it on the floor and then looked Kitty right in the eye. 'I seriously doubt that. She gives me everything I need.'

'What does she give you?'

Rome thought about how he could sum up everything that Freya gave him – from her kindness and patience, the way she made him laugh, how he enjoyed being with her every second of the day – and he smiled as he realised he could capsulate all that in one word.

'Love.'

Kitty looked horrified at that prospect as that was the one thing she could definitely never give him.

'Thanks for coming round, Kitty,' Rome said, picking up two of the boxes and walking back towards the shop without looking back. Only to see that his solicitor, Jim, had arrived and was busily chatting away to Freya.

He hurried in, not wanting Jim to tell Freya why he was here, but he was already too late for that.

'And what is it you're here to see Rome for?' Freya asked, curiously.

'Oh, Rome wants to sell the flat upstairs,' Jim said, clearly not realising that it was supposed to be a secret.

Freya's gaze swung to him accusingly.

Crap.

CHAPTER 21

Freya stared at Rome in shock and the worst thing was how guilty he suddenly looked. She wanted him to tell her it wasn't true, that there'd been some big misunderstanding, but he clearly wasn't going to do that.

'You're selling the flat?'

He hesitated for long enough for her to know it was true, putting the boxes of glass down while he tried to find the right words.

'Freya… it's not. I…' he trailed off, clearly not able to give any suitable answer.

Her heart plummeted into her stomach. That was her home. Where was she going to live when he sold it on? And why hadn't he discussed this with her first before he ripped her home out from under her?

'I'm sorry,' Jim said; clearly he could tell that Freya was less than happy with this arrangement. 'It's quite an unorthodox request, maybe I got the wrong end of the stick.'

'No, Jim, it's OK,' Rome said, awkwardly. 'I haven't spoken to Freya about it yet because I wanted to speak to you first.'

'You didn't think I had a right to know before you made it all legal?' Freya snapped.

'It's not as simple as that. Look, why don't you go and get some lunch for us both while I talk things through with Jim and I'll explain everything when you get back.'

She stormed to the door and Rome snagged her arm before she could leave.

'Trust me,' he said, softly.

She stared up into his gentle grey eyes and realised that she did. He would never do anything to hurt her. He might never love her in the way that she wanted him to but he cared for her and selling her home from under her didn't fit in with that. As upsetting as that news was, she would wait for him to explain it to her before she let her emotions get the better of her.

She nodded and walked out, leaving Rome and Jim alone.

She hurried along the street towards Eden's pottery café, relieved to see that the café was fairly quiet so she could talk to Eden, and happy to see that Bella was there too.

Bella grinned when she saw her; obviously Freya was in for an interrogation about her and Rome's relationship but right now Freya really needed to talk about it so she didn't mind.

Bella got up to hug her and Freya held her tight for a moment, hoping that some of Bella's strength would seep into her. The last few days her heart and her mind had been a churn of emotions and she didn't know what to do about it.

'Not at work today?' Freya asked as they sat back down and Eden came hurrying over to join them so not to miss out on any gossip. Freya was pleased to see Eden's assistant, Clare Crissell, was back and busily helping behind the counter. There was no sign of Dougie, maybe he was out house hunting somewhere, which Freya was glad of; she could do without his sarcastic input today.

'I have the day off. Isaac is taking me to see some show tonight in Penzance, so we are flying out there later this afternoon and staying over. I decided to take the day off so I wouldn't be running around in a mad panic trying to pack in between work.' Bella glanced towards the door and then very innocently asked, 'Rome not with you?'

'No, thank god. That man is going to be the death of me. My head is a mess and I don't know whether I'm coming or going.'

'Something happened when you were in Penzance, didn't it?' Eden said, gently.

Freya nodded. 'I told him I loved him.'

Bella and Eden gave a collective little gasp. Bella's was of surprise, Eden's was of happiness. In Eden's mind, she was already planning the wedding.

'We ended up making love and—'

She was interrupted with squeals from both of them that were loud enough to draw the attention of everyone in the café. She quickly shushed them and when everyone had returned their attention back to the plates and mugs they were painting Freya carried on talking.

'Keep it down. I think everyone on the island will know soon but I don't need them to know all the details. Yes we made love and—'

'And?' Eden said excitedly. 'How was it? I mean, I don't want details. He's my brother, I really don't need that kind of information but was it… OK?'

'It was incredible, as you would imagine it would be when you make love to the man you love for the first time. But it was so much more than that. We shared this connection that was so…' she trailed off, knowing that any words she chose wouldn't even begin to describe what she had shared with Rome. 'Intimate,' she finished lamely. It didn't even come close.

'And then what happened?' Bella said. 'Again, spare me the details.'

Freya smiled as she remembered. 'We kissed. A lot. And then made love again. In fact we've made love many times since then. Each time has been as beautiful as the first time. We ended up making love on Buttercup Beach last night and your dad caught us.'

Eden's eyes widened. 'He was fishing there last night, he loves night-fishing on the rocks between Buttercup Beach and Blueberry Bay.'

'Yes, well he caught more than he bargained for. And he'll obviously tell Lucy and Lucy will probably tell your aunt Cassie and I'm sure there will be an article taken out in the Hope Island newsletter by tonight.'

Bella giggled. 'How embarrassing, especially for Rome. Getting caught is one thing, but no one wants to get caught by their parents.'

'Believe me, it was pretty embarrassing for me too. Though you'll be pleased to know, I've now been invited to the family dinner tomorrow night where I'm sure Lucy and Finn will want to know our wedding plans.'

Bella laughed. 'That sounds like them. So are you two dating now, or is it just sex or…?'

Freya shrugged. 'I have no idea really. Rome says he wants to do this properly and we're going to date each other. And then he slapped some weird sex ban on us.'

'What? Why?' Bella asked.

'He said he doesn't want it to just be about sex with us, like it was for him and Paige.'

Eden and Bella stared at her.

'That's a big step for him. He's always had very physical relationships. The fact that he wants to do this differently is very significant,' Eden said.

'Is it?' Freya said and sighed, swirling patterns in the glass tabletop. She looked up to see that Bella and Eden were still watching her carefully.

'Come on, out with it,' Bella said. 'You've been in love with my brother since you started working with him, you've now made love to him multiple times and you're dating, why are you not happier about this?'

Freya stared back down at the glass tabletop for a moment. 'He never said it back. I told him I loved him and he simply doesn't feel the same way.' And that's how it had been with Jake: he'd never said he loved her, she'd waited for him for eight years and he'd never said it to her. Was it happening all over again?

'You need to give him time. This is all so new to him,' Eden said.

'He's had two years. He knew he loved Paige after a month. If he doesn't love me by now, I don't think it's going to happen.'

'I really liked Paige and I don't want to speak ill of her, but I don't think he was ever in love with her. He was infatuated by her, but I don't think it was ever love,' Bella said.

Freya thought about this. 'He says he has never felt for anyone what he feels for me. I took that to mean that this wasn't love because he doesn't feel the same about me as he did about Paige.'

'No, take that as a positive,' Bella insisted.

'He never wanted to fall in love again after Paige died,' Eden said. 'He guarded his heart so carefully and he never let anyone in, until you.'

'I don't think he *has* let me in.'

'Of course he has, you changed his life. He absolutely adores you.'

'That boy is crazy in love with you,' Bella said. 'He might not know it, he might not want to admit it out of some crazy loyalty to Paige, but he is. Anyone can see that. Just give him some time to figure it out for himself.'

'Don't you think that if it was real love he would know it by now?'

'Not if he has nothing to compare it to. He thought he was in love with Paige, if this feels different for him then it must be confusing,' Eden said.

'The fact that he wants to date is really significant. He hasn't dated anyone since Paige,' Bella said.

'Be patient with him, he's worth waiting for,' Eden said.

'Yes, try to enjoy it. This is what you've wanted for years. If you two had just met and started dating, you wouldn't expect him to fall in love with you straight away.'

Freya nodded. 'You're both right. I suppose in my head I just expected or at least hoped he would say it back. But I guess I need to give him time. Although I might not have that. Did you know he's planning to sell the flat?'

Bella and Eden looked confused by that, so clearly they didn't know either.

'Why would he do that?' Bella asked. 'I thought Through the Looking Glass was doing well, surely he doesn't need the money.'

'How can he sell the flat anyway? He bought the whole building – can you break up parts of it and sell it on?'

'I have no idea. But he's meeting with a solicitor right now to discuss it. He's asked me to trust him, but it's not exactly a positive sign.'

'Maybe he wants you to move in with him,' Eden said, always seeing the happy ending.

'I don't think that's likely if he hasn't even said I love you yet.'

'Rome isn't going to kick you out on the street. There's got to be an ulterior motive,' Bella said.

Freya sighed. 'I just wish I knew what that was.'

❦

The shop door swung open and Rome looked up to see his dad walking in with a big smile on his face. He put down the tool he was using to cut the glass and went to greet him.

'Oh, look at all these wonderful pieces,' Finn said, staring around him like a kid who had walked into a sweet shop. He had been in Rome's shop many times before, but every time he acted like it was the first. 'You are so talented, I don't know where you get it from. All I can do is draw stickmen and probably couldn't do that very well.'

'Well, Lowry seemed to do very well out of matchstick men, so there's probably a market for it.'

Finn picked up a blue lamp that had the sea, sky and the sun on it. 'I love this.'

'That's one of Freya's, I can't take any credit for that,' Rome said.

'Well you did teach her everything you know, so you can probably take some credit,' Finn said, putting the lamp carefully back on the shelf.

Rome shook his head. 'No, she naturally has a talent for this. I may have taught her the basic skills but she has come on in leaps and bounds. Her work is outstanding.'

'Is she here?' Finn asked, peering over Rome's shoulder, and when he shook his head Finn sighed in relief. 'I wanted to talk to you alone actually. I'm so sorry about last night. Lucy said I probably embarrassed you both. I mean, I know it was embarrassing that I was there when you two were...' He gestured with his hands to skate over the fact that he had caught his son having sex on the beach. 'But Lucy said that I probably overreacted about you and Freya getting together and that I should have played it cool because it might not be that you're together at all. She said maybe it was just sex, or just a one night stand or just a fling and there I was congratulating you and saying how wonderful it was that you were together and inviting her round for dinner and telling you how happy I was that you had found love and Lucy said that I might have made things worse for you or scared her off because it might not be that yet.'

Rome stared at his dad. But clearly Finn hadn't finished.

'But I said, I saw with my own eyes how much you loved her, I mean I obviously didn't see anything... rude, I had my eyes closed the whole time. Not that it's rude, there's nothing wrong with sex in a loving relationship, well nothing wrong with sex outside of a loving relationship if that's what you want. Nothing wrong with sex at all. Consensual sex obviously. Which it clearly was. Not that I saw anything. But after, when you were kissing, she seemed happy…with the sex. I mean, of course she was happy with the sex, I'm sure you know what you are doing in that department. You've slept with enough women. I mean not enough. Well a lot. Which is your choice. As long as you are happy. And Lucy wanted to know if you used protection because we had sex in the sea once and the condom just floated off. I didn't know until after we'd finished. I was so worried that some poor seal or dolphin would end up choking on it so we spent ages looking for it and thankfully we found it, and a few weeks later Lucy found out she was pregnant with you so wearing condoms in the sea is not that effective.'

'Dad—'

'Oh god, that makes it sound like you were an accident and that's not true at all. We wanted children, we wanted loads of them. Just not at that time as we were living in this tiny studio flat and we were saving to get a bigger place with a garden so all the children could play outside. But when we found out we were having you, we couldn't have been happier. You were such a beautiful chubby baby. I mean not chubby, I've never thought that you were fat. Just big. And you didn't need a garden when you were first born anyway. And by the time you were running around, we had bought our house which did have a garden so I don't think you were any worse off from living in the flat for the first year of your life. So you see, if you didn't use a condom or it floated away, you don't need to worry because having children is the most wonderful thing in the world and you would make such a fantastic dad and I can't think of anyone better to raise your children than Freya, I think she is perfect for you in every way. And Lucy agrees and last night she was looking up knitting patterns for baby cardigans, just in case. And well, I've rambled on now but I just wanted to say that we're both really happy for you, if you are in fact together and having babies, but if you're not together and just having sex with no babies then we're really happy for you too.'

Rome stared at him, not sure if his dad really had finished or if there was anything more embarrassing to come. He didn't even know which part of the monologue to tackle first.

He cleared his throat. 'It's a lot more than sex. She's really important to me.' He honestly couldn't believe he was having this conversation with his dad. 'And there won't be any babies yet. She's on the pill. But maybe in a few years.'

His dad seemed equally delighted with this. 'So this is really forever for you? Oh god I'm so happy, I can't tell you how relieved I am. We heard all about these women you were sleeping with and we were worried that you would never find love again. And then Freya came along and I told Lucy after we had first met her, I said, "Mark my words, he'll marry that girl." And now you've finally got together. I couldn't be happier. Have you talked about marriage at all? Have you set a date?'

'Dad, it's really early days. I… care about her so much, I adore her. And yes I want forever with her but… how do I know if it's love?'

'You'll know.'

Rome resisted rolling his eyes but he did let out a small sigh of frustration.

'When me and your mum first started dating, it was just sex. She was magnificent in bed and—'

'Dad! I really don't need to hear that.'

'No, quite. Perhaps not. But the thing is, I wasn't ready to settle down. I had just moved here with work, not willingly I might add, and I was just biding my time, having some fun until I could get a job off Hope Island and leave. But just sex became making love and long walks, and making love and lots of talking and making love and so much laughing and I enjoyed those bits as much as the sex. And when a job did come up that would finally take me away from Hope Island, a job that was perfect for me and would mean a massive pay rise, it took me about five seconds to decide. I was having the time of my life with your mum and I never wanted it to stop. I knew that there was no one that would ever make me feel this happy. I knew I wanted forever with her and if you're thinking about forever with Freya, if you're thinking about marriage and children, then it's pretty obvious you do love her.'

'But it feels so different to what I felt with Paige.'

'The heart is a multi-layered, multi-faceted organ. The love you feel for your siblings is different to the love you feel for your parents, and you have a different love for your friends and even your pets. The love you have for a soul mate is completely different to all of those things. It's more intense, more... more everything. Just because your feelings for Freya are different to what you felt with Paige, it doesn't mean you didn't love Paige or that you don't love Freya. You can love more than one person and in very different ways.'

Rome sighed. He was more confused than ever. Mostly because his *Book of Love* told him that love was to do with the dopamine and serotonin levels in the brain, nothing to do with the heart at all. But his dad was right about one thing, he really did want forever with Freya and maybe that was all the answer he needed.

CHAPTER 22

Freya walked back into the shop and saw that the solicitor had gone. Rome was shifting the boxes of tools and things they would need to work on the mural at the beach this afternoon nearer to the door. He broke into a huge smile when he saw her and it was such a genuine, warm smile that it filled her with so much happiness. He put down the box he was holding and came to greet her, cupping her face gently and kissing her sweetly.

'You've been gone a while, I missed you.'

She smiled. 'We've been talking about you.'

There was no need to tell him who the 'we' was. He would know that she had been chatting to Eden at the very least.

'I gathered that I was the topic of conversation when I got a text from Bella saying, "Just seen Freya, for god's sake don't screw this up."'

Freya laughed.

He slid his hands down her back and into the back pockets of her denim shorts, holding her against him. 'And I don't intend to.'

She rested her hands on his chest for a moment. 'Did you have a good meeting with the solicitor?'

She looked up at him and he was grinning. 'Yes, I did in fact. Come over here for a moment.'

He led her over to the workbench where there were some official-looking documents.

'So you really are selling the flat?'

'Yes I am. It's taken a few days to sort this out in order to separate the flat from the shop. It's going to take a while to register the flat as separate at the Land Registry so I was going to wait until that was finalised before I told you but the solicitor has drawn up the contract now so there's no harm in telling you today.' He encouraged her to sit down. 'I thought I would give you the chance to buy it first, before I put it on the market.'

Anger flared up in her. 'What? Do you have any idea what property prices are like round here? I do, because I stopped to look in the estate agent window on my way back here and there's no way I could afford a quarter of the cheapest property on my salary. I would be unlikely to get any kind of mortgage on my salary either.'

He stilled her flapping hand with his own as he sat down next to her. 'What kind of properties were the houses you looked at?'

'Some of them were the old cottages, some were the bigger townhouses on the other side of the island,' Freya answered, not sure where he was going with this.

'Any flats?'

She shook her head. There were so very few flats on the island, certainly no blocks of apartments. The only ones were those like hers which were above shops. Most of the shop owners used these for storage or workshop areas to make the things that they sold.

He shrugged. 'Turns out that flats aren't really worth much on the island – everyone wants a cottage with sea views. You only have a tiny sea view from one of your windows so it's worth even less.'

'Then why sell it at all?'

'Because I don't want it.'

'But I do. That's my home.'

'Then buy it off me.'

'With what? I think I have two thousand pounds in my account, funnily enough I don't think that will cover it.'

Rome grabbed the contract and slid it in front of her. She saw his name and underneath that it said he was selling the property to her, which was ridiculously presumptuous of him, but underneath that it said how much he was selling the flat for.

One pound.

She stared at it, looked back up at Rome who was watching her with patient eyes and then back down at the contract again. She swallowed the lump in her throat, all of her anger fading away.

Eventually she found her voice. 'You're selling the flat for a pound?'

'It's not worth anything,' Rome quite clearly lied.

She looked up at him. 'I don't understand why you are doing this. If you were to sell the flat you'd get hundreds of thousands of pounds for it. Property prices in the Scilly Isles are crazy.'

'I don't need the money, and I don't need the flat.'

'You can't give me the flat.'

'I'm not, you're buying it off me. You said that one of the things you wanted to do in your life was to buy your own home, so…'

Oh god.

Tears welled up in her eyes. 'Oh you daft, silly man. You can't give me the flat. Most men give the women they date a bunch of flowers or a box of chocolates, not a flat that's probably worth a quarter of a million pounds or more.'

He stroked her face, wiping the tears away.

'You said you wanted your own home so you knew it could never be taken off you, something that was just yours. I want to make you happy.' More tears joined the ones he had just wiped away and he laughed, slightly. 'Seems I'm not doing a very good job of that.'

'You are, trust me, but I can't accept.'

He shrugged. 'Then I'll have to sell it to someone else. I'll give the estate agents a call tomorrow, get it put up for sale. I expect it will go quite quickly at that price.'

She rolled her eyes.

'Look, you say you love me?' he said and she nodded. 'And if you love me, then you'll want to make me happy. It would make me deliriously happy if you would stop being so stubborn and just accept the gift.'

She thought about it for a moment. He was going to ruin her. Eventually she nodded. 'OK.'

'Good, you owe me a pound.'

A slow smile spread across her face. She owned her own house. Well, she would when everything was final.

She slid her arms round his neck. 'This is the sweetest thing that anyone has ever done for me. Thank you.'

He smiled and kissed her briefly. 'It's my pleasure.'

'I do love you,' Freya said.

Rome smiled but it was another little stab of disappointment when he still didn't say it back. She had agreed to give him time, but that still didn't stop it from hurting. Maybe he'd never say it back.

'Make love to me,' she whispered. At least when they were making love she could feel that connection between them and in that moment she could pretend that it was love for him too.

'Not now. Making love in the shop in the middle of the day is probably a little more risqué than doing it on the beach after dark, plus I haven't forgotten our sex ban.'

'You're so strange. Most men would never dream of implementing a sex ban.'

He shrugged. 'You've had years to get used to how strange I am, it's too late to back out now.'

'I fell in love with all of you, the strangeness doesn't put me off.' She stared down at his chest and kissed just above his heart. 'Eden says this no sex thing is actually really significant for you.'

'Eden sees everything through rose-tinted glasses, but in this instance she's right. You're too important to me to screw this up.'

Her heart filled at that comment and he leaned his forehead against hers.

'I want this to work more than anything,' he said.

'I do too.'

He bent his head and kissed her and she pushed the doubts away. She would trust him and, as Bella and Eden said, it was time that she started to enjoy what she had with Rome and stop worrying about what might happen.

❦

Rome stepped back from the mural, or the very beginnings of it, to look at what they had done so far. They were in the small marquee just outside the school's wall, slowly building the mural up. They had soldered together several smaller pieces into larger roughly rectangular panels. These panels were all carefully wrapped in numbered bits of paper in the boxes they had brought over from the shop and would then be slotted into the right place and soldered onto the other panels. Like a big jigsaw, they were starting from the outside and working their way into the middle. They had done the corners and had started working their way along the bottom. Although they were right at the very beginning of slotting it all together, and they still had a lot of work to do back at the studio before they would be anywhere near finished, he was really proud of how it was looking so far. The only thorn in his side was how hot it was under the marquee. He wanted to lift the sides to let some air in but the marquee was there to protect the mural from being seen before it was officially revealed. There were currently hundreds of people on the other side of the marquee walls, playing on Buttercup Beach, and he didn't want anyone to see it until it was finished.

'Can you stop staring at it and grab the soldering iron?' Freya said as she was holding two panels together. 'I want to do this piece and then step outside for some air. It's so hot in here.'

Her hair was fluffed out, looking like she'd just been dragged through a hedge, she was sweaty and had a smudge of dirt on her forehead – but to him she looked incredibly sexy.

'Let me grab some water,' Rome said. Scooping two bottles from the cool box, he opened one, took a quick mouthful and offered the other to Freya. She arched an eyebrow at him and he laughed when he realised that both her hands were in use, holding the panels in place.

He opened the other bottle and held it to her mouth, carefully angling it up so she could take a drink. She tipped her head back and drank gratefully from the bottle. A few drips slid out from the top of the bottle and ran down her throat. She squealed as the ice-cold water ran down her hot skin.

He quickly stopped pouring. 'Sorry, here let me get that.' He moved his fingers to catch the drips and then thought better of it. He dipped his head and caught the drips with his tongue instead, sliding it up her throat as he followed the little river of water all the way back up to the corner of her mouth. She groaned with need, which sent a punch of desire straight to his stomach.

When he reached the corner of her mouth, he slid his tongue across her icy lips; feeling the coolness against his own hot tongue was achingly wonderful.

She moved to kiss him properly but he edged back slightly.

She was still holding onto the panels, although he guessed if he was to carry on with what he suddenly intended to do, they would probably be dropped to the floor, so he eased the panels from her hands and put them on the workbench behind him.

He held the bottle against her lips again, slowly tipping it up, and she leaned her head back obligingly. This time he wasn't so careful pouring the water into her mouth and some dribbled down her chin, over her chest heading straight for her breasts. Just as it dipped into the valley between her breasts, he caught the drip with his tongue. Her groan was louder this time as she threaded her fingers through his hair. He kissed the flesh on each breast as he slowly inched his way back up towards her throat.

'Hello!' a voice called, just as the flap of the marquee was pulled back and Bella walked in. Rome leapt away but not before Bella clearly caught him licking Freya's breasts.

'Oh my god,' Bella said, before quickly ducking back out again.

What was it with his sodding family catching him in the act? Freya giggled as she straightened her clothing.

'Go and see what she wants, I don't think I'm in any fit state to go and talk to my sister,' Rome muttered, rearranging his shorts.

Freya wiped the rest of the water off her chest and ducked outside.

'I'm so sorry, I had no idea,' he heard Bella whisper theatrically.

Rome took a long cool drink of water and tried to school his thoughts to think about anything other than how good it felt to lick and kiss Freya like that. Christ, this sex ban was going to be the death of him.

'It's OK, we were just kissing,' Freya said, even though it had been clear for anyone to see that it was a hell of a lot more than that. 'It was hardly going to lead to sex when Rome has banned sex from our relationship entirely.'

She sounded disappointed about that and he suspected she was feeling as sexually frustrated as he was right now. God, he hoped he was doing the right thing with banning sex from their relationship for the next week. It could quite easily go the way his relationship had gone with Paige where they couldn't keep their hands off each other. He wanted more from his relationship with Freya. He wanted to prove to her it was more too. But if he got it wrong, then all that would happen would be they'd be getting angry and frustrated with each other.

'I bought some ice creams for you both,' Bella said. 'Thought you might need some cooling down, though I didn't realise the weather wasn't the only thing that was making things hot and steamy in there.'

Now more appropriately ready to talk to his sister, Rome ducked out of the marquee into the bright sunlight.

Bella was handing over two white chocolate Magnums.

'Thanks Bella,' Rome said, taking his from Freya. 'Sorry about that.'

She shrugged. 'It's OK, you're both at that exciting stage of a new relationship where it's all passion and need and lust. I remember being like that with Isaac when we first started dating.'

'From what I can gather, you're both still like that now,' Rome said.

Bella grinned. 'Yeah, probably.'

He unwrapped his ice cream and took a big bite, realising how sexy it was to watch Freya eat hers.

'I thought we could go for a walk actually,' Bella said and Rome swallowed the mouthful of ice cream that was resting on his tongue.

He tore his attention from Freya and looked back at his sister. She had that look that clearly said that she wanted to interfere. It was very obvious she wanted to talk about him and Freya.

'We're quite busy actually.'

'I'm sure you can have a break for five minutes,' Bella said.

He didn't want to say that he had been enjoying his break immensely before she had come along and interrupted him.

'I only have five minutes anyway,' Bella went on. 'We're leaving for Penzance shortly.'

Freya gave him a little nudge. 'I'll be fine on my own for a while.'

Rome rolled his eyes, recognising when he was outnumbered.

'Come on then.' He indicated for Bella to go ahead of him and he fell in by her side as she walked down towards the shore. The sun was shining hard above them from a cloudless blue sky, the turquoise sea shimmering and sparkling as it lapped gently onto the sand.

As he ate his ice cream, they wandered down to the little jetty and Bella didn't say a word as she hopped up onto it and padded out to the end. He followed her and sat down next to her, their feet just inches above the water.

'It's a beautiful day,' Bella said, shielding her eyes and looking out to the horizon.

'Bella, I love you, but if you've brought me down here so you can interfere in my relationship with Freya then I'm just going to walk straight back up to the marquee again. If you want to talk about the weather or anything else in fact, apart from me and Freya, then I'm happy to talk. But I'm not talking about that.'

'Isaac has asked me to move in with him.'

Oh crap, now he felt like scum. Bella hadn't wanted to interfere in his relationship at all.

'Sorry.'

She shrugged, clearly not offended. She started picking at the wood, scraping the sand that had encrusted itself onto the end of the jetty. Clearly this was something she wasn't comfortable with.

'You don't think it's a good idea?' he asked.

'I'm scared.'

Crap. He wasn't geared up to have these kind of conversations. He was close to Bella, he absolutely adored her, but his role as big brother was always to protect her against getting hurt, physically and emotionally. They so rarely had these kinds of conversations. Bella had Eden or their mum for that, or even Freya for that matter. He was the least likely person someone would go to for advice regarding matters of the heart. He was rubbish with women – the one girl who had shown any interest in him beyond the bedroom he had proposed to and she'd promptly gone off to London for the next eighteen months and their relationship had been based mainly on sex after that. And now he had this thing with Freya, his best friend, his lover? His soul mate? He had no idea how to categorise what they had or if it had any chance of lasting. If he was honest, he was scared too. Scared of losing her like he'd lost Paige, scared of screwing things up and losing her in a different way, scared that one day she would wake up and realise that she didn't love him, that he was too grumpy or too boring or too emotionally stunted and he'd lose her anyway. How could he possibly give Bella advice when he was scared too?

He took her hand. 'What is it that you're scared of?'

'Losing him.'

He thought about that for a moment. Maybe he *was* the right person to talk to her. Maybe he didn't have any pearls of wisdom to give but maybe just talking to her about his own feelings would show that she wasn't alone or wrong to have these feelings.

'I feel like I'm going to screw this up,' Bella said, sadly, staring down into the sea.

'There's nothing you can do to screw this up, that man is crazy in love with you. He accepts you and loves you exactly how you are. You don't need to change or pretend to be someone else. He loves you, this… fragile, vulnerable, scared, feisty, fun, kind, generous, wonderful person, he loves all of you.'

Bella sniffed, her face partially hidden by her long red hair. Was she crying?

'Is that how it is with you and Freya?' Bella said, tearfully. 'You know that nothing you do will ever scare her away. She's been your best friend since she moved to Hope Island, she's seen you at your worst, she's seen you grumpy, angry and stood by you when you were grieving over Paige and she still loves you. It must be so wonderful to have that security in a relationship, to know she will love you no matter what.'

He thought about that for a moment. Bella was right. Freya did know him really well. He had never tried to hide who he was. He had never tried to impress her before, he had been completely himself and she had fallen in love with him despite all that. Or maybe because of all that.

He felt his confidence in his relationship grow slightly. He nodded. 'You're right, it is a wonderful feeling to know you're loved. I'm still scared though.'

'What are you scared of?' Bella asked, returning her attention to the jetty again, picking at the bits of sand.

He looked out at the little white sailboat that was bobbing around in the distance. 'I suppose the thing I fear the most is having her taken from me. I loved Paige, well at least I thought I did, and right before she was supposed to come back here and we were going to start our lives together, she was ripped away from me. I never even got the chance to say goodbye. I fear it happening all over again, of falling in love and losing her. I can't go through that again.'

'What you went through with Paige was heartbreaking and I understand why you guard your heart so fiercely. But does that mean you'll never let yourself fall in love again? Never experience that incredible head-rush, that heart-pounding feeling of being in love and having it reciprocated for fear of what might happen in the future? If Paige's death taught me one thing, it was that life is short and we never know what is around the corner, so we have to make the most of what we have now, not hide ourselves away. Don't save for a rainy day, spend your money now. Don't avoid the puddles, go dancing in the rain and other such "seize life" clichés. The point is, life is for the living so you need to embrace it now, not worry about tomorrow. Isn't it better to spend a few weeks or months in a loved-up relationship with Freya than to not experience that at all? Grab hold of this opportunity with both hands before it passes you by. Stop being scared of the what-ifs.'

He stared at her tearless face, his eyes narrowing in suspicion. 'That sounds like advice you should take yourself.'

'I already have, I told Isaac yes this morning as soon as he asked me. Seize the day Rome.' She leaned over and kissed him on the cheek, before scrambling to her feet and running down the jetty onto the beach.

'Love you,' she called, before she ran off laughing.

He watched her go and shook his head. He'd just been played.

CHAPTER 23

Freya was waiting in her lounge later that night for Rome to come and collect her for their first date. That in itself seemed weird when they had already spent so much time in bed and a lot of time kissing out of bed. But there was a huge part of her that was really pleased that he wanted to date her, rather than just jump into bed with her at every opportunity.

After his chat with Bella that afternoon, he had come back to the marquee and just held her in his arms for the longest time and she had decided then and there that she was going to enjoy what she had with him. She knew he had feelings for her too and those feelings were growing every day. She would be happy with that.

She heard her flat door open downstairs and Rome called up to her as he ran upstairs. He appeared in the lounge wearing a suit and carrying a bunch of orchids.

'You brought me flowers?'

'Well, apparently that's the expected gift to give someone you're dating, giving them a flat is not appropriate.'

She laughed and took them from him. 'Thank you.'

She leaned up to kiss him and he kissed her back hard, gathering her against him. 'You look beautiful by the way,' he said against her lips in between kisses. 'I forgot the prerequisite compliment.'

She giggled as she kissed him. 'Compliments and flowers, you really are spoiling me.'

He pulled back slightly. 'I think we better go. If we stay here any longer, this pretty little dress is accidentally going to come off and then I think the sex ban is going to fall apart shortly after.

'How would my dress "accidentally" come off?'

'These things happen.' He pulled away and took her hand. 'Do you need a jacket?'

'No, it's a lovely night, let me just grab my bag.'

She picked her small holdall off the sofa and turned back to Rome who was waiting by the door.

'That's a big handbag.'

She laughed. 'It's my overnight bag.'

'Oh. I hope you didn't pack any pyjamas.'

She arched an eyebrow at him. 'I don't think me sleeping naked in your bed will help the sex ban.'

'I think it will help it very nicely,' Rome said as he took the bag from her and led her down the stairs and out onto the street. 'If we can't make love, sleeping with each other, naked, is the next best thing.'

The sun was just starting to set above them, although it would be several hours before it disappeared into the sea, and the clouds were painted a candyfloss pink, tinged with gold. It lent a magical air to the evening and with Rome Lancaster holding her hand as they walked through the streets, it felt like anything was possible.

'So you'll be pleased to know I researched what makes a good first date.'

Freya laughed. 'I'd expect no less. What did your *Book of Love* say?'

'Well, *The Book of Love* said that the venue was important, as where I choose says a lot about my personality. I'm not sure I agree with that. Envy doesn't really reflect my personality but it feels like somewhere romantic and the food's great. Plus we're quite limited on classy places on Hope Island.'

'I don't agree that the venue is important either, I'd be equally as happy with a picnic on a beach or a home-cooked meal at your house. It's not about the place, it's about spending quality time with the other person.'

'Well as a first date, it might be a bit forward to invite you to my house. Statistically only thirty-six percent of people expect to have sex on a first date and you might think it was expected if I invited you round to my house.'

'But you did invite me round to your house, I'm sleeping with you in your bed tonight.'

'Well yes, but that's because our first date is unique. It's not a typical first date.'

'Then you can probably forget the typical first-date rules.'

He glanced down at himself. 'So dressing in my best suit was a waste of time.'

She turned to him, and he wrapped his hands round her waist as she placed her hands on his chest.

'It's very sweet that you made an effort but, Rome Lancaster, you're a beautiful man, inside and out. You could wear jeans and a t-shirt, this gorgeous suit or be absolutely butt-naked and I'd still be head over heels in love with you.'

A smile spread on his face.

She slipped her hand back into his and carried on walking along the street. 'What else did your dating manual say? Let's put this to bed right now.'

'That I should be punctual and polite.'

'You're always punctual and… well, politeness is overrated.'

He laughed. 'Are you saying that I'm not polite?'

'Only if grumpiness is a type of politeness, but don't worry, you won't lose any first-date points for it.'

'Good to know.'

'What else should I expect from tonight's date?'

'Well, I did think the advice to ask you about your day was pretty redundant as I spent the day with you.'

'You could still ask?'

Rome glanced down at her for a moment. 'Um, how was your day?'

'I bought a house,' Freya said, excitedly, and she saw the answering smile on his face.

'You did?'

'Yes, I'm so excited. It was on my bucket list and now it's become a reality. You have given me so much and you have no idea what this means for me. I don't think I thanked you properly before. But I appreciate it more than you know. That's two of the things on my list that you've helped to come true.'

'I want to make all your dreams come true,' he said, softly, and her heart filled with love for him.

She thought for a moment. 'The other things on the list are a bit trickier.'

'Going on safari isn't that hard to organise. Maybe once this mural is out of the way we could take a few weeks off.'

Her heart soared. She could think of nothing better than going on holiday for a few weeks with Rome. No interruptions, no work, no one poking their nose into their business, it would be bliss. And to do all that on safari would be a dream come true.

'I'd love that.'

'And as for the other two…' he trailed off and she knew he was thinking about her dream to get married. Going to space was an impossible dream but at the moment so was getting married. 'I'm working on it.'

She didn't say anything. She wasn't sure how he could possibly work on her dream to get married. She needed a groom for that and there was only one person she wanted for that job. And although he had casually asked her to marry him a few days before, that was before they had got involved with each other and there had been no mention of it since, so she could hardly set her hopes too high. She wasn't going to think about that now though, there was no point dwelling on the future, she would just enjoy what they had now. He was making her happier than she had ever been and she would enjoy that.

They had arrived at the restaurant by this point and Rome opened the door for her and the host showed them to their table, a small booth in the corner of the restaurant.

Rome sat next to her, instead of opposite her, and she liked that.

'OK, so we know what the first-date etiquette says we should do, but as we already know each other so well and already had bloody amazing sex, we can probably skip past the "try to impress the other person" protocol. How about we really get to know each other?' Freya said, glancing down as Rome took her hand once more.

'What did you have in mind?' Rome said, and she could see the wariness in his eyes.

'A game of "would you rather" will be a hell of a lot more revealing about your personality than which venue you choose for our date. Do you want to play?'

He grinned. 'OK.'

She thought for a moment just as the pretty waitress who had been chatting to Rome the last time they had been here came up to the table.

'Oh, hey Rome,' the waitress smiled and Freya watched that genuine smile appear on Rome's face as he looked up.

'Hi Amelia, oh you two haven't met. Amelia, this is Freya, my girlfriend, and Freya this is Amelia, my...' he trailed off and Freya was left wondering what he had been going to say. 'Um, cousin?' He didn't sound sure and Freya suddenly experienced a bolt of panic. Was he lying?

'Step-cousin maybe,' Amelia suggested.

'Yes, probably,' Rome said, then turned to Freya to explain. 'My dad's brother was Amelia's step-dad.'

Freya nearly sagged with relief. That's why the smile was so genuine, Amelia was family.

Amelia laughed. 'Yes, for about a year before he and my mum divorced, so I'm not sure what that leaves us as now, ex-step-cousins, maybe.'

Rome shrugged. 'Amelia and her brother lived here for that year and we all hung out and we've sort of stayed in contact ever since. Amelia is over here for a few months working at the observatory at the other side of the island.'

'Oh, I heard that's had some massive funding injected into it, is it going to be open to the public soon?' Freya asked.

'It's had thousands of pounds spent on astral imaging equipment, which means we can take some great photos of deep space. We are in such a dark place over that corner of the island – with no other light pollution between here and Canada it's the perfect spot for a bit of stargazing. It's not open to the public, it'll be a few more weeks yet,' Amelia said, clearly very passionate about what they were doing over there. 'Oh hell, don't get me started on it, I could honestly talk about it all night. Let me get you guys a drink and then I'll leave you alone to enjoy your evening.'

'Shall we get a bottle of wine?' Rome asked Freya.

Freya nodded. 'Prosecco?'

'Sure.'

Amelia nodded and left them alone.

'She seems nice,' Freya said, trying to make up for her earlier slur on Rome's character, even if it had been entirely in her own head.

'She is. She had a bit of a rough time of it when she was a teen. They moved here to be with my uncle and then it all fell apart a year later and they moved away again. Anyway, I'm glad you two have met properly.' He arched an eyebrow meaningfully and Freya blushed, knowing that seeing Rome chatting to Amelia last time had been a very tiny reason for her suddenly storming out.

'So shall we play?' Freya said, skating over that embarrassment.

Rome squeezed her hand and kissed her on the cheek. 'OK, you go first.'

'Would you rather… have duck feet or a beak for a nose?'

Rome laughed. 'I think duck feet, you could swim quite effectively and a lot easier if you had webbed feet, I don't think there would be any benefits for having a beak for a nose.'

Freya smiled at his practicality. 'Good point, I agree.'

'OK, would you rather… fight a hundred duck-sized horses or one horse-sized duck?'

Freya burst out laughing. 'A horse-sized duck would be quite scary, especially if I had to fight one, but there's only one of them, so once I defeated it, the battle would be over. Whereas if there were a hundred tiny horses all fighting me at the same time I think it would be too many for me to stand a chance.'

Rome smiled. 'I love the thought that went into that answer.'

He looped his arm around her shoulders but, as he did so, his fingers touched the back of her neck in the lightest of touches, making her gasp and goosebumps erupt all over her body. How could one tiny touch from him have such an effect on her?

She glanced up at him and he must have seen the effect he'd had on her as his eyes darkened. He continued stroking the back of her neck, his fingers touching the top of her spine and then slowly caressing the hair at the bottom of her head.

She leaned back into him, resting her hand on his chest. He stared down at her with such need for her but there was so much fondness and adoration in his eyes too.

'We should look at the menu and decide what we want, Amelia will be back soon with our drinks.'

'I agree, we should,' Freya said, not moving from her position and Rome didn't move either. Eventually he picked up the menu with his other hand, and as he continued to stroke her neck, he held the menu between them.

Freya tore her eyes from him to briefly glance at the menu. 'I'll have the chicken and pasta.'

'Sounds good.' Rome snapped the menu closed and bent his head to kiss her, just as Amelia returned with the wine.

'Are you guys ready to order?'

'We'll both have the chicken, thanks Amelia.'

She nodded and poured the prosecco into the glasses then left them alone. They both took a sip of the wine and then Freya snuggled back into his arms.

Freya reached up and stroked his face. 'OK, I have one based on our current ban. Would you rather make love to me every night for the rest of our relationship but never kiss me, or kiss me every night but never make love?'

His eyes widened at that question. 'That's a hard one. I love making love to you, it's quite honestly the best sex I've ever had.'

Freya smiled at this.

'But I think I would choose kissing you.'

'Over sex?' Freya hadn't expected that at all.

'I could kiss you for hours and never get bored of it, I could kiss you all night and wake up in the morning and carry on kissing you. I doubt I would have the stamina to make love to you twenty-four hours a day. I could kiss you in the street, on the beach, at this restaurant but I could only make love to you privately. I could kiss you all over your beautiful body, not just on the lips, and I know I'd enjoy that or miss that if I could never do it any more.' He moved his head closer. 'Kissing you is like an addiction and not one I think I could ever break.'

Then he kissed her, not caring who saw. His lips were soft against hers as she ran her fingers through the curls at the back of his head. His tongue slid against hers and she could taste the bubbles and prosecco. He ran his fingers down her cheeks and ever so gently he traced his fingers down her neck and across her shoulders, making her shudder with his touch.

Eventually, he pulled back slightly. 'What about you, which would you rather do?'

She thought for a moment. 'Kissing you is like heaven but I think I would choose making love to you.'

He arched an eyebrow. 'And you were the one that said this was only about sex for me.'

'Hey, I wasn't complaining. Making love to you is wonderful, the way you look at me and hold me, for a little while it feels like you love me too. The connection we share when we make love is incredible, I've never felt that way before with anyone.'

He swallowed as he stared at her. 'I feel that connection too,' he said, softly.

Her heart filled for him. 'You do?'

He nodded. 'And that's what confuses the hell out of me. I was in love with Paige and this feels so different to what I had with her. But so much better. This feels so much closer and intimate with you. And not just the sex – this, what we share. And I know we've known each other longer and maybe that's the reason. I just need some time to figure this out in my head. God, that sounds awful. What kind of idiot doesn't know whether they are in love or not? What kind of idiot would make you wait? You've been so patient with me and I don't deserve it but that's kind of the reason for the sex ban. It would be so easy to fall into that kind of relationship where we're tearing each other's clothes off every second but I had that with Paige and I want so much more with you.'

She placed a finger over his lips. 'You don't need to explain. I know you loved Paige and I know this is confusing for you. But you make me so happy and you've already shown me how much you care, I don't need anything more than that. And although not making love to you for the next week is going to frustrate the hell out of me, I'm happy to wait if that's what you need.'

He smiled with relief and bent his head to kiss her briefly. 'I'm crazy about you and I don't want to do anything to screw this up.'

'And I won't let you.'

His smile grew and he kissed her again and this time he didn't stop until their food arrived at the table.

CHAPTER 24

Rome was lying in bed waiting for Freya to come out of the bathroom. For reasons he couldn't put his finger on, he was nervous.

He had tried to explain to her what he was going through but it all sounded very lame to his ears. Freya had the patience of a saint to put up with this rubbish.

She walked into the bedroom wearing only his t-shirt and the need to make love to her was suddenly so powerful, and not just because she looked sexy as hell dressed in his t-shirt. This was a need to connect with her in every way.

But what kind of restraint was he showing if he couldn't even keep his hands off her for one day?

He lifted the duvet for her and she climbed in next to him. She didn't look at him and as she spent a few moments rearranging the duvet properly, he realised that she was nervous too.

This was ridiculous, they had slept in the same bed together as friends before they had become a couple, they had already made love and it had been wonderful, they knew they were compatible in every way, so why were they nervous?

She lay down next to him and pulled the duvet up, so just her eyes were peering out over the top. He laughed.

'I think it's a bit late to be shy now, I've already seen you naked.'

She pulled the duvet down slightly. 'I'm nervous.' She pulled the duvet back up.

'I am too, why are you nervous?'

She pulled the duvet back down and rolled on her side to face him. 'I don't know, I feel like I have to pass some test. That if this feels right for you, if us sleeping together but not actually making love is good for you then maybe you'll want forever with me. And I want that so much, I want marriage and children with you and if I pass this test I might get that. But I have no idea what I can do to pass this test, how do I study for it, what's the right move to make?'

'Wait, this isn't about you,' Rome said, his heart aching for her that she felt that way. He was an arsehole for putting her through this. He gathered her close against him, pulling her onto his chest as he wrapped his arms tightly around her. 'I'm not expecting you to change or do anything differently. The girl I have laughed with, talked with and spent time with over the last two years is the girl I want to be with, exactly as you are. This is not about you passing any kind of test, this is just me trying to get my head around it all.'

'OK.' She stroked his face. 'So why are you nervous?'

'Because…' He thought about it for a moment. 'Because I don't want to screw this up, you're too important to me for that. I'm scared that I'm not doing the right thing by doing this sex ban but I'm scared to go into a full-blown passionate relationship too in case that ruins things for us. I want this to work more than anything.'

She slowly smiled and then reached up and kissed him and as he pulled her tighter against him, he realised if it really was that important to him, it could only mean one thing.

❦❧❦

Rome woke the next morning and smiled when he saw Freya fast asleep in his arms. He wanted to wake her up with gentle kisses and then make love to her and because he still wasn't sure if that was a good idea, he decided to go for a run instead.

He kissed her on the head and she stirred slightly.

'Baby, I'm going for a run,' he whispered.

'I'll stay here,' Freya murmured and he grinned because she was hardly going to come with him. She hated running. She had gone running with him for a few weeks when she had first moved to the island but she had ended up with pain in her shins, back ache and various chafing issues. She had found it hard to keep up with him and he had ended up jogging really slowly so she could still run alongside him. Looking back, she had obviously only wanted to run so she could spend more time with him and he loved her a little because of that.

He slipped from the bed and got dressed. He pulled on his running shoes and noticed that Freya had already gone back to sleep. He quietly left the house and ran down the steps onto Buttercup Beach. The sun had already started its rise into the sky and the forget-me-not blue was a sure sign it was going to be another glorious day. The sand sparkled in the early morning light, the sea a beautiful teal at this time of the day. It was still early and although there were a few people on their way to get the shops ready for the day and there were quite a few fishing boats on their way back in, the island was pretty quiet.

To his surprise, he saw Dougie running down the beach towards him. He was in his running gear too. Rome did a few cursory stretches as he waited for his friend to come towards him and a few moments later Dougie slowed to a stop in front of him.

'Hey,' Rome said.

Dougie grinned at him as he caught his breath. 'Where's your beautiful girlfriend? You two are normally glued at the hip.'

'I left her in my bed and we're not going to talk about her.'

Dougie shrugged. 'You coming for a run or just going to stand there stretching like a big girl?'

Rome started running down the beach and a few seconds later Dougie caught up with him.

'How's the house search going?' Rome asked.

'Good. I've looked at a few and nothing felt right and then the house next door to Eden came up for sale and I think it's perfect for me.'

'The house right next door?'

'Yes, how cool is that?'

Rome rolled his eyes. Eden had had a crush on Dougie since she was a teenager and that crush didn't seem to have diminished over the years. As far as he could see, Dougie was well aware of his sister's crush and seemed to enjoy teasing her, by insisting on staying with her every time he came over, hugging her and flirting with her constantly, but to the best of his knowledge nothing had ever happened between them. It was frustrating as hell for his poor sister and now Dougie wanted to dig the knife in by moving next door to her. That seemed a step too far. But how could he bring it up without telling him how Eden felt for him? If Dougie genuinely didn't know then Rome didn't want to be the one who told him. Eden would be mortified. She had never even discussed it with him so he didn't have any real confirmation.

'I didn't think a cute one-bedroom cottage would really be your thing,' Rome said as they left the beach and then cut through the alleyway into the park.

'Well, I never thought it would be either but I just fell in love with it.'

'So you're not just doing it to wind my sister up?'

'Why would I want to wind Eden up? I adore her. I would never do anything to hurt her.'

Rome sighed. Dougie clearly had no idea how much his visits affected her.

'I don't know, you guys have always had that kind of relationship. You wind everyone up, including me.'

'That's because I adore you too,' Dougie laughed.

They ran out of the park and up the hills that cut through the middle of the island and made Hope Island look a bit like a Nodosaurus from a distance with its low head and arched back. He shook his head, he was such a geek.

They reached the top of the island with those wonderful three-hundred-and-sixty degree views. Up here he could see St Mary's Island and a few of the other Scilly Isles, but over in the west there was nothing but miles of deep blue sea that disappeared into the early morning haze.

Rome sat down.

'You lacking stamina in your old age?' Dougie said and Rome smirked. He was six months older than Dougie so naturally Dougie tried to use the 'old man' joke as often as he could.

'Do you really want to test who has the most stamina and speed?' Rome said, knowing that whenever they had tested that theory in the past, he had always beat Dougie in any distance race.

'It wouldn't be a fair test today, I've already run to Mistletoe Cove and over ten miles before that this morning.'

Rome smirked. The island had a rough circumference of just over two miles, if you ran right around the very edge. He had measured it once, being the geek that he was. So Dougie would have had to have run round the island five times to cover a ten-mile distance, which he found unlikely.

Dougie threw himself down next to him and for a while they fell into silence as they stared out over the sea.

What was he waiting for with Freya? He loved spending time with her, chatting and laughing with her, he loved working alongside her, she was his best friend and there was no one he would rather spend his time with. They had off-the-chart chemistry and the thought of spending forever with her filled him with so much joy and happiness, so why was he holding back? Why was he bothering with this weird sex ban? Shouldn't he be taking Bella's advice and seizing the day? Shouldn't he be enjoying his time with her while everything was good and perfect between them? Why couldn't he tell her he loved her, what was he so afraid of?

He looked over at his friend. 'You ever been in love, Dougie?'

'Christ, you've changed.' Dougie shook his head. 'We used to talk about beer and football and farts, now you want to talk about love and puppies and rainbows and hearts. I don't know you any more. Is this going to be a serious conversation as I don't think my testosterone can take it?'

'We've never talked about beer and football and farts.'

Dougie sighed dramatically. 'I know, I need to choose my friends more wisely.'

'You're a geek, just like me, so we had to stick together. Only you're a computer geek, which is worse. At least my facts about the world are interesting – you can only converse in computer code, which is beyond dull.'

'Believe me, no one is interested in your stupid facts about sharks or the history of the oil can either.'

'Answer the damn question.'

Dougie was silent for a moment. 'Yes, I've been in love. Once.'

This surprised Rome. There had been a few girls in Dougie's life over the years, but no one that had seemed that serious.

'Who?' Rome asked, trying to get some context for their conversation.

Dougie shook his head. 'It doesn't matter.'

Rome thought about this. 'Was it not reciprocated?'

'I… don't know. Part of me hopes that she loved me too but if she did then I know I hurt her when I kissed her and then nothing else happened between us. Part of me hopes that she was able to carry on with her life without this agonising pain in her chest that I've carried with me for so many years.'

Rome stared at his friend. He'd had no idea. 'Why didn't anything happen between you if you both felt the same way?'

'Wrong time, wrong place, thousands of miles apart. I don't know, these all sound like lame excuses but I wasn't sure how it could work.'

Thousands of miles? Was it someone he left behind when Dougie left Hope Island? Was it *his sister*? If Dougie had actually loved Eden at some point, Rome might have to beat him up for causing her so much heartbreak for no reason.

'How did you know it was love?'

'When I lost her. When everything was new and exciting and fantastic in my life and all I could think about was her. She filled my every thought, she still does if I'm honest. I think if it's real love, it never goes away.'

Rome thought about this. If that was true then maybe he had never really loved Paige at all. He didn't miss her, hadn't thought about her in any kind of sexual way since he'd been having those nightmares about her as the grim reaper, and he knew what he felt for Freya was so much more than what he had felt for Paige.

'You've not told her you love her yet, have you?' Dougie said.

And because Dougie had bared his soul and for once in his life was being sincere, Rome decided to talk to him.

'No, I just…' It sounded so stupid when he had to vocalise his madness. 'I'm scared.'

'Because of Paige?'

'Partly.'

'You feel disloyal to her?'

'No... Yes. No it's not that. This is so different to what I had with Paige and if this is love then what the hell did I have with Paige? And I do feel guilty about that, maybe I never loved her at all.'

'Don't feel guilty. You adored Paige, you gave her everything. You had an amazing eighteen months, you had a lot of fun and a lot of great sex, but maybe that was all that it was, just a bit of fun. Tell me, if she had come back and you had lived together and after a few months it all just fizzled out, would you regret the time you had together?'

'No, I'd never regret that. We had a blast.'

'And I bet she wouldn't regret it either. Do you think she would be hurt or angry to see you moving on with Freya after all this time?'

'No, she told me once that she expected me to find someone else if she died. It was one of those silly conversations but I know she was sincere.'

'So what's the problem?'

'It's not Paige. I mean, that's a tiny part of it.'

'Do you love Freya?'

'Yes. I... I think I do.'

'Oh Jesus Rome, no girl wants to hear, I think I love you.'

'I know, that's the problem. I don't want to tell her if I don't. I won't hurt her like that.'

'If you're waiting for some life-changing lightning-bolt moment of clarity, a definitive sign that shows you love her, then you'll be waiting around forever.'

'I just don't want to lose Freya. It would destroy me if I screwed this up and lost her. I want to do this right.'

'She has been head over heels in love with you since she met you, the only possible way you are going to screw this up is by not grabbing her and telling her you love her too. She's not going to wait around for you forever.'

Rome sighed. Dougie was right.

Dougie got up and stretched his arms above his head. 'Don't cock this up.'

He turned and ran down the hill, leaving Rome alone with his thoughts.

❧

'Right, I think that's enough for today,' Rome said, stretching, and Freya enjoyed the flash of toned stomach as he raised his arms.

They had spent another day in the tent on the beach, putting the mural together. It had been hot and unbelievably sweaty and she was filthy. She wanted to just go home, take a long bath and lie on her sofa for the rest of the night, preferably wrapped in Rome's arms, but she had to go to dinner with Rome's family and, while she absolutely adored his parents, she now felt like she had to impress them too.

Rome was in the process of packing all the tools away, and she started helping him. While it was very unlikely that anyone on Hope Island would steal Rome's tools, she knew he wouldn't leave them in the tent overnight. Ordering new tools to be delivered to the Scilly Isles always took a lot longer than anywhere else in the UK. It wouldn't take long to pack everything away, they didn't have a lot of tools with them, as they had already done most of the work with the pieces of glass they were using that day back at the shop.

He picked up the tool box and they stepped outside into the cool sea breeze. The beach was still quite busy, though lots of families that had been there at lunch time had already packed up and gone back to their guest houses or holiday cottages for dinner.

He secured the flap with the piece of rope, which was completely redundant as it would have taken seconds for someone to untie the rope and peer inside if they wanted to have a look. When they had arrived that morning, the rope had already been undone, proving that the curiosity of the islanders was so great that a little piece of rope wasn't going to stand in their way.

Rome took Freya's hand as they walked back towards the shop and she couldn't help but smile at his sweetness.

'I need a shower,' Freya said, pulling at her t-shirt to stop it sticking to her.

'I do too,' Rome said, and when she looked up at him he arched an eyebrow at her.

She laughed. 'Don't look at me like that.'

'Like what?'

'Like you want to have a shower with me and want to do rude and dirty things to me in the shower.'

'Wow, you got all that from one raised eyebrow?'

'Was I right?'

'One hundred percent.'

'I know you, Rome Lancaster. And I don't think us getting naked together is going to help your sex ban. We're just going to end up getting sexually frustrated.'

'Is this ban making you sexually frustrated?'

'Of course it is! Two years I've been waiting for this to happen between us and then twenty-four hours of making love and it's suddenly stopped. I feel like a contestant on one of those cheesy eighties game shows, "Here's what you could have won." I've seen the fabulous prize, I've even got to experience it for a while, and now it's been whisked away. If this is what you need then I'm prepared to wait but I don't think this is going to do anything to strengthen our relationship, the only thing it will achieve is driving us crazy.'

'Well, if it's making you frustrated, we'll have to do something about that,' Rome said as he let them into the shop. Still holding her hand, he led her inside, dumped the tools on the workbench and then pulled her upstairs without breaking his stride.

She followed him into the bathroom and he started to undress her. She stared at him for a moment, wondering if she should stop him. A naked hot kiss wasn't going to do anything to quell her need for him. But then she decided against it. If he really was going to make her wait a week, then she'd take any little sniff of action she could get.

She pulled his t-shirt over his head and he quickly wrestled himself out of his shorts so they were both naked and then tugged her into the shower.

The hot water poured over his shoulders and chest and he pulled her into his arms so the water covered her too. Steam billowed between them and she immediately thought about the wonderful first time they made love. He kissed her deeply, holding her face between his hands.

He pulled back and grabbed the shower gel, poured it into his hands and then started washing her body. He was stroking her, caressing her, taking care of her, and it was hot as hell.

She grabbed the shower gel too and started washing his chest and arms, and was rewarded with a dazzling warm smile as she took care of him. God, she wanted nothing more than to take care of him for the rest of her life if only he'd let her.

As he continued to stroke his hands across her body she reached up and kissed him. She suddenly gasped against his lips as his fingers slipped between her thighs. He didn't take his lips off hers for a second as he worked his magic on her. As tension built in her stomach, he pulled back slightly so he could watch her when she fell apart. It was so sexy and so intimate to have him look at her so intently in that intense moment that she quickly tumbled over the edge. Before she had caught her breath he was kissing her again, hard, seemingly as turned on by watching her as he would be if she had been touching him.

'Is that better?' he whispered against her lips.

'A little.'

'I promise, when we do make love again, it'll be worth the wait. For now, we have a family meal to endure and I don't think they are going to make it easy for us.'

Freya frowned slightly. 'What does that mean?'

'It means, if we can get out of there without my parents mentioning marriage, weddings or babies, it will be a bloody miracle.'

Freya laughed. 'Really?'

'Oh yes, they've been badgering me for years to ask you out. "Freya's a nice girl, when you going to ask her out?" and "I really like Freya, I think you should take her out" and then more recently, "When are you going to marry Freya and give me some grandchildren?"'

Freya laughed as Rome turned the shower off.

'She didn't say that?'

'That was my dad, but Mum is just as bad.'

'That's hilarious. But the question is, if you've had feelings for me for so long, why didn't you ask me out before?'

'Because you're my best friend and I didn't want to do anything to damage that.'

She smiled with love for him as Rome wrapped a towel around her and tugged her towards him so he could kiss her on the forehead.

'So what do I say when they start asking me about when I'm going to marry you?'

'You say, "soon".'

Freya laughed. 'Isn't that giving them false hope?'

He stared at her for a moment. 'I don't think so.'

Her heart soared with hope herself.

'Well, we better go and face the music. Isaac has just asked Bella to move in with him so with any luck they'll be asking them about marriage, not us.'

CHAPTER 25

Freya walked up the garden path of Rome's parents' house feeling slightly nervous. The last time she had seen Finn hadn't been in the best circumstances and to know that he had immediately come home and told Lucy all about their late night swim didn't lessen her awkwardness about the situation.

Rome was holding her hand, which made her feel slightly better. She loved how affectionate he was with her, always taking every opportunity to touch her in some way. It gave her such hope. She knew he had strong feelings for her and she was hopeful that those feelings were love or at least would be eventually. He just hadn't figured it out or wasn't prepared to admit it yet.

Rome knocked on the door and she heard Lucy inside practically whoop for joy.

'They're here, oh my god, I can't believe she's really here with him. Everyone, play it cool, don't ask them embarrassing questions. Just act normal,' Lucy bellowed at everyone else who had already arrived.

'Just act normal?' Freya giggled.

Rome rolled his eyes. 'Welcome to my life.'

The door opened and, before Freya could utter a word, Lucy had yanked her into a giant bear hug.

'Oh my dear, we're so pleased to have you here for dinner. We're so glad the two of you have finally got together. Come in and tell us all about it.'

Freya suppressed a giggle as she was dragged inside. What on earth was she going to tell them?

Rome shut the door behind them just as Finn came barrelling out and grabbed Freya into a big hug too.

'I hope you're not embarrassing them by talking about the beach incident,' Finn said. 'We agreed we weren't going to talk about that.'

'I'm not talking about it, you are,' Lucy scolded.

'Well, it was just a bit of a shock,' Finn said. 'There I was fishing, thinking about making some kind of fish curry, and then suddenly I was interrupted by two people getting naked. It was all just a bit embarrassing really. And when I realised it was my own son and Freya, well I didn't know where to look.'

'Stop talking about it,' Lucy said. 'You're embarrassing them. I want to hear all about how you finally told each other you loved each other. I think it's so romantic. Two best friends, falling in love after all this time. I want to hear all the details.'

'And that's not embarrassing?' Finn said. 'Maybe they don't want to share that with everyone. If it was anything like the beach incident then maybe it's better left unsaid.'

'Nonsense, we are all family. We don't have any secrets. Come through, everyone is here.'

Finn and Lucy disappeared back towards the kitchen and Freya looked up at Rome.

'This is playing it cool?'

'My parents don't have that setting. They have enthusiastic, over-enthusiastic and "this is the best news ever". I think if the day comes when Dougie and Eden ever get together, my mum might actually explode with happiness. Look, we won't be staying long so just try to grin and bear it for a few hours.'

'I think it's wonderful that they're so excited for us. I love your parents, it's totally fine.'

'Well, I actually have a plan for afterwards, so we really can't stay long. We have somewhere we need to be at nine o'clock.'

'Sounds intriguing.'

'I'm hoping you'll think it's romantic.'

Lucy came back out, clearly too impatient to wait. 'Come on dear, you can sit next to me.'

She took Freya's hand and tugged her into the kitchen. Bella and Isaac were already sitting on one side of the table and Dougie and Eden were sitting opposite them. They all grinned at her as she was dragged in. Clearly this was totally normal behaviour from Lucy.

Lucy sat down next to Dougie and pulled Freya down beside her, leaving Rome to sit down opposite her.

Finn came over holding a bottle of champagne which he popped and the sweet foam poured from the top before he managed to get a glass under it. 'We were saving this for a special occasion but I think we've got to celebrate you two getting together,' Finn said as he filled everyone's glasses.

Freya smirked. Actual champagne to celebrate that they were dating and having sex. It was so cute it was laughable.

'We want to know everything,' Lucy said. 'How did it happen?'

How could she describe what had happened between her and Rome over the last few days? Would she start from the fateful night at the restaurant when she had cried because Rome had asked her to be his business partner and not his girlfriend? Should she include the part where she and Rome had had a row at the hotel in Penzance and then ended up having the hottest sex of her life in the shower?

'Umm… we went to Penzance, we ended up kissing under the fireworks. We won the best float award and part of the prize was a night in the Under the Sea suite where I told him I loved him and… well, the rest as they say is history,' Freya said, trying to skate over that he hadn't actually said it back yet.

'You told *him*?' Lucy said. 'That's so romantic. He's been in love with you since you came to the island, though he's always been too scared to admit it or do anything about it, but any idiot could tell that he was head over heels in love with you. And you, clever girl, you knew it too and instead of waiting for him to pluck up the courage to tell you, you took matters into your own hands. Did he just say it straight back to you?'

'Wait, what do you mean? You knew I was in love with her?' Rome asked.

'Of course, everyone knew.'

'What do you mean, everyone knew? We were friends, that's all it was in the beginning.'

'Yes dear, for the first few weeks, then you fell in love with her. We all knew that.'

'How did you know?'

'Because she was all you would talk about, all the time, and the way you looked at her, it was obvious. Dorothy from the WI said you didn't know it and one day you would suddenly realise it. We all had bets on how long it would take for you two to get together. No one expected it to take this long when you were so besotted with her.'

Rome didn't say anything, he just frowned as he focussed on his glass of champagne. Well, this was a bit awkward. The whole island thought Rome had been in love with her for years and he hadn't. Unless he was and he really didn't know it.

'We have some news,' Bella said, breaking the silence and beautifully taking the attention away from Freya and Rome.

'Oh my god, Isaac's proposed. I knew it, I knew he would.'

'No, not yet,' Bella laughed. 'We've only been together three months.'

'You're pregnant then, I'm going to be a grandmother.'

'No.' Bella shook her head affectionately at Lucy and Isaac laughed. He was clearly used to this by now. 'Isaac has asked me to move in with him.'

Lucy leapt up from her seat so fast she nearly sent Freya flying.

'That's wonderful news,' Lucy said, running round the table and pulling them both into a big hug.

Bella glanced at Freya through the hugs that Finn and Lucy were plying her and Isaac with and winked.

'Thank you,' Freya mouthed and Bella just grinned.

❦

'Right, we need to go,' Rome said, standing up.

Freya looked up from the wedding magazine that had been *casually* placed on the table, clearly in the hope that either Rome or Isaac would suddenly be inspired to propose. When neither men had given it even a second glance, Lucy had pushed it gently in Bella's direction and, when Bella had pushed it firmly back into the middle of the table, Lucy had gently pushed it in Freya's direction instead. Not wanting to offend Lucy, and not having that relationship with her that Bella did where she could be firm with her, Freya had obligingly flicked through the pages, which seemed to make Rome increasingly uncomfortable. And now he was on his feet saying goodbye to his parents.

'Oh yes, you two have your wonderful date,' Lucy gushed. 'I'm so excited for the two of you. It's so romantic.'

Rome smiled and bent to kiss his mum on the cheek. 'Bye Mum, thanks for dinner.'

Lucy hugged him and then whispered in his ear, loud enough for everyone to hear. 'Are you going to propose tonight?'

Freya snorted as she tried to keep the laughter in, then turned it into a cough.

Rome shook his head at Lucy and Freya saw the visible disappointment in her face.

'Well, you two have fun anyway,' Lucy said.

Freya stood up and Eden came to give her a hug.

'Don't pay any attention to her,' Eden whispered. 'She means well.'

Freya smiled. 'I love your mum.'

Bella hugged her too. 'Well, at least you took the heat off us a little bit.'

Freya grinned. 'And thank you for sharing the load.'

She turned back to see Lucy finishing her conversation with Rome and she came over to give Freya a hug goodbye. 'So good to see you tonight, you'll come again next week, won't you? I promise there'll be no more talk about weddings. I just got a bit carried away tonight.'

'It's totally fine. I love how happy you are for us. I think Rome was more bothered by it than I was.'

Lucy waved away her concerns. 'He's always held himself back. With you he can truly be himself. You're the best thing that has ever happened to him, I truly believe that. He'll realise it soon enough.'

Rome appeared at her side and took Freya's hand. They said their goodbyes and then Rome ushered her out onto the street.

'I'm sorry about them.'

'Don't be. Your parents are wonderful. We didn't have to leave just because the wedding magazine came out.'

'We didn't leave because of that. I told you I have a date planned.'

To Freya's surprise, they didn't walk down the hill towards the town but up the hill and then along the footpath that would take them towards the western corner of the island. Freya was intrigued. There wasn't a lot up that end of the island, a few cottages, a few boats were kept there, but as they came to the end of the path and the field opened out in front of them, she saw the big white domed building ahead of them and she gasped.

'Are we going to the observatory?'

'Yes we are.'

'I didn't think it was open to the public yet.'

'It isn't. Amelia is letting us look around before the grand opening in a few weeks' time.'

'That's fantastic, how exciting,' Freya said, a huge smile spreading across her face.

'Well, you said you wanted to see space. I know part of that dream was to travel through space and as that's a bit tricky to accomplish for you at the moment, I thought this would be the next best thing.'

'Oh.' Freya's heart filled with love for him as she realised the significance of the venue. This was not just a romantic date, this was about making her dreams come true. It was not possible to love him more than she did right then. She swallowed down a big lump in her throat.

He stroked her face and held her close. 'I thought tomorrow we could spend some time booking our safari holiday too. I want to make sure it's the right one for you, that it ticks all those boxes for you in terms of the animal experiences. So I thought we could book it together.'

'Thank you, this is amazing, thank you so much. That will be four out of five things on my list you've made come true for me.'

He kissed her on the forehead. 'I'm working on the fifth,' he whispered.

He looked into her eyes and she knew he was just asking for more time. Right then, she would have given him all the time in the world.

'Come on, let's go inside.'

Amelia was waiting for them inside and Freya noticed several computers and large telescopes. On the roof of the dome a huge, detailed photo of the moon was projected into the darkened room, so it was gleaming down upon them.

'Hey guys, good to have you here. As you can probably tell, we're not quite ready for the public yet and if you both come back in a few weeks, I'll give you a proper guided tour and talk to you a little bit about what we do here, but I have some great photos to show you. These are all ones we have taken from here using our astral imaging equipment.' Amelia turned to Freya. 'Rome thought you might want to watch one of the videos we have made for the public of all the photos. The one you're about to watch is called, "Travelling Through Space".'

Freya smiled. Oh god, this man.

'I've got some things I need to take care of in my office, so I'll leave you guys to it. Just give me a knock before you go,' Amelia said, handing Rome a remote control. She smiled at Freya and then left them alone.

'This is incredible, look at that moon,' Freya said, staring up at the great orb in wonder. She could see every crater, every lump and bump in glorious detail. She felt like she could reach out and touch it.

'Shall we sit down and watch the video?' Rome said and indicated two leather recliners that were positioned so they could lie back and look at the photos on the dome above them.

Freya sat down and lay back as Rome did the same next to her. Rome pressed a button on the remote and the video started playing. Several different images of the moon passed by on the ceiling above them and Freya stared in awe at the wonderful detail the camera had managed to capture.

The next few photos were of vibrant nebulas that looked like coloured clouds or arcs of bright lightning in space. It was beautiful and unlike anything she had seen before. Because the domed roof stretched all round them, it felt like they were actually there as the pictures changed while they travelled through the dark wilderness.

'It's a shame there's no commentary, I'd like to hear more about these photos and what we're actually looking at,' Freya said, settling back into her chair.

'There is, but I have it on mute,' Rome said. 'I thought it would just be more romantic to look at the pictures.'

'No, I want to hear all about it. I want to learn it all,' Freya protested. 'Can you go back to the beginning and play the commentary this time?'

Rome obliged and the commanding voice of the narrator filled the dome as the film started again.

Freya giggled because Rome was right. There was nothing romantic about this. But she didn't care. As the narrator launched into his spiel about the moon and the other images, Freya sat listening to every word.

※✿◎

Rome watched Freya with wonder. She was a geek just like him. She was loving listening to all the facts about space, finding it as fascinating as he would, though right now the only thing he could look at was her. He smiled at her. He had seen elements of this geeky side before – she was always fascinated when he came out with some little nugget or fact and she would often quiz him about the book he was reading whenever he brought a new one into work. This little detail was something else he loved about her.

The smile slid off his face as he thought about that. He was in love with her. He *was* in love with her.

He thought back to what his mum had said about everyone on the island thinking that he loved her for the last two years. Had he really been in love with her all this time and he just didn't know? How could he not have known?

He had nothing to compare it to, that was the problem. He had this belief that he had been in love with Paige and he knew this didn't feel like that. Looking back, maybe he loved Paige but he wasn't in love with her. Or maybe it had only been lust. But suddenly it didn't matter any more what he had felt for Paige. It had been six years and she would have wanted him to move on. He certainly wasn't going to feel guilty about it any more. The only thing that mattered was his feelings for Freya.

He thought about what Bella had said about love, that it was this warmth that spread through her every time she thought of Isaac or he did or said something nice. It was this powerful feeling that had hit her so hard and so fast, that was so much more intense than anything she had felt before.

He thought about what his mum had once said about falling in love with his dad. How she had felt so much excitement about getting to know him, about having him in her life. Somehow knowing, after just a few hours, that this was forever for her.

He had felt these things. He had felt them for the last two years. The warmth he had felt in his chest when he thought or talked about her. The affection he had for her whenever they spent time together. He had made sure Freya knew she could stay in the flat as long as she wanted, rent-free, because he didn't want her to ever leave. He had started really looking forward to going to work because he would get to see her and spend time with her, so much so he remembered actually being excited about going into the studio, going to work earlier and leaving later just so he could spend more time with her.

He really had been in love with her for two years and he'd just never known before? As Dougie had said, he had been waiting for some light bulb defining moment that would prove to him that he loved her when it had been there all along.

He wanted forever with her. He wanted marriage and children with her and the excitement of spending the rest of his life with her filled him.

Freya glanced over to him, obviously aware he was just staring, and she had the biggest grin on her face.

Her smile slid off when she saw how he was looking at her.

He leaned over and hooked an arm round her waist and pulled her onto his recliner with him.

She giggled. 'You'll tip us up.'

'I won't let you fall,' Rome said and, under the light of a million stars, he kissed her.

❦

Rome couldn't stop smiling as he lay in bed waiting for Freya to come out the bathroom later that night. Life couldn't be more perfect right now.

He had been going to tell Freya he loved her as soon as they left the observatory but he had stopped himself. He wanted to get it right, he wanted to use the right words, at the right time, maybe in some big sweeping romantic gesture so she would know how much she meant to him. He would come up with some kind of romantic date tomorrow and he would tell her then and after he would bring her back here and make love to her. For now he would just enjoy spending the night with the woman he loved wrapped in his arms.

Right on cue, Freya walked into his room wearing only his t-shirt. As she climbed into bed next to him and he turned out the light, he felt like he was the luckiest man alive.

He rolled her into his arms and pulled her t-shirt off so she was completely naked. The feel of her skin against his was heaven and the desire to tell her he loved her was so strong, but he wanted to do this properly and telling her he loved her when she was naked in his bed seemed closer to lust than to love. He didn't want there to be any misunderstanding.

He would just content himself with kissing her until neither of them could remember their own name.

CHAPTER 26

Rome was sitting on the beach with Freya, looking out at the sunrise. She was cuddled up against his shoulder, when he realised there was a dark shadow standing over them.

His heart suddenly thundering in his chest, he looked up to see the same cloaked figure that had plagued his dreams for years. The cloaked figure suddenly made a grab for them but, instead of grabbing him, it seized Freya and started to drag her away from him. He leapt up and started to push the grim reaper away from her as Freya fought against it too, screaming and reaching out for Rome in desperation for him to save her.

In the struggle, the hood fell from the grim reaper's head and, sure enough, the cold dead eyes of Paige stared back at him as he tried to stop her from taking the woman he loved.

No matter how hard he fought against Paige, he couldn't get Freya back. He was going to lose her.

'Paige, no, please,' he begged but it was no use.

He turned to Freya, grabbing her hand. 'Please don't go.'

But she was snatched from his grasp and dragged away from him and there was nothing he could do.

He woke with a jerk, his heart thundering in his chest so hard he could barely breathe. It was dark but he knew he was in his bedroom and to his utmost relief Freya was next to him, stroking his shoulder and trying to soothe him.

'It's OK,' she whispered, in the darkness. 'It was just a dream.'

He gathered Freya to him, holding her tight and kissing her hard, a desperate need for her erupting inside of him.

'Let me make love to you.'

'Of course.'

That was the only encouragement he needed. He rolled on top of her as he kissed her again and as she wrapped her arms and legs around him he slid inside her.

'Christ, I thought I'd lost you,' he said as he thrust inside her. 'I dreamt you were taken from me, that I'd lost you and it destroyed me. I love you so much, I always have and I always will. You need to know that.'

He felt her still beneath him, he had never meant to tell her like this but he needed her to know. 'I love you. You are everything to me. There will never be anyone who means as much as you do to me. I love you so much.' Two years of not saying it and now he couldn't stop. 'I love you.'

God, sex had never been like this with her, this was frantic and desperate and filled with fear over losing her and a relief to find he hadn't. It was hard and fast and urgent and he knew it wasn't going to last long. He slid his hand between them, stroking her and coaxing her over the edge, and as she shouted out his name, he lost his grip on any kind of control he had been clinging to. As he came inside her, all he could do was shout out 'I love you', over and over again.

❦

Freya watched as Rome slept peacefully. One arm was around her shoulder but he wasn't really aware she was there now. He had a big grin on his face and she presumed he was dreaming about Paige again. Only this time he was clearly thinking nice things about her, probably the sex he'd just thought he'd had with her.

She slipped from the bed and quickly got dressed, wanting to be out of the house before she burst into tears.

He didn't even stir.

She left him in bed with his dreams and exited the house, running along Buttercup Beach back towards her house.

She played the last half hour in her head over again. He had been having a bad dream, that much was clear. And she had tried to comfort him but then the words he had shouted out turned to ice in her veins.

'*Paige, no, please don't go.*'

He had obviously been thinking about Paige dying. It had broken her heart to hear him begging for her to come back. It hurt her to see him in pain, but it hurt for herself too, knowing he would never love her as much as he loved Paige. When he had woken up and started making love to her, she had thought he was looking for comfort from her, but it turned out he thought he was with Paige the whole time.

'*I thought I'd lost you. I dreamt you were taken from me, that I'd lost you and it destroyed me. I love you, I always have and I always will.*'

A sob tore from Freya's throat. He hadn't been making love to her, he had been making love to Paige, thinking that the pain he had gone through over the last few years had just been a dream – that's why the sex had been so different, so frantic, just like he'd said it had always been with Paige.

Freya had said she would wait for him, that she would be patient, but in reality he was never going to get over Paige.

A shadow loomed out of the darkness towards her and she leapt back.

'Freya, it's me,' and she recognised the voice of Dougie a few moments before her eyes adjusted and she could see him. He was the last person she wanted to see right now, with his sarcastic remarks. 'Are you OK?'

'I'm fine,' Freya sobbed and tried to get past him but he caught her shoulder.

'No, you're not. Where's Rome, have you just come from his house?'

'He's in bed fast asleep. I need to go.'

'What happened? Are you hurt?'

She couldn't stop herself from bursting into tears. To her surprise, Dougie suddenly hugged her, holding her tight and rubbing his hands down her back as he tried to soothe her. 'Come on, let's go back to Eden's house.'

'It's the middle of the night,' Freya protested.

'And she would want to know if her best friend is upset.'

Dougie guided her back onto the road with his arm round her shoulders, making sure she didn't run away from him. He let them back into Eden's house.

'Wait here, I'll just go and get her,' Dougie said, gently.

She sat down on the sofa and Dougie disappeared upstairs. She heard soft voices and a few moments later Eden came running down the stairs.

'What's happened, are you OK?'

Eden enveloped her in a big hug as Freya cried against her. It was over. She didn't think there was any going back after this.

❦

Rome woke to a hammering on his door. He looked around and realised the bed was empty and, judging by how cold it was, it had been empty for some time.

'Freya?' he called out, but there was no answer.

As the hammering on the door came again, he quickly pulled on his jeans and ran downstairs to answer it.

There was Dougie standing on his doorstep. It was still dark outside. What the hell was going on?

'Did you and Freya have a fight?'

'No, where is she?'

'Currently at Eden's house sobbing her heart out. I couldn't sleep and went for a walk and I found her on the beach running away from your house. What did you do?'

Rome's heart leapt with fear. What had he done? He had been so careful not to screw this up with her and somehow he'd messed it up anyway. What had happened? He'd had the bad dream about Paige taking away Freya, he'd woken up and made love to Freya, told her he loved her and then kissed her until he had fallen asleep. What could possibly be wrong about that? He *had* told her he loved her. It wasn't supposed to come out like that but surely it was a good thing?

Suddenly he felt sick. The way they had made love had been so different to how he had made love to her before, it had been fast and hard. Christ, what if he had hurt her? He quickly grabbed his trainers, pulling them on, scooped up his keys and stepped out onto the street.

'I need to talk to her,' Rome said.

Dougie gestured for him to go ahead, knowing that he probably couldn't keep up with him when Rome was running flat out.

Rome arrived at Eden's house a minute later and banged on her door. Eden opened it straight away.

'She's gone back to her flat, she said she wanted to be alone,' Eden said before Rome could even get a word out.

Dougie came running up behind him.

'Please, if she's here, I need to talk to her,' Rome said, urgently.

Eden shook her head. 'I promise she's not. I could barely get a word out of her. She kept mentioning Paige but then she said she wanted to be alone and left.'

'And you let her?'

'What did you want me to do, tie her up?'

Rome sighed. He just needed to talk to her.

'Thanks, both of you.'

He quickly ran down the street towards the shop and let himself into her flat and then ran up the stairs.

He heard crying coming from the bedroom and he quickly walked in there. His heart dropped into his stomach as he saw Freya. She was sobbing uncontrollably as she moved around the room and he could clearly see that she was packing, throwing any clothes and belongings that she could grab into a suitcase. She was leaving and panic ripped through him at that prospect. He couldn't lose her but what the hell could he do to stop her?

CHAPTER 27

'What's going on?' Rome asked and Freya looked up from her packing, tears filled her eyes again as she saw him.

'I need to go.'

He stepped towards her. 'Go where?'

'Anywhere, I just need to get away from you.'

She heard him gasp softly. 'What did I do? Did I hurt you when we were making love, was I rough with you?'

Freya shook her head, throwing the last few things into her suitcase and zipping it up. 'It's not that.'

'Then what the hell is it, what did I do?'

Freya grabbed her bag off the bed and hoisted it onto the floor. 'I need to go.'

Rome slammed the bedroom door, trapping her in the room. 'Not without giving me an explanation. You owe me that much.'

'I don't owe you anything.'

'Wait a minute. We're friends, you're my best friend, and before we started seeing each other, you promised me that that would never change. So before you walk away from us, you at least need to tell me why.'

A sob tore from her throat. 'Because you're still in love with her.'

Rome looked confused for a moment. 'Who?'

'Paige.'

He looked alarmed. 'No I'm not. I don't think I was ever in love with her actually, but I'm certainly not in love with her now.'

Freya shook her head. 'I was in love with you for two years, and I kept waiting and hoping that one day you would fall in love with me too. Just like I hoped Jake would one day fall out of love with his ex and fall in love with me. But you still love her.'

'What the hell are you talking about?'

'You dreamed about her.'

Rome paled and then he nodded. 'Yes. I did.'

'You called out to her, begged her not to leave you and then you woke up and thought I was her. When you made love to me, you were really making love to her, telling her you were scared that you had lost her, telling her how much you loved her, that you've always loved her and always will,' Freya sobbed.

He looked horrified. 'Wait, that's not what happened. I was making love to you, I knew it was you the whole time. When I said I was in love with you, I meant it. I love you Freya.'

'Bullshit. Why would you say that you've always loved me? I told you I loved you and you never said it back, despite knowing how much it hurt that you didn't say it back to me, but now you're telling me that you've been in love with me for two years.'

He pushed his curly hair from his face. 'It's complicated.'

Freya shook her head. 'This is all lies. You just don't want me to go so now you're saying anything to keep me here.'

She moved to the door.

'I didn't know,' Rome blurted out. 'I didn't know I was in love with you because I never felt like this with Paige. I thought I was in love with her, I was going to marry her, so then when I fell in love with you, I didn't know this was what love was really supposed to feel like. Everything with you was so much better, so much more wonderful. We were closer in the first few weeks of our friendship than I ever was with Paige. I thought what we had was friendship in the beginning but it was so much more than that. I thought it might be lust but it was more than that too. I've been asking people how they knew they were in love and I realised I have all of that with you, I always have. I realised at the observatory that I've always been in love with you.'

'But you never told me.'

'I wanted to do it somewhere romantic, I didn't want to just blurt it out, or mention it in passing. I wanted to do it right.'

'But you called for Paige in your dreams, you begged her not to leave.'

'I was begging you not to leave, not her.'

Freya shook her head at the lies, opened the door and stepped out into the lounge.

'You really want to know what my dream was about? What it's always about. You really want to know how messed up I am? As a child I had nightmares about the grim reaper taking me away. They stopped when I got older but when Paige died the nightmares returned, but this time when the grim reaper comes, it's always Paige. You want to know how I remember my ex? I see her as bloodied, mutilated zombified corpse and she comes to take me away. Sometimes she has even come to take away my loved ones instead of me: Eden, Bella, my parents or, in the case of tonight's dream, she came to take away you. In my dream I was begging her not to take you and then I was begging you not to leave me. Just like I'm doing now. You have to believe me. I love you and that dream messed me up so badly because I cannot cope with the thought of losing you.'

Freya hesitated for a moment. It sounded so implausible.

'But this isn't really about me not being over my past is it, this is about you not being over yours,' Rome said. 'Jake never loved you. He couldn't have if he was sleeping with his ex the whole time you were together. He betrayed you and you've never got over that, which is why you are overreacting about my dream.'

Anger boiled up in her. 'I'm not overreacting.'

'You're leaving here with a suitcase filled with jumpers during one of the hottest summers we've had in years. You have no place to go to and you don't think you might be acting a little irrationally? Why are you so quick to believe I'm lying to you? I have never lied to you since I've met you. You just need to calm down and think about what I'm saying, and if you need space to do that, I can give it to you, but please don't leave. This is your home.'

'I can't stay here hoping one day you'll love me as much as I love you. You love me as a friend but you're not in love with me. Real love is not something that takes you years to realise, real love hits you with the force of a ten-ton bus, it takes your breath away, you can't sleep at night because the other person is all you think about. You're fond of me, you like working with me, that's as far as it goes. Now it's time to let me go. Let me move on and get over you once and for all.'

She turned away and walked down the stairs and he didn't call her back.

Freya hurried down the street towards the ferry that would take her to St Mary's and away from the man she loved. She wiped the tears from her eyes that wouldn't stop falling.

Her head was a swirl of emotions. Rome's weird dreams, his sudden declaration of love that came from nowhere, the fact that, if what he said was true, he had loved her and never told her.

But then, she had never told him how she felt either.

Rome was right about one thing though, he had never lied to her before, never given her any reason to doubt him.

As she joined the back of a small queue of people waiting for the five o'clock ferry, the phone rang and she quickly fished it out of her bag and saw it was Eden.

She answered the phone.

'Freya, are you OK?'

More tears fell from her eyes at her friend's kindness. How could she tell Eden she was leaving, she'd be so upset. Not only was she walking away from Rome, she was walking away from Bella and Eden too and the thought of that hurt almost as much as leaving Rome. Maybe it wouldn't be forever, she just needed some time to think.

Up ahead, Bob, the ferry captain, was starting to let people on board and she shuffled forward in the queue.

'I don't know,' Freya said, quietly, mainly because she had no idea how to describe what was going on in her head at the moment. 'Eden, has Rome ever told you about the dreams he has of Paige?'

There was silence for a moment and Freya stepped aboard the ferry, flashing Bob her ferry pass and dragging on her suitcase.

'Are you talking about the horrible dreams he has of her as the grim reaper?'

Freya's heart sank as she sat down. It was true. 'Yes.'

'He's had them since he was little. Rome read everything he could get his hands on when he was growing up, including a ton of stuff that was way too old for him. The hazards of having a library at the end of our road. That was Rome's playground – while the other little boys were out playing football, Rome was in there reading books about anything and everything, including a load of books about death after our gran had died. For some reason he fixated on the image of the grim reaper and had terrible nightmares about it. They went away after a few years but they came back after Paige died, with her in the starring role.'

Freya closed her eyes as the boat suddenly juddered into life. Why had she doubted him? He had been telling the truth. Well, at least about that.

'Eden, I need to go. I'll call you later.'

'You better do.'

'I will.'

'He loves you, you know. Mum was right about that. Anyone can see he is crazy in love with you. Please don't do anything rash.'

She was just about to defend herself but Rome had been right about that too. Throwing anything she could grab into a suitcase and running away was how she had handled the thing with Jake and now she was doing the same thing again.

'I just need some time to think.'

'He's your best friend, don't forget that. I know how it feels and, however much it hurts to have Dougie back and know he will never be mine, I would rather have him home and to see him every day than to never see him again. So before you do anything stupid, please think what your life will be like without Rome in it at all.'

Freya thought about this.

'Call me later,' Eden said.

'I will, I promise.'

Freya hung up and stared out at the inky sea, as Bob manoeuvred the boat out of the harbour. A pink glow lighting up the horizon indicated the sun was going to rise soon.

Was Rome right about her issues with Jake? Had Jake really messed her up far more than she realised?

The problem was, her relationship with Jake had begun in a similar way to how her relationship with Rome had started. They had been friends first then one night they had ended up sleeping together. Jake hadn't been keen to start a relationship either but they'd slept with each other a few more times. When her nan had died and she'd had nowhere else to go, Jake had offered her his place as somewhere to stay until she sorted herself out and she had been so pathetically grateful and so stupidly in love with him that she had made herself indispensable, cooking, cleaning, working her arse off for him at his company. He'd never said he loved her and she told herself she didn't need to hear it because she thought he did love her in his way. And although he talked about Lizzie a lot she had naïvely assumed that if he wanted to be with Lizzie he would be. She'd had no idea he was having his cake and eating it. When she had found out it had hurt her so much.

She realised now, that experience had tainted her relationship with Rome. She had been waiting for Rome to betray her too. Maybe not in the same way; she knew she could trust Rome to be faithful to her, though that hadn't stopped the green-eyed monster when he had been talking to Amelia, that first night at Envy, and whenever Kitty had come round and flirted with Rome. She had been expecting him to betray her by not loving her back but had he really been in love with her the whole time, falling deeper in love with her every day they were together?

She thought about the connection they shared when they made love. It had never been like that with Jake. You couldn't fake that level of intimacy. They could only really have shared that connection if he had deep feelings for her too.

She thought about all the dreams he had made come true for her, and how incredible it was that he wanted to do that for her. He said he wanted to make her happy. Tears filled her eyes again.

She replayed the events of the last few hours in her head now she knew what Rome was saying about the dream was true. Everything he had said fitted with his version of events, which meant that when he'd been making love to her and had kept repeating that he loved her, he really had been saying it to her.

He loved her.

And actually the signs had been there all along.

Oh god what had she done? She had allowed what Jake had done to ruin what she had with Rome. It wasn't that Rome was hung up on his past at all, it was all her.

Fresh tears filled her eyes as the boat came in to dock at St Mary's. She needed to talk to him.

Bob tied the boat up and the small number of passengers slowly started to disembark, some of them stopping to chat to Bob on the way out. Freya had to stop herself from screaming in frustration, she had to get back to Hope Island.

Suddenly there was a commotion on the jetty as someone shoved past the small queue of people patiently waiting. People were protesting but the man didn't care.

Freya's heart leapt into her mouth as she recognised the dark curls and the huge frame of Rome Lancaster. She stood up, wiping her tears away so she could see clearly. It was him. How the hell he was here when she had just left him on Hope Island, she didn't know, but he *was* here.

She ran to greet him as he suddenly stepped on the boat and gathered her into his arms. 'I told you, I'm never letting you go,' he said, fiercely, as he kissed her hard.

She protested feebly against his lips, desperate to talk to him, but then she didn't care any more and she melted into the kiss.

Rome shuffled her backwards onto the boat out of the way of the people still departing or getting on.

Oh god, he was here. He was kissing her. She hadn't messed everything up with him at all.

He pulled back slightly to look at her. Her brain was a mush of emotions and questions. 'How are you here?' she blurted out.

'I stole Isaac's speedboat,' Rome said before kissing her again.

He held her to him tightly, clearly afraid to let her go. When he did pull back, she could barely catch her breath. But there was so much she wanted to say to him.

The boat was already pulling away from the jetty, taking them back to Hope Island, taking them home, when suddenly Rome dropped to his knees in front of her.

The small crowd of passengers gasped and went quiet. Any words she had wanted to say caught in her throat as he produced a small black box from his pocket.

'Freya Greene, I love you so much. You are everything to me. My best friend, my soul mate, will you do me the honour of becoming my wife?'

She quickly sank to her knees in front of him. 'No, no, no. Rome you don't need to do this. I love you. I made a mistake. I cocked up. I didn't believe you when I had no reason not to trust you. You were right when you said that I was letting my past hold me back. This wasn't you at all. I was on my way back to apologise, you don't need to propose to me to get me to stay.'

He looked at her in confusion. 'You don't want me to propose to you?'

'Of course I do, I want forever with you. The day we get married will be the happiest day of my life. But I want this when the time is right for you. Not because we had a silly row.'

He sat back on his heels, clearly unsure of what to do next. No book of love could prepare him for this. She stroked his face and he held her hand against his cheek.

'I held back too,' Rome said, softly. 'When I first met you I was so afraid of getting hurt again, of falling in love and losing you, that I pushed the possibility of love away. I wouldn't even consider that I was falling in love. I ignored the signs, ignored the feelings building up inside of me. And when the feelings became too much to ignore, when they would keep me awake at night because I was thinking about you and I ended up at your flat too many times to count, not because of the nightmares but because I just needed to be close to you, I was still too cowardly to do anything about it. Not because I was afraid of getting hurt, but because I didn't want to cock it up and lose you. You were, and you still are, my best friend and that was way too important to me to do anything that might damage that friendship. I would much rather we were friends forever than lovers for a few weeks and then lose you because I'm an idiot. I should have told you sooner, I do love you.'

'I love you too,' Freya cried.

He wiped the tears from her cheeks. 'I wasted two years, confused by my feelings, and too afraid to admit the truth. I don't want to waste another day. This, right now, is the right time for me. I want to marry you.'

He opened the black box. She stared at the ring and gasped. The stone was not diamond or opal, it was made from glass just like he said it would be. Swirls of gold, blue, caramel and pink twisted around each other in a tiny bead of fused glass.

It was at that moment the sun peeped above the horizon and the light picked out the tiny fragments and bubbles of different colours that surrounded the swirls. It was like looking at a tiny galaxy of a million stars, the swirls and the gases of the nebulas in space.

'I started making this for you after our conversation outside the jewellers that night. I didn't know when I was going to give it to you, but I wanted to see if I could make something as beautiful and special as you are. The gold and blue is for your hair, the toffee strand is for your beautiful eyes and the rose is the exact shade of your lips, which I could kiss forever and never get tired of it.'

Freya stared at it, unable to take her eyes off it.

'If you want a traditional diamond or an opal or a sapphire or a ruby, I'll get it for you, but I wanted something that captured how uniquely beautiful you are. I love you, will you marry me?'

Freya nodded, unable to hold back the tears now. 'Yes. Yes, of course I'll marry you.'

Rome slid the ring onto her finger and Freya couldn't stop sobbing as he gathered her to him and kissed her.

The passengers cheered and clapped and she pulled away from him slightly, giggling, and realised they had arrived back at Hope Island. The streets were quiet and peaceful, the island still seemed to be sleeping, the street lights twinkling in the early morning light. But she knew she was home now.

'You've made all my dreams come true now,' Freya said.

'And we'll make new dreams together.'

Freya looked out at the sun rising over the sea. It was a new day, a new beginning. 'Shall we go home?'

Rome shook his head. 'I would love nothing more than to go home and take you back to bed right now, but I need to go back and get Isaac's boat.'

Freya laughed.

'Will you come with me?'

'I'd follow you to the moon and back.'

EPILOGUE

'Ten, nine...'

'Are you nervous?' Freya asked, leaning into Rome. He let go of her hand and wrapped his arm round her shoulders, kissing her forehead.

'No, I know this is our best work yet. It's been months of hard work but I'm incredibly proud of what we've achieved.'

'Two, one...' the mayor of Hope Island shouted, the crowd joining him with the countdown. He pulled the red curtain off the school mural and, as it fell to the floor and the glass glinted and sparkled in the sunlight, the crowd gasped and then cheered and clapped.

She smiled at all the children on the mural, playing in the playground and on the beach, she loved the dolphins jumping out of the waves and was most proud of how the sea had turned out, with its fused glass and metallic ribbons of gold weaved through it. That had been her idea and her part of the project and it couldn't have turned out better. It really was beautiful. But the thing that made her smile the most was some of the people standing on the edges of the mural. Rome had the idea that they should put their loved ones into the mural to show how important they were to them and to the island. Bella, Isaac, Eden, Dougie, Finn and Lucy had all been immortalised on the mural. And although most people on the island would only see them as figures, non-descript people, Freya and Rome knew who they were. Freya grinned at the figure of Rome that she had put into the mural with his arm around the figure of her that he had put in. She was a part of this island now and it meant the world to her to see that symbolised in the mural too.

The school was opening for the new academic year the next day, it had been hard work getting the mural finished in time, working almost every day over the summer holidays and they had only just finished two days before, but Freya was so pleased with how it had turned out.

People came up to them and congratulated them and then started to drift off towards the barbeque that was being held to help celebrate the unveiling of the new school wing and the glass mural.

'I didn't mean about this,' Freya said, once most of the people had moved into the school grounds for the celebrations.

'Oh,' Rome grinned. 'Not one bit. You?'

'No, not at all.'

They started to slowly walk down the beach away from the school. A few other stragglers were heading down the beach ahead of them.

'You look so beautiful today, have I told you that?' Rome said.

Freya looked down at the creamy strapless beach dress that sparkled with blue sequins, offset with a satin blue belt. She loved seeing Rome's look of delight when she came downstairs in it before they came out.

'Yes you have, and you're looking pretty bloody hot yourself, Rome Lancaster.' He was wearing a suit jacket over a pale blue shirt that was open at the collar. He looked so happy and relaxed.

'And have I told you how much I love you?'

She smiled. 'You tell me ten times a day.'

That was probably an understatement. Since the first time he had uttered those wonderful words, it was like a dam had burst and he couldn't stop saying it. He didn't care about saying it in public either, he was quite happy to shout his love to anyone and everyone who would listen. It was so genuine though, she knew that he meant it.

'Does your *Book of Love* tell you to say it so often?'

'I gave that book to the charity shop, I don't need a book to know how I feel for you. There are no words sufficient to describe my feelings for you. And you seem to love me regardless of what I do or say. There are no rules any more.'

'I do love you, very much.'

He bent his head and kissed her, smiling against her lips.

She looked ahead to the small round marquee that was billowing in the sea breeze. Out in the sea, she could see the dolphins frolicking in the waves. It was a perfect, sunny, September day.

'I can't believe tomorrow we fly out to Africa for our safari. I'm so excited. That's my last dream coming true.'

He'd made every one of her dreams come true for her. Rome had insisted on going ahead with the sale of the flat, despite that she had moved in with him, pretty much straightaway. He'd told her it was her dream and he wasn't going to go back on that.

'Not all your dreams have come true. I believe you wanted four children by the time you're thirty. We might have our work cut out having four in the next year, but we can give it a go. We'll have lots of time on our safari for baby-making.'

She stopped him and looped her arms round his neck. He wrapped his arms round her back and held her close against him. He leaned his forehead against hers and moved his hands to caress her stomach.

'I can't wait to see you carrying my baby,' he said, softly, his thumbs dancing across her belly.

Pretty much as soon as he'd slid the engagement ring on her finger, he'd started talking about trying for a baby and at first she'd thought he was doing that for her, trying to make all her dreams come true, but when he'd started reading books about babies and being a dad and getting really excited about the prospect, she knew he wanted this as much as she did.

'You won't have too long to wait,' she whispered.

He frowned slightly, his smile falling off his face. He looked down at her stomach and then back up at her. 'You're pregnant?'

'We're pregnant,' Freya giggled. 'Just a few weeks so it's still really early, but yes, you're going to be a dad.'

She watched the huge smile spread across his face and then he kissed her hard.

'We're having a baby?' Rome said, pulling back slightly.

She laughed and nodded and he kissed her again, his hands on her belly the whole time.

He pulled back again and he was still grinning.

'But we can still practise for the next one while we're on safari,' Freya said and he laughed.

He gestured to the marquee at the end of the beach and Bella and Eden waiting outside in their long blue dresses.

'We better get on with this then, I don't want anyone saying we had a baby outside of wedlock.'

Freya laughed. 'Yes, because all the islanders honestly believe we've been sleeping in separate bedrooms up until now.'

'That's true. Still I better make an honest woman out of you.'

He took her hand and led her up to the marquee. She greeted Eden and Bella and with her hand still in Rome's they ducked inside. Fairy lights lit up the inside, interweaved with flowers and gold chairs filled with their friends and family were arranged in a circle around the edge of the marquee. Dougie was waiting in the middle with the registrar and Rome led her over to them, Bella and Eden bringing up the rear.

As the guests' chatter died down and soft music started playing, Rome bent his head and kissed her on the cheek.

'I love you both,' Rome whispered.

'We love you too,' Freya said, unable to stop the smile from spreading on her face.

He smiled and they turned to face the registrar.

The registrar smiled at them.

'Friends and family, welcome and thank you all for being here on this important day. We are gathered together to celebrate the very special love between Rome and Freya by joining them in marriage…'

Freya looked up at Rome and smiled, knowing all her dreams had come true.

The End

A LETTER FROM HOLLY

Thank you so much for reading *Summer at Buttercup Beach*, I had so much fun creating this story and I hope you enjoyed reading it as much as I enjoyed writing it.

One of the best parts of writing comes from seeing the reaction from readers. Did it make you smile or laugh, did it make you cry, hopefully happy tears? Did you fall in love with Freya and Rome? Did you like the beautiful Hope Island? If you enjoyed the story, I would absolutely love it if you could leave a short review. Getting feedback from readers is amazing and it also helps to persuade other readers to pick up one of my books for the first time.

If you haven't read *Spring at Blueberry Bay* yet, the first book set on Hope Island, then you can get your copy today, I'm sure you'll love Bella and Isaac's story.

Thank you for reading.

Love Holly x

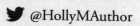 HollyMartinAuthor

@HollyMAuthor

hollymartinwriter.wordpress.com/

Summer at Buttercup Beach
Dairy-Free Ice Cream

While lying on a beach this summer, or even in your back garden, you want a sweet, summery treat to cool you down. And as our fictional beach is Buttercup Beach it probably needs to be something yellow.

INGREDIENTS:
- ♥ 2 bananas
- ♥ 2 mangoes
- ♥ Toppings, (optional) pineapple, mango, raspberry or strawberry juice. Star fruit or pineapple.

1. We all buy bananas and then not get around to eating them before they go over-ripe and speckly. Well, when they are at that slightly speckly stage, peel two of them, chop them into inch-long chunks and place on a baking tray in the freezer for around half an hour. Do this with the mango too; chop, scoop out the flesh and freeze. You don't get a lot of flesh from a mango because of the big stone in the middle, so you will probably need two large mangoes for this.

2. Once the fruit is frozen, add both portions to the blender and mix until creamy. Pour into a tupperware box, put the lid on and return to the freezer. Now you can scoop out the mixture and serve, just like you would do with ice cream.

3. Toppings (optional): Pour mango or pineapple juice into star-shaped ice cube trays, pour raspberry or strawberry juice into heart-shaped ice cube trays and freeze them both. Then you can pop them out and add a little bit of romantic magic to your banana and mango dessert. Alternatively, you can add a slice of star fruit or chopped pineapple to the dessert for that magical touch.

Tip: Buying whole fruits like a pineapple can sometimes be quite expensive but most supermarkets will sell packets of chopped fruit which might be a bit cheaper. They also sell frozen chopped fruit that might work out cheaper too.

ACKNOWLEDGEMENTS

To my family, my mom, my biggest fan, who reads every word I have written a hundred times over and loves it every single time, my dad, my brother Lee and my sister-in-law Julie, for your support, love, encouragement and endless excitement for my stories.

For my twinnie, the gorgeous Aven Ellis for just being my wonderful friend, for your endless support, for cheering me on, for reading my stories and telling me what works and what doesn't and for keeping me entertained with wonderful stories and pictures of hot men. I love you dearly.

To my friends Gareth, Mandie, Angie, Jac, Verity and Jodie who listen to me talk about my books endlessly and get excited about it every single time.

For Sharon Sant for just being there always and your wonderful friendship.

To my wonderful agent Madeleine Milburn and Hayley Steed for just being amazing and fighting my corner and for your unending patience with my constant questions.

To the lovely Claire Bord for putting up with all my crazy throughout the whole process, for replying to every single email and for listening to me freak out with complete and utter patience. To my new editor Natasha Harding for being so excited about working with me, I'm really looking forward to working with you too. My structural editor Celine Kelly for helping to make this book so much better, my copy editor Rhian for doing such a good job at spotting any issues or typos. Thank you to Kim Nash for the tireless promoting, tweeting and general cheerleading. Thank you to all the other wonderful people at Bookouture; Oliver Rhodes, the editing team and the wonderful designers who created this absolutely gorgeous cover.

To the CASG, the best writing group in the world, you wonderful talented supportive bunch of authors, I feel very blessed to know you all, you guys are the very best.

To the wonderful Bookouture authors for all your encouragement and support.

Thank you to Catherine Packham at Catherine's Glass and Dean Tothill at Glow-worm Glass Studio who gave me loads of advice about stained glass work, fused glass and everything else I needed to make Rome and Freya's glass work as accurate as possible.

To Tracey Gatland who patiently answered all my questions about life in the Scilly Isles.

To Cathy Bramley and her husband Tony for giving me loads of advice about astronomy and what exactly I would see through a telescope from the Scilly Isles in July. The scene didn't make the final cut, but the advice about astral imaging equipment really helped when writing the scene in the observatory.

To anyone who has read my book and taken the time to tell me you've enjoyed it or wrote a review, thank you so much.

Thank you, I love you all.